WILD LIFE PUBLISHING

"A CAPTIVATING READ...
PACKED WITH DRAMA, ACTION AND
SUSPENSE!"
- ALFRED ADAMS, JR.
BEST SELLING AUTHOR OF
MY BROTHERS KEEPER

MOVING TARGET

A NOVEL BY

NOW BORN

AUTHOR OF *PROMISE*

PUBLISHER'S INFORMATION
Wild Life Publishing presents,
MOVING TARGET

ISBN-10 Number: 0615666167
ISBN-13 Number: 978-0-615-66616-7
Library of Congress Catalog Card Number: TXU-1-789-488

Wild Life Publishing, P.O. Box 78964
Atlanta, GA 30357
Wildlife.publishing@yahoo.com

Edited by Denise Keese and Trina Lucky
Cover Design/ Graphics by Drea Delgado for KTL Graphic Designs

Paperback Design by eBook Bakery.com

Manufactured in the United States of America

ACKNOWLEDGEMENTS

First, I want to recognize and give praises to the most high. I would like to thank my mother, father and all of my siblings for their unconditional love and support throughout all of my trials and tribulations.

Thanks to my very close friend Shalonda Holmes, who has been a motivating force in my life. I want to dedicate this book to my nieces: Timesha, Nija, Jayla, Nailah, Laiah and my nephew Keyshawn. I just want to encourage all of you to always remain close with one another, always follow your dreams and know that you can achieve anything that you can imagine. This book is also dedicated to my friend Shaquake Scott, who has given me much inspiration. May all of your days be blessed. I've lost a bit of family members and friends who were dear to me. I would also like to dedicate this book to them. "Rest in Peace" to all of my grandparents, my aunt Betty Ann Pringle, and to all of my fallen soldiers: Travis "Fresco Dolla" Kirkland, Lamont "Rampage" Clark, Timothy Bolling, Amar Allah, Wayne "Bloody Bust" Durant, Marwin Gainey, Mario Johnson and Mario Stokes.

Finally, I want to dedicate this book to all of the brothers and sisters who are serving time in State or Federal prisons, those on death row, and those of you who are fugitives on the run. This book is for you.

Peace.

PROLOGUE

Baseer Watson was born on June 4th, 1978 at the Bronx-Lebanon Hospital in the Bronx, New York. He grew up living with his immediate family in a fifth floor three-bedroom apartment on Morris Avenue between 169th Street and 170th Street. Growing up, he was your typical black kid in New York City. He was very inquisitive and seemed to pick up on things very fast. His earliest passion was drawing wild style graffiti, an art style that derived from the hip-hop culture. He also liked to animate people and different things from his surrounding environment. He always made excellent grades in school and his teachers always took a liking to him because of his modesty and his charming personality.

Baseer was the third child and only son of Catherine and James Watson. Catherine, originally Catherine Anderson, was a Bronx native. She grew up on Teller Avenue between 161st and 162nd Street. James was originally from Fayetteville, NC where he spent most of his childhood living in various low-income housing complexes throughout the city. After graduating from high school in 1969, James moved to Brooklyn, New York and stayed with his uncle Isaiah. He enrolled in Medgar Evers University located on Bedford Avenue. In his Sociology class is where he met Catherine Anderson who later became his wife and bore four children from him in the order as follows: a daughter named Carmin, a second daughter named Lashawn, a son named Baseer, and a third daughter named Alana. Catherine worked as a nurse's assistant at Lincoln Hospital in the Bronx. James never could maintain a steady job but he always managed to

1

conjure up enough money to make ends meet within the household. The couple married each other in 1971 and moved to Morris Avenue in the Bronx, just two blocks from the Grand Concourse.

James was a slender-built dark skinned man who stood about 5' 11" tall. He always dressed nice. He spoke with a smooth deep voice and a rich southern accent. Life in NY City seemed fast to James. The people that he chose to befriend rarely had much going for themselves. His friends were mostly unemployed alcoholics and a great many of them began to smoke crack-cocaine as it became popular in the 1980's. James started smoking also but he appeared to be somewhat of a functional smoker. His only shortcomings began to show when he would return home over-intoxicated from a mixture of alcohol and crack co-caine. That's when he would violently take his failures and insecurities out on his wife Catherine. On many oc-casions, the children were present to witness their moth-er being abused. They were too young and small to do anything about it, so they would go ignored and he would continue doing what he did until he felt that his point was made. Most of their fights would escalate from ar-guments that usually began with Catherine's complaints that James wasn't pulling his weight as the man of the house. Catherine was forced to play the role of the mother and the father because James' addiction caused him to slack on his responsibilities tremendously. Instead of ac-cepting her advice as constructive criticism, James would accuse her of crossing her boundaries by questioning his authority-thus being his selfish justification for her pun-ishment.

Baseer developed a hateful feeling towards his father and constantly reminded himself that he would never abuse a female. After every fight, James would storm out of the apartment and run the streets of the Bronx, Brook-lyn and Harlem for hours and sometimes days. Catherine never once called the police to arrest James for his at-tacks. She blamed his temper on his uncontrollable drug addiction and simply preferred that he sought for recov-ery. When Baseer was seven years old, James and Cath-erine finally divorced. James' lifestyle then became like that of a vagabond. His tunnel focus was getting high and he began doing things that young Baseer never dreamed to see his father succumb to – stealing and pan-handling. After learning of his father's activity in the streets, Baseer began to feel embarrassed by him and grew to despise him even more. Frequently, James would visit the children on Morris Avenue but he would never have money or gifts for them. His visits were always brief, only long enough for him to say how much he loved them and their mother. The children always turned a deaf ear to him because they chose to side with their mother and reflect her disdain for him.

In elementary school, Baseer loved to draw. He also enjoyed playing basketball at Claremont Park, just a couple of blocks away from his apartment building. He had many friends in his neighborhood but his two best friends were Tramal "TK" Kennedy and Kevin Clarke. The both of them lived one block away on Sheridan Avenue and they met while in the second grade at Public School #53. TK was a good kid, originally from Lafayette Gardens in Brooklyn. He was deliberately sloppy with a nappy afro, untied shoe-strings and baggy clothes. Everybody liked him because of his keen sense of humor. From the outside-looking in, anyone could see that his parents instilled in him the importance of setting goals and securing a future for himself legally. He never got into trouble. Kevin was originally from Tompkins Projects in Brooklyn but he and his single mother moved to the Bronx when he was only five years old. Kevin was more of a rebellious spirit and trouble always seemed to follow when he and Baseer hung out together. Still, their loyalty to one another was genuine. Catherine knew that TK and Kevin were good friends to Baseer so she treated them like sons. When Baseer reached the age of 10 years old, he fell in love with hip-hop music and he began writing song lyrics of his own. His older sister Lashawn played clarinet in her middle school band, and her band director gave her instrumental cassette tapes to use for practice at home. Baseer, being without the necessary equipment to compose his own instrumentals, would borrow Lashawn's cassettes and write lyrics to recite over them. His oldest sister Carmin had a small Karaoke machine that he would borrow to record his songs.

Baseer's lyrical content surrounded the social ills and the poverty that he understood at his age. Catherine had an older brother named Gerald Anderson who lived down in Glen Burnie, Maryland. He was the lead guitar player in a Blues/Jazz band known as "Black Soul". He and his wife Mary never had children because she was barren. They lived in a two-bedroom apartment so the guest bedroom was made into a pre recording studio. He had Mackie mixing boards, Yamaha Keyboards, Tascam digital 8-track recorders, Boss drum machines, lead guitars, bass guitars, Peavey amplifiers and studio standard cassette tape recorders. During that era, that was an aspiring musician's dream. During the winter holidays, Gerald always visited the Watson family in the Bronx for a few days. He would always take his lead guitar and his amplifier. Whenever he was in town, Baseer could always stay up late and listen to his uncle sing and play the guitar. Gerald was illiterate but he was a professional guitarist. He was self-taught as a teenager and he never learned to read music. He played everything by ear. When he noticed Baseer's love for music at such a young age, he began to encourage him to continue writing songs and he promised that he would always support what he did. He saw traits of himself in Baseer and wanted to see his own personal dreams come true through him. He knew that he was up in age and that the chances of him ever becoming famous for his work were very slim. The music industry was more acceptable to the younger generation. In 1990, when Baseer was 12 years old, Catherine bought him his very first piece of musical equipment for Christmas. It was a Yamaha Keyboard. He continually practiced with it and learned to create different melodies.

TK soon developed a similar desire to make hip hop music. Baseer would often call his Uncle Gerald and complain that he felt extremely limited, having only one keyboard. In order to make hip hop music he needed equipment that would enable him to sequence multiple tracks and combine drum patterns with other sounds or instruments. That following Christmas, Gerald surprised Baseer with a Porta-02 Tascam 4-track recorder as a gift. He practiced day and night until he mastered the art of creating drum patterns and sequencing tracks. All of this, he did while maintaining a "B" average in school. Baseer used to earn money from his mother by doing chores in the apartment. He would earn extra money from their landlord by volunteering to sweep and mop the staircases on both sides of the building, and cleaning up trash from the courtyard in front of the building. He saved his money until he was able to purchase other equipment that he saw in a show window on Fordham Road. He bought a microphone, a mic stand, headphones, a drum machine and a digital sampler. By the age of thirteen, Baseer had the necessary equipment to produce his own songs and pre-record his vocals in the privacy of his bedroom. That's when he and TK decided to form a rap group called "The Terrible Two". Kevin was always around but he wasn't interested in making music. He found more pleasure in being mischievous. He skipped school, smoked cigarettes, and he loved to shoplift. He also liked to hop over subway turnstiles without paying his fare. Whenever Kevin was around, Baseer would often engage in devilishment as well. Kevin liked to make fun of TK for being so obedient, and the two really didn't get along. They always ended up in the presence of one another because they both hung around Baseer. Eventually, they learned to ignore their differences.

In 1992, Morris Avenue became more dangerous than usual. More robberies were occurring, more gunshots were being heard and the sidewalks were more often stained with trails of blood. In September of that year, a 22-year old Puerto Rican man's body was discovered in the basement of the Watson Family's building. Catherine decided that their neighborhood wasn't safe enough to raise her children in. She began saving her money until the summer of 1993. That's when she was finally able to move her family to a 3-bedroom apartment in Harlem on 114th Street between 8th Avenue and Adam Clayton Powell Blvd. Life in Harlem was a big change for Baseer because TK and Kevin weren't around as much. Whenever he got bored he would walk up and down 7th Avenue and listen to his walkman/cassette player. Even though his passion was for making Hip Hop music, he preferred listening to soul and R&B songs. His favorite cassette tape was "The Very Best of Sade". He would listen to her songs for hours and analyze her song structure. In that era, hip hop productions were far simpler than her complex style of music – thus teaching Baseer to be more musical. Being that TK was hardly ever around, Baseer began recording solo compositions but he would always give recognition to his other half (TK). By then, his lyrical content consisted of a more political commentary.

In January of 1994, Baseer became involved with a girl from his school named Darlene. She lived in St. Nicholas Projects. In order to walk to St. Nicholas Projects, Baseer had to pass by "Allah Youth Center in Mecca" located on 126th Street and Adam Clayton Powell Blvd (7th Avenue). Every time he walked pass that building he noticed groups of sharply-dressed black men standing under the awning of the building. Their vernacular always sounded impressive and their dialogue was always about God, the poor social condition of the black man in New York City, and the desire to properly educate the black youth. Baseer soon learned that these men were members of an organization known as "The Five Percenters" or "The Nation of Gods and Earths." He then started to attend their academy and became an active member in their movement.

The founder of the Nation of Gods and Earths was a former member of the Nation of Islam, named Clarence 13x Smith. Their cause was to teach all black families what they considered to be the proper knowledge about their history, the cause of their poor conditions, the misconceptions that they've been taught to believe during slavery, self purification, and the upliftment of the black race throughout the world. Their doctrine contained certain ideologies that would seem extreme and radical to some people. For instance: their referral to all Caucasian people as "devils" and their belief that every Blackman is "God" in essence. To Baseer, these teachings never seemed very far fetched. They actually sounded plausible after he learned different sciences and history to substantiate these theories. He then began to incorporate those very same teachings into his music. On weekends he would visit his friends in the Bronx. Eventually he persuaded TK and Kevin to adopt the same teachings. TK began calling himself "KMAR" and Kevin began calling himself "Powerful". That same year, Powerful decided to join the rap group and they changed their name to "The Terrible Three". For their songs, Baseer liked to sample melodies from Catherine's old soul, gospel and Jazz albums. She had a huge collection. Baseer preferred using sad and somber melodies because they made it easy for him to lyrically express his contempt for the social condition of Blacks in America. Some of their songs would promote violence but there was an evident revolutionary undertone even in those songs.

Baseer's personal educator at Allah Youth Center in Mecca was a man named Amar Allah. He was permanently paralyzed from the waist-down as a result of his participation in the Attica Prison Riot in the 1970's. He became like a father figure to Baseer. He was very supportive of his musical talent and he always reminded Baseer that he would be great someday. He helped Baseer with his school work and even sent him home with a belly full of food everyday. Catherine noticed the positive change and mental growth in Baseer, so she approved of him attending the youth academy as much as he chose to. Elders in the Youth Center were referred to as the "older Gods." They would go to the wholesale district in mid-town Manhattan and purchase balloons at wholesale. The price was $15.00 for 1000 balloons. On weekends, the young Gods would go down to 110th Street and sell these balloons to local families and tourists in Central Park for $1 each. Catherine appreciated what the older Gods were doing because they kept Baseer out of the streets, and they also taught him legitimate ways of getting money before he was of the legal age to work a job. On weekends he always brought at least $125 home. Some of his money he gave to his mother to assist with her bills. The rest of his money was used to purchase musical equipment from a store called Beat Street, located in Downtown Brooklyn. There he bought another keyboard, 2 automatic-drive turntables, and a DJ mixer.

By the summer of 1995, Baseer had become somewhat of a professional at composing Hip-Hop instrumentals. His ability to express his emotions and life experiences in rhyme-form exceeded most young artists his age. Majority of the songs that he recorded were solo compositions. He was making a name for himself, musically, in the streets of Harlem and the Bronx. He accumulated extra money by selling his unwanted beats to other aspiring artists in his school, William H Taft High School in the Bronx. In the final months of that year, two events occurred almost simultaneously and the effects were psychologically damaging. The lesser of the two was when his girlfriend Darlene was caught cheating with a Puerto Rican kid named Raphael. The second tragedy was the unexpected death of Amar Allah. Baseer then took a break from making music and less frequently visited the youth center on 126th Street. Instead, he resorted to hanging out in the Bronx with his old friend Powerful and getting into trouble. He began drinking alcohol and smoking marijuana everyday. He and Powerful would stay out all night getting high and they would often skip school. TK, on the contrary, remained focused on school and the principles that he had learned from the youth center. He also began buying musical equipment of his own.

Baseer's father, James, finally developed the strength to overcome his drug addiction and started working as an electrician for the union. He was now living with his uncle Isaiah in the Pink Houses Community in East New York. Catherine's best friend, Janice, saw James one day on Jerome Avenue in the Bronx getting off of the #4 train. She noticed how good he looked and the obviousness of his recovery. Janice always liked James and she believed that Catherine was still in love with him because she often spoke about him over the telephone. That's when Janice told James that if he wanted to find Catherine, he should go down to Harlem on 114th Street and 7th Avenue. She never gave him the number of the building that she was living in, but that was all of the information that he needed. A few days later, James went to 114th Street and coincidentally arrived on the block while Catherine was parallel parking her car after a busy day at work. When he approached her car she immediately noticed how clean and sober he looked so she granted him the respect of listening to what he had to say. He apologized for his abusive past and admitted that she was always right about him not pulling his weight as the man of the house. Then he went further to explain how difficult his recovery was and how happy he was to finally be clean for an impressive two years. Deeply within, Catherine was lonely and she longed for the marriage that she once had before the abuse ever started. When James explained that he was living with his uncle and working for the Union, she asked him if he wanted to move into her home. The initial agreement was that he was only allowed back to help provide for their children; not to reconstruct their marriage. Naturally the couple decided to reconcile as a family after a short while. Still legally divorced, they were a happy pair once more.

Baseer was the only one in the Watson family to hold a grudge against James. That was because of his attachment to Amar and the other elders from the youth center who criticized James after learning of his failings. Baseer continued to hang out in the Bronx with Powerful and he stayed out all night like his father used to. James found it hard to control Baseer because he was heedless to his father's instructions. He would argue that he had missed his opportunity at fatherhood when he was using drugs. James' guilt and empathy combined always left him lost for words when those types of comments were made. That type of reaction caused Baseer to feel even more justified in his insubordination. Catherine had a sincere love for her only son and he always gave her the utmost respect.

Baseer graduated from high school with a borderline grade average. That following September, James' father Julius Watson became very sick from cirrhosis of the liver. He was an alcoholic for many years. He died only 2 months after learning that he had this disease. When Baseer's grandfather decided to write out his will, he considered the fact that all of his other children (besides James) were well-established and financially secure. That's when he decided to leave his home and his property to his youngest son, James. His home was a 4-bedroom brick house located in a suburban neighborhood in Fayetteville, North Carolina. It was always Catherine's dream to move away from New York City. In February, after receiving her income tax returns, Catherine and her family migrated to Fayetteville. Her two oldest daughters, Carmin and Lashawn, chose to remain in New York with their boyfriends. Baseer and Alana moved to the south with their parents. Alana had two years remaining in high school so she transferred and completed high school in Fayetteville. Baseer started working part-time as a stocker at the PX on Fort Bragg's military base in Fayetteville. In his leisure time, he would smoke weed, write songs and make beats. After a short while, Baseer began to feel like the lifestyle in Fayetteville was too slow for him. The money earned from the PX was never enough and there was very little demand for hip hop music production.

After only 4 months of working at The PX, Baseer decided to resort to robbing local drug dealers for jewelry, cash and product. This seemed promising until he was arrested on counts of assault and battery and possession of a firearm. He was sentenced to two years in the North Carolina Department of Corrections. While incarcerated, Baseer had many altercations with the administration after they learned of his affiliation with The Nation of Gods and Earths. He was labeled as a security threat and was frequently harassed. Most of the high-ranked officers were members of the Masonic order and the teachings of The Nations of Gods and Earths exposed their secret practices. Baseer avoided those officers as much as possible. He occupied his time by writing songs and studying books on conspiracy theories, Black History, science and astronomy. He also learned brick masonry and earned a certificate which stated that he was "now a certified brick mason". In NCDC, Baseer had a number of students in which he taught the lessons that he learned at the youth center in Harlem. His method of teaching was almost identical to that of his former enlightener, Amar Allah.

After being released from prison, Baseer was placed on intense parole under the supervision of a 33 year old black man named Hugh Garrison. Mr. Garrison was also a mason and had learned of Baseer's involvement with The Nation of Gods and Earths, after reviewing Baseer's institutional records. His parole conditions were that he was required to have a job, refrain from using drugs, report weekly and pay a $75 supervision fee monthly. Upon Baseer's release, James had it arranged for Baseer to be employed as a laborer for his childhood friend, Gillespie. Gillespie was the foreman of a brick masonry company. Baseer lived with his parents until he finally saved up enough money to rent a 2-bedroom apartment in a complex called Cambridge Arms. During that same time, Baseer became involved with a beautiful female named Nicole. She attended Fayetteville State University and she was majoring in Accounting. She was a special kind of woman. She came from a very poor family in Hamlet, North Carolina. She reminded Baseer very much of his mother, Catherine. She was deeply in love with Baseer; so much to the point where she referred to him as "God". She willingly adopted his belief system and accepted the title as his "earth". The male Five Percenters call their women "earths" for a number of reasons. One of the most popular reasons is because the Planet Earth is the only planet in our solar system that's capable of reproducing human life. They also teach that, since the Earth is ¾ covered under water, ¾ of the black woman's body should be covered with clothing whenever she's abroad.

Baseer gave Nicole the nickname "Zanasia". She respectfully submitted to Baseer and was willing to do whatever it took to satisfy him. She was a perfect homebody and she preferred the life of a housewife. Baseer, on the other hand, was still running the streets and dealing with lots of other women. He always respected Zanasia enough to prevent her from finding out about his other women. After two years, Baseer began doing more things to jeopardize their relationship. He was making a decent amount of money in the streets but he would spend it recklessly. Instead of budgeting like a true family man, his money was spent on jewelry, clothes, sneakers, clubs, weed and other women. He had totally taken for granted the virtuous woman that he had at home. Some nights he would stay out clubbing until sunrise and leave Zanasia alone in their apartment. She tolerated his disrespect but their relationship slowly began to die after he struck her in the face with the palm of his hand for the first time. It was one of those nights when he had stayed out all night. Zanasia was up all night awaiting his return so that she could confront him about her suspicions of him cheating. When he entered the apartment at 6:00 the next morning, he was drunk. Zanasia began to question him immediately. In his drunken stupor, he decided to use aggression and disrespectful words as a defensive tactic because he knew that he was indeed guilty. His threatening manner didn't succeed at silencing her. After she continued to question him he slapped her and she fell to the floor. Then she ran into their bedroom to cry. The realization of his mistake caused Baseer to sober up immediately. Then he followed her into the room to apologize and beg for her forgiveness. She forgave him and decided to stay with him but over time the disrespect and the abuse continued.

The domestic violence was never as intense as that of Baseer's mother Catherine from James but was always enough to remind Baseer of what he witnessed as a child. After each incident with Zanasia, Baseer would go into the bathroom and stare at himself in the mirror while hearing her cries through the wall. He would silently say to himself, "I'm behaving just like my father, what's wrong with me?" He would notice how much he resembled his father and how his eyes would be bloodshot red just like his father's used to be.

In the following year, Baseer violated his parole conditions and was revocated by Mr. Hugh Garrison. He was sentenced to one year in NCDC. Zanasia wrote Baseer a letter during his first 2 weeks of incarceration. In this letter she explained that she really loved him and how she believed that his abusive temper was fueled by drugs and alcohol. She agreed to stay with him under three conditions: 1) that he promised to never hit her again. 2) That he promised to refrain from using drugs and alcohol and 3) that he promised to marry her upon his release. Prison seemed to give Baseer a clearer outlook on his life. He understood that finding Zanasia was the best thing that ever happened for him, so he promised her the things that she asked for. He spent that entire year doing things that he considered to be constructive like writing music, exercising, studying, and writing letters to Zanasia. Zanasia spent that year working, paying bills, planning and preparing for their wedding. She visited Baseer every weekend and on holidays. She would often visit Catherine and discuss her wedding plans. In the final months of Baseer's incarceration, Zanasia and Catherine began making payments on different things that were needed for the wedding ceremony. When Baseer got released, the entire wedding was paid for. There were 5 lay-a-way payments left on their wedding rings. On the day that Baseer got released, Zanasia gave him $1000 so that he could hustle and get back up on his feet. His only contribution to the wedding was to pay the remaining balance on the wedding rings. The wedding was scheduled for June 12th, just 3 months after Baseer's release date. After only 5 weeks, Baseer started to second guess his decision to marry at what then seemed to be "such a young age". He then decided to go out and enjoy the clubs and the nightlife a few more times before the wedding. Baseer was very popular around the Fayetteville area so when he stepped back on to the club scene he was overwhelmed with attention from the females. Eventually, he found himself dealing with other females, drinking alcohol and smoking marijuana again. Just two weeks prior to their scheduled wedding, Baseer raised his fist to strike Zanasia during an argument. That's when she packed up her belongings, called off the wedding and moved into her mother's home in Hamlet.

Baseer spent the following year trying to make amends with Zanasia. By that point, Zanasia had made up her mind to move forward without him. She didn't even want him back as a friend. Baseer did everything that he could think of to bring her back. Then he started to believe that money and flashy things would attract her attention and convince her that with him was where she needed to be. Almost naturally, he resorted back to robbing local drug dealers. After each robbery he would go to Zanasia's job to flaunt his money. Unfortunately, she was never impressed. His biggest heist was when he seized 1.5 kilos of cocaine from a local dealer named Ace. Baseer sold the cocaine and used the money to open a hip hop clothing store called "Seerious Fashion" located downtown Fayetteville. He then met another beautiful woman named Desire'. She was initially a customer. In appearance, she was far more beautiful than Zanasia. She was the materialistic type, wearing lots of jewelry and fancy clothes. Even though she was exceedingly beautiful, Baseer's heart was still with Zanasia because of their long history together. Shortly into their relationship, Desire moved in with Baseer in Cambridge Arms Apartments. Unknowingly, she was only serving as a substitute until Zanasia returned. For years Baseer had placed his music career on hold, and he lost contact with his childhood friend "Powerful" after learning of him being incarcerated in Clinton Correctional Facility.

CHAPTER ONE

(Ring, Ring, Ring)

"Baby please answer that loud ass phone!" yells Desire.

Baseer picks up the telephone with a rude greeting, "Talk".

"Peace, I'm trying to get in contact with Baseer".

"This is Baseer. Who's speaking?"

"C'mon, you don't recognize your own brother's voice?"

"I don't have a brother, who the fuck is this?"

"I'll give you one hint; I make up one third of the terrible three."

".... Powerful?"

"Yea nigga- what up?"

"Ohhh Shiit! Peace God, where have you been at my nigga?"

"It's a long story"

"Yeah real long, it's been almost six years."

"Yeah I just came home from doin' five joints up north."

"That's wild; I just did three joints myself."

"For what?'

"Gun possession, how did you get my math anyway?"

"I bumped into TK in Vims this afternoon and he gave it to me. I'm surprised that you're still down South."

"Yeah I'm still down this bitch, where are you calling me from?"

"I'm on East 23rd and Newkirk right now, walking to the corner store on Ditmas to get some dutches. I just copped some sour diesel."

"Oh yeah? What's on Flatbush?"

"My bitch stays over here; I've got my own pad uptown in Foster."

"Word? I've got a little kingdom down here with my shorty. . Her name's Desi."

"She's from out there?"

"No she's from Allentown, PA"

"How many seeds?"

"Zero"

"Damn Kid you must be shootin' blanks down there."

"I don't know what the fuck's going on; it might be the sour deez."

"I've got two sons, one is three years old and the other one just turned two."

"Say word, I thought you just did five joints."

"I did, I was locked up when I got my wife pregnant."

"Oh you're married Dunn?"

"Honestly I did it for the conjugal visits. I hope you don't mind but I named my oldest son Baseer, after you."

"My nigga"

"But anyway, when are you coming back up top?"

"Actually, I'll be there Monday morning, but I'll be in and out. I'm just coming to cop some sneakers."

"What?! North Carolina doesn't have a Dr. Jay's?"

"Yeah stupid, I have a store down here called Seerious Fashion. I get my Jordans from the Africans on 27th and Broadway plus I've gotta pick up some gear from Canal Street. By Monday night, I need to be back on I-95 because my store opens from Tuesday through Saturday."

"I know you're killin' em down there."

"Yeah Homie, the flip is crazy. How is money in Harlem right now?"

"Everything is slow motion because of this parole bullshit. My PO made me find a job so I'm working at Pathmark. But I'm still getting my hands dirty in the streets. I can't complain." Interrupting, Baseer then says

"Ayo Power, I hate to chop your build but is this your cell phone number?" Power replies, "Indeed so." Then Baseer says, "I'm gonna have to hit you back later because I have to handle something." That's when the conversation ended and the call disconnected.

When Baseer hung up the phone, Desire was in the kitchen washing the dishes. Baseer took a quick shower and got dressed. He put on a pair of stone-washed Azzure jeans, a white T-shirt, a pair of coffee-brown suede construction Timberlands and a coffee-brown NY Yankees fitted cap. As he was getting dressed, Desire entered the bedroom. She then asked "Who was that on the telephone?" and a brief conversation followed.

"That was my nigga Powerful."

"Who?"

"You don't know him; we grew up together in the Bronx. Do you remember when I told you about me being in a rap group called The Terrible Three? Well that was me, TK and him."

"What's he talking about?"

"C'mon boo you're blowing my high with all the questions. Look, I need to go and gas up the truck plus get my oil changed. Do you need anything while I'm out?"

"Baseer, why don't I just ride with you?"

"Cool, I have to go by my store to do an inventory count – you can help me."

"Never mind baby, I'll chill."

"Yeah, chill, I won't be long."

Baseer spent the remainder of the day getting prepared for his trip. He was able to make love to Desire and spend four hours of quality time with her before pulling out at 7:30 that evening. He was driving a navy blue Ford Expedition with factory rims and a factory paint job. He left all of his jewelry at home with Desire and the only things that he brought along with him were his money, his gun, and his book of CDs. His pistol was an all black .45 ruger which he kept stashed under the hood of his truck. He rolled himself two dutch master cigars with sour diesel, only enough to last him until he arrived in New York where he could buy more. Shortly after Baseer got on I-95 to begin his trip, he felt his Nextel flip phone vibrating in his pocket. When he looked at the screen, Powerful's name appeared so he answered it.

"Power, what's good?"

"Damn son, turn your music down."

"Hold fast. – yeah whattup?"

"What time are you leaving God?"

"Oh I'm on I-95 right now; I just pulled out so I should be there around 8:00 in the morning."

"That's what's up; I'll meet you on 27th and Broadway around 8:30." "Aiight Peace."

"Peace."

Baseer then turns the music back up and listens to "Hold On" by Trick Daddy on repeat until his phone vibrates again. This time the screen read "my baby," so he answered. "Desi-baby, what's good?"

"Hey Boo, how's the traffic?"

"Not too bad."

"I'm almost in Baltimore, about to grab some food from the Travel Plaza."

"And be careful."

"I will."

"You're clean right?"

"I brought my hammer but it's invisible to the cops if I get pulled over. And I'm smoking this last blunt of sour diesel, it's almost gone."

"Okay, goodnight, kiss kiss."

"Kisses"

Then Baseer turned up the music and skipped through the CD until he found "Feel it In the Air" by Beanie Siegel.

After leaving the Travel Plaza in Maryland, Baseer drove non stop and arrived in Manhattan at 8:15 Monday morning. He parked his truck and walked to the Sbarros restaurant on 28th Street and Broadway to meet with Powerful. Powerful looked a lot different than he looked when Baseer last saw him. Instead of a low ceasar, he now had dread locks that hung down to his back. Together, they walked to the warehouse on 27th Street to meet with his African connects. It took Baseer one hour to buy everything that he needed. He no longer needed to go to Canal Street because he ended up overspending on Broadway. Afterwards, the two drove uptown to Harlem to visit "Allah Youth Center in Mecca." This was where they were educated at during their early teenage years. They parked the truck on Adam Clayton Powell Blvd., directly in front of the center. Powerful walked to St. Nicholas projects to find some weed to smoke, while Baseer went inside of the Youth Center for a brief visit.

When Baseer walks into the center a bell sounds and calls attention to his direction. Then he began greeting everyone in sight. "Peace C-Allah, Peace Najee, Peace Prince" "Peace Baseer, how's the God?" "Oh I'm gaining and maintaining," Baseer responded. C-Allah then asked him "how is your wisdom doing?" "Oh she's fine. I'll bring her with me when I come to the Show-n-Prove in June" replied Baseer. "That's peace Gee; do you need any of this month's power papers?" "Yeah, I need 200 of them." "Just give me knowledge add two ($100)" "nice lookin', ayo C-Allah, I'm about to say Peace because I have to drop the God off and jump back on 95." "Alright Blackman, travel in harmony." "Peace to the gods" said Baseer while exiting the building. Powerful was waiting in the truck when Baseer went outside.

"Damn God you took long enough." "You know how old man C-Allah can get. If I would've stayed any longer, he would've sold me the whole school." "Hah, you're crazy. Let's find a spot where we can grub and discuss business" "Alright, we can go to the Juice Bar on 125th Street." Baseer then drove to the Uptown Juice Bar and parked his Expedition in an empty parking spot in the front of the building as they smoked the last end of their blunt. Powerful put $1 in the parking meter and they proceeded into the restaurant. The Uptown Juice Bar was a vegetarian restaurant ran by a Caribbean family. Most of their customers were members of The Nation of Islam, The Rastafarian Community, or The Nation of Gods and Earths. The walls were decorated with paintings of historical black innovators such as Malcolm X, Martin Luther King, Jr., and Marcus Garvey. The cashier was a very beautiful Caribbean woman wearing a white head wrap. She spoke with a foreign accent.

"Good afternoon, what will you two gentlemen be having today?" "Give me 4 slices of spinach and mushroom pizza with white marinara sauce, and I'll have a Nantucket Nectar to drink" said Baseer. "And you sir?" asked the cashier after placing her eyes on Powerful. Then he replied, "I'll have the same order." "That will be $9 for each of you." "Here's a dub, keep the change," said Powerful as he handed her a $20 bill. The two of them spotted a table in the back of the lobby and seated themselves. After being seated, they began stuffing their faces. In the middle of his meal, Powerful looked over at Baseer and asked "so, when can we do a juxe down south, I know that you are down to put in this work with me like we used to get it back in the day." Baseer responded "My nigga, the last juxe that I pulled was when I robbed this clown for a brick and a half. That was my Roc-a-Fella start up money. Since then, I've been running my store down south. But I'm still down for a juxe whenever." With a mouth full of pizza, Powerful then mumbled "What are the banks like down there?" Without hesitation, Baseer replied "sweet". "That's peace, you got hammers?" "All night long." "Beautiful, I'll be down there in a few weeks. I can't eat anymore of this shit." "I'm good too, let's bounce." Baseer then reached into his pocket and left a $5 tip before exiting the restaurant.

Baseer and Powerful then drove up West 125th Street and made a left turn on 7th Avenue. Being pressed for time, Baseer asked Powerful "Do you want me to bring you to Foster, because I have to get back on the road?" Powerful answered "No-drop me off at the train in front of Kennedy's Fried Chicken on 116th Street and Adam Clayton. I'm going back to Brooklyn to chill with wifey." Baseer then dropped Powerful off and got back on the interstate. He had a smooth trip back to Fayetteville and the trip took exactly 9 ½ hours. He arrived at his apartment in Cambridge Arms at 3:34 a.m., Tuesday morning. Being exhausted, he left all of his boxes in the truck and headed straight for his bedroom.

"Desi-baby wake up, daddy's home." "I missed you boo, when are you gonna stop taking so many trips? I'll be glad when we can spend more time together. You'd better be ready to fuck my brains out because I've been thumpin all night waiting for your black ass – now come and get this pussy." Baseer slips out of his clothes and the two of them began to have intercourse. Desire considered the fact that he was probably tired so she decided to ride on top of him until they both climaxed, almost simultaneously. Baseer rolled over on his stomach and Desire massaged his back and his shoulders until he fell asleep.

Desire was a beautiful Puerto Rican girl from Allentown, Pennsylvania. She was 22 years old and she spoke English as well as Spanish fluently. Baseer woke up several hours later to Desire preparing breakfast in the kitchen, wearing nothing but one of Baseer's black t-shirts bearing the Universal Flag of Islam on the front. She looked over at him in an expecting manner and said "Good Morning boo, that's your plate already fixed. Your cherry Limeade is in the freezer." Baseer said "Thank you baby, you're too good to me." "Nothing's too good for my man." "Don't flatter me. I was thinking about what you said last night about me taking so many trips. I'm planning on doing this job in a few weeks. If it pulls through, then I won't have to work so much and take as many trips without you. We can take a vacation and the whole nine". "What type of job?" "The type that's gonna pay me enough to shut you up from crying so much." "Don't be funny. What time are you opening the store this morning?" "As soon as I take a shower because I have to unpack these boxes and put everything out on display. Tell your girls at work that I have some new bags too." Then Baseer pulled out a wad of money. "Take this $250 and buy some groceries today. I'll probably be back home around 3:30 because Tuesdays are usually slow."

After eating his breakfast, Baseer gets dressed and drives downtown Fayetteville to open his store. When he got there he keyed in his security code to his alarm (1-4-2-1). He spent most of the morning unpacking boxes and stocking. That entire day, his thoughts were about the Bank of America located in a small town nearby called Hamlet. Money was slow that afternoon and also through the duration of that week. Baseer and Powerful conversed everyday over the phone for the next three weeks. By then, they were both highly enthusiastic about their plan and were more than ready to pull off the heist- just like old times. Baseer decided to take Desire on a vacation to Jamaica if everything went as planned. He also wanted to buy more modern studio equipment so that he and Powerful could resume making music. Powerful decided to go to Fayetteville on Thursday after he reported to his parole officer just to case out the bank.

On Wednesday night, Baseer was watching "Scarface" on his flat screen television when his cellular phone rang. After the third ring he answered it. "Peace" "Peace, it's Powerful. I'm leaving New York in about 20 minutes. I'm at Port Authority waiting on my bus." "Alright, what time are you scheduled to arrive at the Greyhound terminal here in Fayetteville?" "My ticket says 10:00 am., so be there to pick me up around 10:20 or 10:30." "Alright Gee!" "One" When Baseer hangs up the telephone, he tells Desire to clean up the guest bedroom and change the sheets on the bed. After she does so, the two of them fall asleep. Powerful's bus ride was approximately ten hours long and he arrived in Fayetteville at 10:27 am. Baseer was already waiting in the Greyhound station's parking lot in Desire's silver Lincoln LS. Baseer noticed Powerful looking around when he stepped off of the bus so he honked his horn, let down his window and yelled "Over here God, C'Mon." Powerful then hurried over to the car after noticing the cloud of smoke that was released when Baseer let his window down.

"Peace, I didn't recognize you in this car." "I know, this is my shorty's shit." "Where's the weed at dunn?" "All that's left is that clip in the ashtray, you can smoke that. I'm on the way to the trees spot right now." Baseer drives for 2 miles and makes a right turn into the projects known as Mount Sinai Apartments on Murchinson Road (The Murk). After he parked, a young light skinned kid with dreadlocks, named Bullet, leaned into the driver's side window and said "Baseer, what's good my G?" Baseer replied "You, sometimes me. What's on deck?" "All I have is this fruity shit called Mango Pina." "Give me a gram of that shit, I smoked some yesterday." "I've gotta get $30 for a gram." "So here, get it." "My bad New York, as a matter of fact here's about 2 grams. I should have some more sour later on today." "Alright Bullet, I'm ghost." "One." Baseer then backs out of his parking space, turns the music up and makes a left turn onto Murchinson Road.

"Powerful, roll this shit up fam. There's a box of dutches in the glove compartment" said Baseer as he passed

Powerful the small bag of Mango Pina. In less than 2 minutes, Powerful was wrapping the leaf and putting the finishing touches on the blunt. Then he asked Baseer, "So where is this bank at?" "I'm about to show you right now. It's like 20 minutes away, here's my lighter." ". . . Swwwww. This shit is smoking kid, it's so fruity we don't even need air freshener – hit this." "swwww. . . (cough cough)". Baseer turned the music back up. The song playing was "All I Know" by Field Mob featuring Cee Lo.

A few seconds after passing the "Welcome to Hamlet" sign, Baseer tapped Powerful on the arm and said "That's the Bank of America joint right there." Powerful exhaled the smoke that he was holding in his lungs and said "Word. That shit does look sweet. Circle around it, where are the cameras at?" "There's one over the entrance door, and I see one on top of that light pole in the parking lot. Those are all the cameras that I see." "You're right kid, this is gonna be easier than I thought. You know tomorrow's Friday, we should just go all out and do this shit in the morning." "That's how you feel?" "Actual fact!" "Well bet that up, it's goin down like a plane crash. Now let's go to the rest and get ready for the next day." "Stop by this Dollar General Store, I'm gonna buy some garbage bags and rubber gloves. We can just rip an old t-shirt to tie over our faces. Do you have paper tags for the whip?" "I have some stolen tags to throw on my Bonneville, that's what we're driving tomorrow. The tags came off of a Bonneville that looked identical to my shit in Laurinburg." "Beautiful."

Baseer sat in the car while Powerful went inside of the Dollar General Store. Then he grabbed his cellular phone from inside of the cup holder and dialed 910-862-7731. "Hello." "Baby, I'm on the way home right now and I've got the God with me. Did you cook anything? Because I can pick up a few pizzas while I'm out and about." "I cooked vegetable lasagna, corn on the cob and I baked some potato wedges with red and green peppers." "alright Desi, well I'll be home in about 1200 seconds." "Okay Baseer, I love you." "I love me too," "Boy you're so crazy." "Nah. . . nine twelve twenty-one (I love you)." Baseer hung up the phone just as Powerful was getting in the car. Baseer drives off and unmutes the radio. (All I know is I done been down this road before. It ain't the first time it won't be the last.

I've gotta slow-down because I'm living too fast.)

When Baseer walked into the apartment, Desire was in the kitchen setting the table. Both guys took off their shoes at the door because the living room floor was white carpet. Baseer announced himself "Baby, I'm home. This is Powerful and Power this is Desi." Powerful extends his hand to shake hers and says "Nice to meet you sis." Desire generously replied, "Likewise. Well Baseer, I'll be in the bedroom. I already fixed your food and your drinks are in the freezer." Desire kisses Baseer on his right cheek and proceeded into the bedroom. Powerful sat down at the kitchen table and said "Ayo Baseer, this is a nice Kingdom." Baseer responded, "Yeah Desi decorated this shit. Look, your room is the second door on the left and you have your own personal bathroom. The Hennessey is in the cabinet over the microwave and the TV remote is on your lamp stand. I'm about to lie down and get my mind right for the next day." "Alright, Peace almighty."

Baseer went into the bedroom and set the alarm on his cell phone for 7:30 the next morning. Desire was in the mood to have sex and so was Baseer, but he felt like it was important for him to conserve all of his energy for the heist the next morning. To prevent Desire from complaining, Baseer performed oral sex on her until she had an orgasm. Then he went into the bathroom to clean his mouth and returned to bed to go to sleep.

At 7:30 am the alarm on Baseer's cellular phone sounded. It was the ringtone for "Juicy" by the Notorious B.I.G. That's when Baseer woke up and went into the guest bedroom to wake up Powerful. Desire didn't have a clue as to what Baseer had planned that morning so she jumped straight into the shower. When Baseer knocked on Powerful's door, he was sitting on the bed and he invited him in. "Ayo Power, get ready for start time." "I was born ready." "Look inside of that Timberland box, there's a .45 ruger with two clips and a box of food. Do what you have to do because I'll be ready to pull out as soon as the Bonneville warms up. I'm going to start the whip right now" Baseer carries a garbage bag, gloves and an old t-shirt to the backseat of his Bonneville and starts the car. Then he goes back inside to get his fully loaded German Luger .380 and places it in the holster on his waist. After telling Desire that he would be back shortly, Baseer and Powerful got in the car and headed to Hamlet. Baseer skipped through 50 Cent's "The Massacre" Cd until he found song #10 and turned the volume up really high. He was driving a silver 1986 box model Bonneville with mirror tints on the windows and factory rims. The song "Ski Mask Way' was his preferred theme music for what he was getting ready to do.

"Baseer, pull over in this hotel parking lot so we can switch the tags." "Alright, go ahead and move fast before somebody comes outside." "I did it, drive!" As the car neared the bank Baseer told Powerful "I'm about to park in this parking lot behind the bank and we can walk over to those apartments across the street. We can watch the bank from that staircase right there. When those five cars leave then I'll be ready to run up in there." "That sounds good to me," agreed Powerful. They both grabbed their gloves and Powerful put the garbage bag in his back pocket. They then ripped the t-shirt into two strips and put them in their coat pockets. Next, they walked to the apartment complex across the street and carefully watched the bank for about seven minutes. That's when Baseer said "Alright, let's tie our masks around our faces and put on our gloves. The fifth car is getting ready to leave right now. Are you ready?" "Are you ready?", Powerful mirrored nervously. "Yeah, lets get it!" said Baseer as the two of them began to jog towards the entrance door of the bank.

Baseer and Powerful entered the bank quietly and were barely even noticed until Powerful was hopping the counter with the garbage bag in his left hand and the .45 Ruger in his right hand. He handed the bag to the teller at the drive thru window and calmly said to her "You know what it is." There were a total of four tellers, all Caucasian women who looked to be over the age of 35. As Powerful held the garbage bag open, the window teller emptied all of the money from her station into the bag. Meanwhile, Baseer told the other three tellers "alright bitches, I need both hands in the air like 11:05. And you, here in front of me, empty your drawer on the counter – Now!" Baseer didn't have a bag so he folded the bottom part of his shirt upward and began to rake stacks of money into his shirt from the countertop with his right arm; while still hold-

ing the .380 in his right hand. By then almost 60 seconds
had passed. Baseer looked over at Powerful and noticed
that his bag looked almost 1/5 full. Then he looked down
at the money in his t-shirt and it appeared to be at least
$10,000 to him. That's when he yelled "This is enough,
Henry let's go!"

The two of them quickly exited the bank with their
guns still drawn, and their masks still covering their faces.
There were no police around so they made it to the Bonneville without any complications. Baseer sped off quickly
and headed back to Fayetteville immediately. As he was
driving, Baseer emptied the money from his shirt into the
bag with the rest of the money. Everything happened so
fast that when they arrived back at the apartment, Desire
was just cooking breakfast. They went straight into the
guest bedroom and emptied the money onto the navy blue
comforter on the bed. They were both very excited, then
Baseer said "Kid this is a lot of gwop! Help me separate
it. Put all of the hundreds over here, fifties right here,
twenties right there, tens here, fives over there , and singles right there." While Baseer was separating the cash,
Powerful went outside to place the original tags back on
the Bonneville. After separating the bills, Baseer equally
divided each pile one bill at a time. "One for you, now one
for me – two for you, now two for me." After the count
was done they both had $17,480 each. Then they took
showers and rested until 6:00 pm. They didn't want to go
anywhere until they watched the 6:00 news to see what
leads the Hamlet Police Department had on the robbery
suspects. The news reporter stated that over $75,000 was
reportedly taken and that the subjects were masked and
currently remained unidentified. That's when Baseer suggested that they went to the mall and did some light shopping, so they went to the Cross Creek Mall that was just
minutes from Cambridge Arms apartments.

Powerful wanted to buy a new pair of boots, so their
first stop in the mall was Foot Locker. Upon their entry,
they were greeted by one of the female employees. "Welcome to Foot Locker, how can I help you guys?" Powerful unattentively answered "we're fine thank you. Ayo
Baseer, look at shorty behind the register – do you know
her?" Baseer replied "No but you can bag her though."

"Go figure" "Just buy something and leave the rest to me." "I'm gonna buy that brown Timberland sweatsuit and those brown construction Tims right there." "Cool, I'll meet you at the register." Powerful then grabs a 3x sweatsuit from the rack and a Timberland boot from the display shelf, and walks to the register. The cashier was a beautiful brown skinned girl with light brown eyes and a million dollar smile. She stood about 5'2" and she was really thick. Powerful placed his sweatsuit on the counter and greeted her with a simple "Hello Miss". In a gentle voice, she replied "Good evening sir – are you ready to check out?" "Yes I want this sweatsuit and I need these boots in a size 10." The cashier then waves down one of the male employees and says to him "Robert, can you go to the back and find a size 10 in these?' "Just a minute", he answered. "Sir, your total will be $344.07. Will this be paid with paper or plastic?", asked the cashier. "Paper" he answered confidently.

Baseer then walks up and says to Powerful "damn Big Time, since you're ballin like that why don't you buy me a pair?" Powerful asked, "Do you really want a pair?" "Yeah my nigga." "What size?" "Size 10". "I'm sorry Miss but could you get my dog the same shoe in the same size?" Then she answered him, "No problem, dang since you're in the giving mood you might as well buy me a pair too." "That's funny Ma" replied Powerful just before he pulled out a wad of money that appeared to be well over $20,000. The cashier stared down at his cash with a look on her face like she had to vomit. Noticing, Baseer broke her attention by saying to Powerful "hold on, I never paid you back for the $500 that you gave me yesterday. I'll pay for my own boots." Baseer pulls out his wad of cash. Powerful's money was neatly folded in layers. Baseer was very disorganized, dropping a few hundred dollar bills on the floor when he pulled his bankroll from his pocket. Powerful, playing the big brother role, says "Damn Bro, didn't I tell you to be more neat with your money." Baseer smiled and said "Yeah, my bad. Hey Miss do you have a rubber band?" "Sure your total is $147.73", she answered as she dug into a cup on the counter to find a rubber band for Baseer. Baseer hands the cashier a crispy hundred dollar bill and a fifty dollar bill and tells her "you can give my homey the change." Baseer exits the shoe store with his bag while Powerful falls back to get more acquainted with the cashier.

"So what's your name beautiful?" "Myra", "Powerful and Myra, that's got a ring to it." Myra smiled and then said "Nice to meet you Powerful. You're not from around here are you?" "No, I'm from the Bronx, New York. I'm in town visiting my nigga but I'll be leaving on the next day." "That's too bad because tomorrow is my day off and I'll have to spend the evening all alone." "What time do you knock off tonight?" "I leave here at 9:00" "Do you drive?" "Of course I do." "Well I'll be in Cambridge Arms apartments tonight if you want to drop through." "Should I?" "Of course you should. Take my number." "Here save it into my phone. I know where Cambridge is so I'll call you around 10:30." "That's what's up." "Alright, I guess I'll see you later."

Powerful then goes looking for Baseer and finds him in the Golden Calf jewelry store. The clerk was a young Arab man named Ali. He remembered Baseer from the few times that he came to purchase jewelry for Desire before. When Powerful walked up, Baseer was asking Ali "Poppy, how much for this rope right here?" Ali said "That rope alone is $800." Most customers would try to convince Ali to reduce the price, but without hesitation Baseer said, "I want that. Plus I need a charm, preferably a religious piece." Then he looked over to Powerful and asked "Yo, which charm should I get?' Powerful looked at the selection and said "I like that Angel right there with the crushed diamonds on her wings." Baseer agreed, "I like it too. Give me that Angel too." Ali then tapped a few buttons on his calculator and said "Alright, your total is $1850." When Baseer pulled out his wad of money, the jeweler asked "damn homeboy, what did you do rob a bank?" Then with a smirk, Baseer replied, "Hell no, I'm a rapper. Me and my partner here just signed a record deal." When Baseer gave Ali the cash, he told him, "Keep your bag, I'm putting my shit on right now". As they were walking out of the jewelry store, Ali yells "thank you and be sure to bring me a copy of your record!" Baseer looks back at him with a smirk and says "sure thing".

As they were leaving the mall, Powerful couldn't restrain himself from laughing. "Ayo Baseer, you're crazy son. That Arab nigga really thinks you're a rapper. And one more thing. . . " "What's that?" "Why the hell did you call me Henry in the bank earlier?" "That was to throw the tellers off, but it was also a joke. Your robbery outfit made you look like crack head Henry that used to sleep on your roof on Sheridan Avenue." "Oh that's fucked up gee, he had lupus – I can't believe you still remember that nigga." "How could I forget? That old bastard gave me nightmares until I was 14 years old." "God we need more trees before we go back to the apartment, I want to get nice before shorty comes through." "Word, I'm about to swing by Bullet's crib, he was supposed to have some sour deez for me." Baseer drove to Mount Sinai apartments where he and Powerful equally split the cost of 7 grams of sour diesel weed from Bullet. Baseer was so high when he arrived back at his apartment that he went directly into the bedroom and fell asleep alongside Desire. Powerful chilled out on the couch in the living room and watched the movie "American Me" while he waited on Myra's call.

CHAPTER TWO

Powerful passed out on the couch as he was waiting for Myra to call. At 10:23 he was awakened by his cell phone's ring tone "Tear the Pussy Up" by Young Jeezy. When he looked at his screen he noticed that the area code was "910", so he knew that it was Myra calling. Then he pressed "send" and answered the call in a deep and intoxicated voice –"Hello" "Hello Powerful?" "Yeah" "This is Myra, I'm about two minutes from Cambridge right now. Which apartment are you in?" "Drive all the way to the back and I'm in the last building on the right, Apartment 4F." Powerful put his boots back on, walked outside and asked "Where are you now?" "I just turned into Cambridge." "I think I see you, I'm standing on the sidewalk" said Powerful as he waved his right hand in the air. She replied "alright, I see you too." They both hung up their phones and Myra parked her red and silver Avalanche Truck in an empty parking space in front of Baseer's apartment.

After noticing that Myra was hesitant to get out of the truck, Powerful opened the passenger's side door and sat in the passenger seat. The interior of her truck looked like it had just been vacuumed and it smelled like Pineapple air freshener. She was listening to "Come Over" by Aaliyah; and she was wearing a pink and white nylon Baby Phat outfit, with some all white Nike Air Force Ones. Her hair was in a doobie-wrap style. In his most charming voice, Powerful asked "Hey Sexy, you don't want to step up?". She answered, "Actually, I was hoping that I could show you my place. I know that your homeboy probably doesn't want too much company at this time of night."

Powerful paused for a moment as if he was wondering if Myra was plotting to set him up to get robbed. When he looked into her eyes, he sensed that her intentions were pure so he replied "That's fine, let me go and tell my nigga what's up. I'll be right back." As Powerful walked off, Myra looked at herself in the mirror and put on more lip gloss. Powerful went into the apartment and pulled the Timberland box from under the bed that he was sleeping in. He grabbed the .45 ruger and put it in his right pants-pocket. Then he peeled two hundred dollar bills from his bank roll, stashed the rest of his money in the box and pushed it back under the bed. Just before going back to the truck, he tapped on Baseer's bedroom door and told him that he was going out with Myra. Baseer simply replied, "alright Gee, be careful." Powerful locked the front door of the apartment, got back into Myra's truck and the two of them drove to her house. When they pulled up in Myra's driveway, there was an all white Mitsubishi Galant with 22" Hypnotic rims parked directly in front of them. That car also belonged to Myra. Her home was a three bedroom brick house in a suburban neighborhood approximately 20 minutes away from Cambridge Arms apartments. Upon his entrance, Powerful could not avoid noticing how clean her home was. It almost looked to him as if she had hired a professional home interior decorator to decorate the entire house.

Powerful seated himself on her black leather couch in the living room while she went into the bedroom to put away her purse and slip into her bedroom slippers. Then she yelled out to him "Powerful come back here. You don't have to stay in there." Powerful proceeded down the hallway and into her bedroom where he found her sitting on the edge of the bed, watching the 11:00 news. Myra said "You can kick off your boots and get more comfortable if you want to." As Powerful began to take off his boots, he noticed two magnum condoms sitting on top of the television. Myra surprised him by asking "Do you want a show?" Now confused, Powerful asked "What type of show?" She replied, "I wanna dance for you." "That's fine by me" he nonchalantly replied. Myra walked towards her bathroom, looked back at Powerful and said "Don't come in here, I'm about to change into something that I bought just for you." When she closed the bathroom door, he loosened his belt and raised one foot up on the bed with his back against the headboard. After about three minutes, Myra came out of the bathroom wearing nothing but a green, black and brown camouflage bra and thong set with a pair of brown Timberlands that were identical to the one's that she sold to Powerful earlier that evening. With a devious grin and a model-like spin, she asked "You like?" Powerful instantly got an erection and then he answered "Hell yeah, is all that for me?" She replied "Yeah, I'm your thug-girl tonight."

Myra walked over to the stereo system that was right beside her television and turned on the music. Her song of choice was "Pop That Pussy" by Pastor Troy. Then she grabbed the remote control that controlled the lighting and dimmed the lights. After setting the mood, she commenced to giving Powerful a lap dance. Her entire body shined as if she was covered in baby oil, and she smelled like "Sex on the Beach" body oil. She first sat on his lap and started to grind on him backwards, while looking back at him. Then she turned around and began grinding on him from the front while rubbing his face in adoration. Next, she slowly pushed him back onto the bed, straddled him, placed both of her hands on his chest and began grinding down on him as if she was riding him while he was still fully dressed. Myra got up, unzipped Powerful's jeans and pulled them off. She then started sucking his fully erected penis and stroking it gently with her hand. Powerful was then ready to have sex with Myra so he halted her from performing oral sex and got up to grab the magnum condom from the top of the television. When he got to the television, the condoms had disappeared. That's when he looked back at Myra. She was sitting up on the bed with her legs gapped wide open and a condom sitting between her breasts, smiling from ear to ear. She opened the condom wrapper with her teeth and motioned for Powerful to come to her with her index finger. Powerful took off all of his clothes, put the condom on and made love to Myra for over two hours. They tried almost every position possible and Myra loved every second of it. When they finished, they were both dripping wet from sweating. Myra then fell asleep with her head on Powerful's chest and one arm wrapped around him.

At 7:15, the following morning, Powerful was awakened by the ringing of his cell phone. When he noticed that the caller was Baseer he answered it. "Peace" "Peace God, what's the science?" "Oh everything's peace – I'm at shorty's crib like 20 minutes away" "Alright. I was just making sure that everything was good. What time are you coming back?" "Probably in a few because I need to get back to the city." "Well I'm not opening my store today so I can take you to handle your business. Just call when you're on your way." "No doubt, Peace." "Peace."

When Baseer hung up the phone, Desire had already began taking a shower because she had to be at her job by 8:30 am. She still had no idea about what Baseer and Powerful had done on the previous day. She drove Baseer's Expedition to work and left him the keys to her Silver Lincoln LS. As soon as Desire left, Baseer rolled another Dutch Master Cigar with sour diesel and pulled his money from his stash to recount it. He had approximately $15,500 of the robbery money left. As he began smoking he went into a deep meditation about everything that had transpired on the previous day. Suddenly, he began to feel extremely paranoid about Ali, the jeweler, asking him if he had robbed a bank. The question kept replaying in his brain, in Ali's voice. He then decided that it was wisest for him to leave the Fayetteville area for at least two weeks until the heat cooled down. In a small town like Hamlet, their heist would have been a high profiled case and would've received a lot of media attention. In turn, he called his right hand man named Peru. Peru was one of Baseer's Peruvian friends that he used to hang out with before he moved to Fayetteville. Peru was originally from Harlem. He was living in Clarkston, Ga on the run for a murder that occurred in Ashbury Park, New Jersey – linking to him as the primary suspect. Before Peru moved to Clarkston, Baseer allowed him to hide out in his Fayetteville apartment for approximately four months. That was until he was arrested for driving without a driver's license. Baseer immediately bonded him out of jail the same day because Peru had given the officers at Bookings an alias name, and it would've taken three days for his fingerprints to come back.

After he was released, he packed up all of his clothes and went to Clarkston to live with his cousin named "Stax". Stax was very prominent in the drug business in the Atlanta area. As soon as Peru moved in, Stax gave him two pounds of mid-grade weed and introduced him to some of his own personal clientele so that he could get up on his feet quickly. In a matter of two months, Peru had accumulated a decent amount of money. He then rented a two-bedroom apartment on Memorial College Avenue, directly across from Georgia Perimeter College. He became involved with a girl named Monique who was a registered nurse at Grady Hospital, located in the heart of downtown Atlanta. Her job paid $27 an hour and she had her own apartment in a nearby town called Tucker, where she was originally from. When Peru gave Baseer the okay to stay with him for two weeks, he decided to leave on the following day. He didn't know what time Powerful's bus was departing for New York. Plus he needed time to pack up all of his inventory from his store and carry it to his apartment.

At 12:00 that afternoon, Powerful and Myra came back to Baseer's apartment in Cambridge Arms. This time, Myra didn't hesitate to go inside because she wanted to hang out with Powerful until it was time for him to go to the Greyhound station and depart for NY. His bus left at 5:30 pm. He spent the most part of the afternoon smoking weed and watching movies with Myra. In that small period of time, Myra started to display an attachment to Powerful so he promised to visit her again during the following month. Baseer told Powerful to take his .45 Ruger with him on the bus because he was carrying entirely too much money to be unarmed. Being that Baseer had a busy day scheduled, Myra honorably gave Powerful a ride to the bus station and waited with him until the time of his departure.

Baseer stashed his money in the light fixture in his bathroom, then drove to his store to pack everything. He had to make three trips to and from the apartment because Desire's Lincoln LS was small and had very limited trunk-space. He finished around 7:00 and returned to his apartment. Desire got off from work at 4:30 and went home to prepare dinner for Baseer. Baseer waited until he and Desire were sitting down at the dinner table before he told her that he was going to Atlanta on the next day. She didn't approve of his sudden idea, especially when she found out how long he was planning to stay. She began questioning him about having another female friend in Atlanta. He refused to tell her his actual reason for leaving. Instead, he said that he was going on a business trip. Unconvinced, Desire continued to accuse him and argue vehemently. Baseer excused himself from her presence and locked himself in the bathroom. That's when he unscrewed the light fixture and dislodged his wad of money. He took $2000 out of his bank roll and placed the rest back in the light fixture. He put $1000 in his pocket and exited the bathroom with the other $1000 in his hand. Then he went into the bedroom where he found Desire lying across the bed, finally silent. That's when Baseer said "Baby, here's a $1000 for you to go shopping while I'm gone. Buy yourself a few outfits and be ready to go on a vacation when I get back."

That simple comment seemed to pacify her instantly, as she reached out her hand to receive the money. She asked anxiously, "Where are we going boo?" Baseer answered, "It's gonna be a surprise. And since you're such a fuckin' cry baby, I'll be back in a week. Have you taken any vacation days from your job this year?" "No baby, but I'll have to inform my manager seven days in advance." "All right, well, let him know tomorrow that you'll be needing a full week starting next Monday." "Alright, I will." "I know that you will, you spoiled little bastard," responded Baseer with a smile.

Baseer felt guilty about leaving Desire home alone for an entire week so he spent the remainder of the night making love to her and sharing pillow talk. He also gave her a full body massage for 2 hours until she fell asleep. That night, he explained how he wished that Desire would exhibit more trust and tolerate him having to take care of his business. He also promised to make her breakfast before she left to go to work on the next morning.

When Baseer awoke, it was 6:52 am and Desire was still asleep. She had to be at her job at 8:30. When he looked over at her she was lying on top of the covers, wearing nothing but a Spongebob T-shirt with matching panties. She was looking so delicious that Baseer eased down to the foot of the bed and began to perform oral sex on her while she was still sleeping. At first she seemed to be un-aroused, but after a few moments she was winding her body and moaning in satisfaction. After an early orgasm, she realized that it was getting close to the time for her to get dressed for work. That's when she unwantingly asked Baseer to stop so that she could get dressed.

As Desire got prepared to take a shower, she asked Baseer "Boo are you still gonna make me breakfast?" Then he sarcastically answered "Shit, you already were breakfast.... No, I'm bullshittin. It will be ready when you come out of the shower." Desire took a twenty minute shower and went back into the bedroom to retrieve an outfit from her closet. As she was looking through her wardrobe, she realized that she didn't smell any food cooking. Then she yelled out to Baseer in the kitchen and asked him if her breakfast was ready. When he responded "Yes" she finished dressing and walked into the kitchen. Baseer was sitting at the kitchen table with two bowls in front of him. Desire asked "Baby what's that?", then he replied "Cereal." Desire then looked at Baseer as if she wondered if he was serious. "C'mon baby cereal?" "What do you mean, Fruity Pebbles is the shit. Plus I had the milk in the fridge getting cold for you all night." She smiled then shook her head, just before uttering, "Boy you're lucky that I love your black ass." Baseer winked his left eye at her and said "I know" with a smile. They both ate their cereal, then Desire had to rush off to work. Before leaving, she gave Baseer a long kiss goodbye and told him to be careful in Atlanta.

One hour after Desire left for work, Baseer was dressed and ready to get on the highway. He drove his Expedition and, as usual, he concealed his gun under the hood. While driving, Baseer decided to call Powerful to make sure that he had made it back to New York safely. When Powerful answered his cell phone, he was in Brooklyn – lying beside his wife in bed. The two of them only spoke for about 60 seconds, then they agreed to talk at a later hour that day. Baseer's trip took 5.5 hours. He was sober and drove at the speed limit for the entire trip, so he didn't have any complications from the police. When he arrived in Clarkston, he didn't have the directions to Peru's apartment. So he parked in a Publix grocery store parking lot and dialed Peru's cell phone number into his Nextel flip phone (678-887-3341) "Baseer, what's goody?" "I'm at the Publix on Memorial Drive." "Oh you're not far, just stay right there. Me and Monique will be there in a minute." "What are you driving?" "The new Navi – all black." "Yeah and I'm in my Expo." "Aiight, Out!" "Out"

Baseer went inside of the grocery store and bought two six-packs of Heineken beer. When he returned to his truck, he opened a bottle of beer with his teeth and began drinking it. Suddenly he started hearing bass pounding from a car stereo system nearby. That's when he noticed that the music was coming from a shiny-black Lincoln Navigator at the traffic light. The truck had a left turn signal on, getting ready to turn into the Publix parking lot. Baseer stepped out of his truck to greet Peru who was sitting in the passenger's seat. When Monique parked the navigator, Peru stepped out and greeted Baseer with a pound followed by a hug with one arm. Then Baseer said to him "Yo, I haven't smoked any weed all day. Where's the tree spot?" Peru laughed and replied "C'Mon Ba', you know I sell trees. Just follow us."

Peru's apartment was a five minute drive away. His apartment was decorated in all black – everything from the leather couches in the living room to the bathroom set. He had a movie-theater style projector in his living room and the movie Goodfellas was on the screen when they walked into the apartment. Baseer took his luggage into the guest bedroom. Then he went back into the living room, opened a box of Dutch Master's cigars and removed one cigar from it's plastic wrapper. Next, he licked his cigar and began unraveling the leaf from around it. He asked Peru "Where's the izzy at son?" Peru walked into the kitchen and opened a cabinet door above his refrigerator. Then he pulled out a clear garbage bag containing eight pounds of mid-grade weed. He peeled off a ¼ an ounce and gave it to Baseer to roll up. Peru reached into his cabinet once more and withdrew a second garbage bag with 2.5 pounds of Kush, then he pinched off about two grams and told Baseer, "Mix this with it, this is some different shit." Baseer then rolled two cigars and they smoked individually.

While Baseer and Peru were smoking and listening to music, Monique had to leave and get ready to work at the hospital that night. As soon as she walked out of the apartment, Baseer looked over at Peru and asked "So what can we get into tonight?" Peru calmly replied "Oh God, you already know. We're gonna live that life tonight. I'll probably take you to Prime Time, that's Deion Sanders' club." After Baseer got a nice buzz from the weed, he went into the guest bedroom to choose an outfit to wear because he felt like riding around the city. All of the clothes that he had brought with him were brand new outfits that he put aside for himself when he was packing up his inventory from his store.

Baseer dressed in a blue and gold Evisu outfit. The gold glitter on his shirt accented the gold rope and Angel charm around his neck. So did the gold thread that bordered around his Yankees emblem on his blue and white fitted cap. On his feet were the coffee brown Timberlands that he had purchased at the Cross Creek Mall. When they got into Baseer's Expedition, he flipped through his CD book and inserted the "War Report" CD by Capone-n-Noreaga. When Peru and Baseer hung out as teenagers in Harlem, that entire album was like an anthem to them. Baseer lit up a blunt of Kush and began driving his truck in route to the Lenox Mall.

The guys' original intentions were to go to the mall but the plans changed when Peru received a phone call from one of his weed suppliers. He was a 25-year old Mexican man named Calin. (telephone ringing) Peru then answered his cell phone using the Spanish language: "Que Pasa" (what's up?) "Donde estas" (Where are you?) "Ando en la ciudad" (I'm riding around the city) "Me puedes encontrar en parke de colejio en el Taco Bell en Old National Highway?" (Can you meet me in College Park at the Taco Bell on Old National Highway?)

"Si, puedo estar ahi en 10 minutes?" That's when Baseer asked "who do we have to meet in ten minutes?" Baseer understood Spanish because many of his friends during his childhood were Puerto Ricans and Dominicans. In response to Baseer's question, Peru replied "That was my connect. I don't really know what he wants but he probably needs to build with me about some paper. Anything else, he would've said over the phone."

Baseer turned off of I-85 at the Old National Highway exit. Then they rode over the bridge to their left and turned into a Taco Bell parking lot on their right, one mile later. Calin was there waiting in a cocaine-white Hummer, so Peru stepped out of Baseer's truck and sat in Calin's passenger seat. They began to discuss something that appeared to Baseer to be important. Now feeling like Peru could take a few minutes, Baseer decided to call Desire. When she answered her telephone she said that she was in the Cross Creek Mall shopping with her friend named Dana. The phone call only lasted for a couple of minutes. That's how long it took before he trustfully said "Alright baby, have your fun. I love you." Then Desire, responded "and I love you more." They said their goodbyes and then Baseer called Powerful. When Powerful answered, he was downtown Brooklyn shopping with his girlfriend, "Tiffy". He and Baseer only spoke for a few seconds, then they hung up their phones, only seconds before Peru finally stepped back into Baseer's Expedition with a disturbed look on his face.

CHAPTER THREE

When Peru returned to Baseer's truck, Baseer was dialing his mother's phone number into his cellular phone. When he noticed the expression on Peru's face, he immediately stopped dialing and asked him "What's good G?" Peru remained paused for a few moments, then he uttered "Everything's good. Ayo – fuck Lenox Mall right now, let's go back to my pad for a second. Just follow son in the Hummer".

Calin was driving in the same direction that they had to travel in order to get back on I-85, so they began following him down Old National Highway. When Baseer turned onto the interstate, Peru pressed the horn because Calin had continued driving forward. After about twenty seconds, Peru turned down the music and began to explain what had him in such deep thought. "That was my son Calin back there. I've been coppin' work from dunn for a minute. The nigga just came to me with a mean proposition but I turned him down." Baseer remained silent as if he was waiting for Peru to further expound on the matter. Peru continued, "Calin just offered me twenty grand to murk some rattin ass nigga who just got his brother Raul sent up for 30 joints. He had the bread in the truck with him and everything."

Before Peru could explain any further, Baseer asked "What would make him ask you something like that? I know that you're not down here telling niggas about what you did up in Allah's Paradise" (Ashbury Park). Peru answered, "Hell no, he must recognize a real goomba when he sees one. You know that real bad boys move in silence. But, on some real shit, I was tempted to accept that offer. It's just that stakes are high right now and I can't risk it. Fuck that though, I'm ready to get some drugs in me. Let's just go back to the rest, burn a tree, and get fresh for the club."

Baseer and Peru returned to the apartment ten minutes later. Once inside, Peru poured two glasses of Patron Silver and Baseer rolled 2 blunts of Kush. They sat for about an hour discussing ways to get money together while getting stimulated and listening to "The War Report" by Capone-n-Noreaga. During that same hour, Baseer called Desire but they only spoke for a couple of minutes, because she was eating dinner at the Applebee's restaurant with her girlfriend Dana. Afterwards, Baseer searched through his black Samsonite suitcase to decide on which outfit he should've worn out to the club that night. He decided to wear a brand new pair of gray stone-washed Enyce jeans, and a black wife-beater tank top underneath a white and black Enyce T-shirt. Next, he dug into his bag to retrieve a connoisseur jewelry rag to buff and shine his golden Angel charm on his chain. Just before taking his shower, Baseer rolled another blunt of mid-grade weed mixed with Kush for them to smoke later on that night in the club.

Baseer finished getting dressed before Peru did, so he went outside to remove his pistol from under the hood of his truck and placed it beneath the driver's seat. They were both comfortably intoxicated and they proceeded to the Prime Time nightclub. Before arriving at the club, Baseer stopped at a local convenience store to buy condoms and a box of Gemstar razor blades. Then he drove through a 24-hour drive thru car wash to wash his Expedition. The truck was already clean but he wanted the truck to be dripping wet when he pulled into the club's parking lot. It was 12:30 am when they arrived at the club. Baseer paid $20 to park in the V.I.P. parking lot directly in front of the club's entrance. When parked, Baseer opened the box of razor blades and placed one into his mouth, outside of the upper right side of his gum with the razor edge facing downward. Baseer had been carrying razors in his mouth for many years and he knew how to drink, smoke and talk without cutting himself. Peru did the exact same thing and the both of them went into the club. The metal detectors did not detect their razors.

The club was filled with beautiful women who out-numbered the men five to one. The smell of exotic weed was circulating through the building and the women were dressed like supermodels. Only about twenty percent of the people were dancing and they were all doing the tra-ditional "Pool Palace" dance which originated in Atlanta. There was a local rap artist named "O.J. the Juiceman" performing on stage. Baseer had never heard his music before, but the crowd was reciting the words to his songs and making A's with their fingers like gang signs. Almost every male in the club had gold teeth and big gold chains around their necks. Every couple of minutes, there was at least one of them in Baseer's view throwing stacks of one-dollar bills into the crowd.

When Baseer and Peru walked into the club, Baseer walked directly to the bar and bought four cups of Hen-nessey and Coca-Cola while Peru went to find a vacant table. Two of the drinks were for Peru and the other two were for himself. Baseer was enjoying himself and the la-dies were paying him a lot of attention because he was a new face in the club. Peru's girlfriend Monique was going to be at Peru's apartment when they left the club so their main objective was to find a girl to be Baseer's company for the night. Baseer decided to aim for the sexiest female in the club, in his opinion. That's when he noticed a petite red-boned girl with sandy-red micro braids watching him from a nearby table with two of her girlfriends. He didn't react hastily because it was still early and he didn't want to appear to be desperate. So, he pulled the blunt of Kush from his pocket, lit it with his Zippo lighter and began smoking with Peru.

After Peru took two drags from the blunt, he stood up and told Baseer "I'll be right back, I'm gonna get us some change so we can make it rain on these niggas"; in a tone as if he was holding his breath. Then Peru exhaled his smoke and passed the blunt back to Baseer. Baseer placed the blunt into an aluminum ashtray that was on the table and pulled a wad of money from his pocket. Then he handed two hundred dollar bills to Peru and said

"Fuck it, bust this up for me." Peru then grabbed one of his cups and walked to the bar to get $400 in one dollar bills. Baseer remained seated and continued to observe the scenery.

A few minutes later, the dj played the song "Circles" by Crime Mob. The red-boned girl and her friends stood up as if that was their favorite song, and they began walking towards the dance floor. In order to get to the dance floor, the three of them had to walk by Baseer's table. As they started walking, she allowed her friends to walk a few feet ahead of her because she wanted to give Baseer the opportunity to speak to her. When Baseer saw a full-body view of her, her beauty made it hard for him to refrain from staring. She was wearing an all-white Baby Phat dress with a gold Baby Phat emblem in the bottom-right corner. She also had on a pair of Baby Phat heels with her toes exposed and they were pedicured with white tips. She had a natural beauty that didn't require make-up and she was draped in gold jewelry – rings, bracelets, bangles, and a gold chain bearing a heart shaped locket with the word "love" inscribed in diamonds. As she walked pass Baseer, she looked towards the dance floor because she was bashful. All along, she was certain that Baseer was watching her.

When she got within Baseer's arm reach, he gently grabbed her left hand and pulled her towards his chair. She didn't show any resistance, so Baseer leaned towards her ear and initiated a conversation by asking "Damn, who are you looking so delicious for?" Blushing, she replied "Nobody, this just me." "Oh yeah, well who you is?" Baseer replied, mockingly in a southern accent. Then she laughed and said "My name is Yahnis, what's yours?" "Baseer." "That's cute. I've never heard that name before. You don't talk like you're from around here." "I'm not. I live in North Cak but I'm from the Bronx. I'm out here for a week with my nigga. But anyway, put your number into my phone and we can chop it up later because I saw you getting ready to go and shake your little ass wit your homegirls." Yahnis was surprised by his boldness but she liked it, so she simply said "you're a trip. Give me your phone." Baseer pulled out his cellular phone and said "Just dial your number and press "send". "I'll save it into my phonebook later".

As Yahnis was dialing her number, Peru returned to his seat and placed two stacks of $1 bills on the table in front of Baseer. Then Yahnis told Baseer "You better call me too. I don't usually give my number out." Baseer smirked and asked, sarcastically, "So what, I'm special?" "I guess so." "Word? So what's good later on tonite?" "You already know." "Alright, well go ahead and cut a rug. I'll send you a text when I'm ready to bounce." "Alright Shawty, make sure you do that." Before she turned to walk away, Baseer handed her $100 in singles and said "Go and make it rain on them hoes." Baseer winked his right eye at her and she walked to the dance floor to reunite with her girlfriends. Baseer placed the other stack of money into his pocket. Peru retrieved the blunt from the ashtray, lit it and said to Baseer "Damn Kid, You blend right in. That bitch wants to give you some trim."

When Baseer finished drinking his second cup of Hennessey and coke, he went to the restroom because he felt like his bladder was about to explode. He left Peru sitting at their table. When he walked into the restroom, there were four guys there standing against the wall and selling ecstasy pills. Another man had an opened briefcase on the counter filled with candy, cigarettes, condoms, and cigars for sale. After Baseer used the restroom he walked over to the sink to wash his hands. That's when he noticed that the man with the briefcase was selling chewing gum, so he asked "Ayo money, how much for a five-pack of Big Red?" The man replied "$2". Baseer said "True. I respect your grind G, give me two," then he gave the man a $5 bill. When the man gave Baseer his chewing gum along with his change, one of the other four guys said "Ayo dog, I got them beans for you too." Baseer then looked back, distastefully, at the man and said "What nigga? Do I look like a fuckin crack head to you son? You don't have shit for me." Baseer exited the restroom. As he was leaving, he overheard that same guy telling his partners "man fuck that pussy ass nigga," obviously in reference to him. He pretended not to hear the comment and continued back to the table where he had left Peru.

Peru passed the blunt to Baseer as soon as he sat down but he refused it. Then Peru asked "What's up dunn?" Blatantly upset, Baseer replied "Some fuck ass nigga just tried me in the bathroom. I should go back in there and eat his food." "Tried you how?" "Talking that gangsta shit, but I can tell he aint shaped like that. He said that shit all low. I wanna go back and blow this nigga; give his bitch ass a smiley face." "A smiley face?" "Yeah man, chop 'em from ear to ear." "Oh word? I always gave niggas telephones –from the ear to the mouth." "Whatever homey. I'm about to blast this nigga, are you comin'?" "C'mon dunn, what type of question is that?"

The two of them left their table and walked to the rest-room. As Baseer was walking, he removed the razor blade from his jaw with his tongue and blew it into his right hand. Peru did the exact same thing, simultaneously. When they entered the restroom, the guy that made the comment to Baseer had his back turned and his attention was on a man who was buying ecstasy pills from him. The other three guys seemed as if they didn't realize why Baseer had returned to the restroom because they continued talking and laughing amongst themselves. Baseer calmly walked over to the man with his razor blade cuffed tightly in his right hand between his thumb and his index finger. Then he tapped him on his shoulder twice while saying "Ayo, main man." The guy turned to see who had just tapped him on his shoulder. That's when Baseer raised his hand and chopped him with the razor blade from his right sideburn to the corner of his lip. The spontaneity of it all caused the man to freeze momentarily in a state of shock. The cut didn't look very severe in the beginning. It looked like a paper-thin red line. Then he opened his mouth to yell something. That's when the cut zipped wide open and blood began to pour down the right side of his chin like a waterfall. The razor blade went completely through his skin; so from the outside of his face, the interior of his mouth was visible.

The man then collapsed to the floor in panic. Baseer and Peru both began to stomp and kick the man in his face and upper torso with their boots as he curled up on the floor of one of the bathroom's stalls. Peru then swung his blade down and sliced the man across his forehead. The fight and the sight of blood caused everyone else to evacuate the restroom, including the victim's three friends. Baseer and Peru stopped stomping the man as he seemed to be lying unconscious. There were about two cups worth of blood already on the floor and the man was still leaking. Baseer's white and black Enyce T-shirt was badly stained with blood. That's when Baseer said "Yo God, we've gotta boat before security comes in here." Then they flushed their razor blades down the toilet next to where the man was lying motionless.

Baseer decided to remove his t-shirt and he threw it into the toilet so that the water would destroy all possible fingerprints. He exited the restroom with his gold chain swinging across his black wife-beater tank top which didn't appear bloody because of the dimness in the club. The club's exit door was approximately twelve yards away from the restroom. The security guards didn't seem to be aware of what had just transpired so the two of them made their way through the club without any complications. Baseer spotted Yahnis talking to her girlfriends as he was leaving but she didn't look in his direction. Once they made it outside, they began to walk in double-time because the blood stains on their clothes were more visible under the lights in the parking lot. Baseer then pressed the buttons on his keychain to deactivate the alarm on his truck before they got inside. He drove out of the parking lot slowly as if there was nothing wrong. As he was leaving, he looked back at the club through his rearview mirror to make sure that no one had followed them outside and tried to learn his license tag number.

When Peru recognized that they had escaped safely, he began to talk. "Ayo, Ba, you blew that nigga's head off kid. He was leaking like a muthafucka. Do you think we killed him?" Baseer replied, emotionlessly, "I don't know. If we did, fuck-em, more oxygen for us. Yo, look through my CD book and find a CD that has TK written on it." "What's that, Tragedy Khadafi?" "Hell no, that's my nigga Tramal from BK. I used to rhyme with son back in the day. He stuck with the shit and my nigga's about to blow real soon." "Word? Give me a minute."

While Peru searched through Baseer's cds, Baseer decided to call Desire. Her cell phone rang 4 times before she answered it because she was asleep prior to the call. "Hello," Desire answered in an exhausted voice. Then Baseer asked "Baby are you sleeping?" "No. Not anymore, where are you?" "I'm still in Georgia, just leaving the club. A nigga almost went to jail tonight." "For what?" "We had to mash some young nigga out. He started running his suck muscles and shit, I was drunk so we pounced him out in the bathroom." "You see, that's what the fuck I mean Baseer. You said this was gonna be a business trip and you never said anything about going to the club. Where did you go, to the Magic City strip club or something?" "Baby, breathe easy – you're making a big deal out of nothing. I didn't call to get my ears chewed off, I was just checkin in to let you know that I was alright."

Their conversation didn't last longer than four minutes. As usual, she complained that she was lonely and wished that Baseer would stop taking so many trips without her. Peru inserted TK's demo cd and they listened to it until they arrived back at Peru's apartment in Clarkston. When they went inside, Peru went directly into his bedroom where Monique was lying in wait for him. Baseer went into the guest bedroom to take a hot shower and change into some clean clothes. After taking his shower he placed his bloody clothes into the plastic Publix bags that his six-packs of Heineken came in, then he carried the bags out to the dumpster in the parking lot. When he went back inside, he sent a text message to Yahnis' cellular phone that read "This is Baseer. Something came up and I had to bounce early. HMB when you get this message." Then Baseer attached the charger to his phone and plugged it into the wall. He began watching "Fist of Fury" starring Bruce Lee, as he waited for Yahnis to return his call. After thirty minutes without hearing a response, Baseer set his ringer to silent mode and fell asleep.

*****

CHAPTER FOUR

Powerful woke up on Saturday morning thinking about a gold chain that he had priced in Harlem on the previous day. He was spending the weekend with Tiffy and his kids in Flatbush, Brooklyn. He got dressed earlier than he usually would. He gave Tiffy $1000 to take their sons shopping, then he left her to go Uptown to Harlem to buy his chain. He actually had his eyes on that chain ever since the week before he and Baseer committed their robbery. When Powerful left Tiffy's apartment, his first stop was the bodega on the corner of Flatbush Avenue and Newkirk Avenue. He went there to buy a bag of sour diesel from some Blood members that he knew who always posted up by the payphone outside of the store. Next, he walked to the subway train station on East 17th street to catch the Q-train to 34th Street in Manhattan. There, he would transfer to the B-train and go to 125th Street in Harlem. The Q-train was pulling off as Powerful made his way downstairs, which left him with about 8 minutes that he had to wait for the next train. He walked to the very end of the platform where nobody was standing and rolled a blunt to smoke. There were no police officers in sight so he ripped off a small piece of his blunt and smoked until his train arrived.

Powerful got off of the B-train on the corner of 125th Street and St. Nicholas Avenue. He walked into the KFC restaurant directly across the street from the train station to eat breakfast. Then he walked to the Kings and Queens Jewelry store on 7th Avenue, where he had priced

49

his chain. The charm was a six-inch 14 Karat gold Jesus head wearing a halo of thorns. The thorns were colored in crushed diamonds and the blood emitted from his head was represented by red rubies. As he was on his way to the jewelry store, he noticed a light-skinned man with braids standing in front of Jimmy Jazz wearing a smaller replica of the charm that he was about to buy. That's when he smiled, nefariously, thinking about the attention that he would soon be attracting when wearing his bigger one. He paid $1700 cash for the chain and walked out of the store wearing it tucked underneath his hoodie sweater. He was still carrying Baseer's fully-loaded .45 Ruger. After that, he flagged down a yellow cab that was driving down 7th Avenue and paid the cab driver six dollars to drop him off at the park in front of Foster Projects. That's when he retired to his apartment where he ended up smoking the rest of his blunt and admiring his new chain in the mirror for about 30 minutes.

Two hours later, Myra sent a nude picture of herself to Powerful's cellular phone with a text message attached that read "call me." So, he called her to see what she was doing. She was driving her Mitsubishi Galant on her way to work at Foot Locker. She told Powerful that she was already beginning to miss him and that she was willing to fund his next trip to visit her in Fayetteville, NC. He promised to visit her in 30 days. In the meantime, he was planning to invest the remainder of his robbery money in cocaine from his Dominican connect in Washington Heights. He could pay him $13,000 for 3/4 of a Kilo. He had planned to mix it with 9 ounces of Procaine and sell it as an entire Kilo to his younger cousin named Mario from Baltimore, MD for $23,000. After another week, he could repeat that same cycle and guarantee himself an extra $10,000 weekly without having to scramble in the streets much at all. Mario was even willing to drive up to Harlem every week instead of having Powerful drive himself and risk a parole violation for leaving the state without his Parole officer's consent. Mario was an ex-army kid turned wanna-be hustler who was really gullible and green to the drug business. He was just trying to solidify a name for himself in the streets.

Mario still wasn't losing because he was hustling on

a notorious Baltimore block known as Reisterstown and Ruskin, on Reisterstown Road and Ruskin Avenue. The entire block was filled with abandoned apartment housing tenements. This particular block was the dead end block on Ruskin Avenue. Near the "Dead End" sign is where one could always find at least four serving lines. Two lines were for weed customers and the other two lines were for cocaine customers. Everything from pounds of weed to Kilos of cocaine could've been purchased on that block in broad daylight. There were armed men who stood on every rooftop on that block, ready to open fire on any cop or robber who tried to disturb the order of their operation. Young teenage boys were armed on every stoop with the same instructions. There were even adolescent kids who were paid to post up on every corner with Nextel walkie-talkies to warn the others of any sort of infiltration.

During the week, Powerful planned to continue working as a stocker at PathMark to keep his parole officer satisfied. The majority of his business with Mario would've been conducted on the weekends when Powerful was off from work. In the remaining hours of the week, he planned to spend quality time with Tiffy and their sons – as he normally would. For the next three weeks, everything went according to plan and Powerful accumulated $50,000. People in his neighborhood were starting to suspect that he was making a lot of money. He wasn't being flagrant, but it was noticeable that he was making a lot more moves than usual.

*****

Baseer had remained in Clarkston with Peru until that Friday, then he returned to his apartment in Fayetteville. Yahnis never called or responded to his text message so he deleted her phone number from his call log and never bothered to contact her again. Since the club incident occurred, he spent the remainder of his trip relaxing at Peru's apartment while Peru sold weed everyday. Peru didn't serve any of his customers at night, no matter how large of a quantity his customers wanted. His hours were from 7:00 am to 7:00 pm strictly.

When Baseer returned to his apartment, the very first thing that he did was unscrew the light fixture in his bathroom and count the money that he had stashed there. It was all there; approximately $13,500. He returned home on Desire's final day at work before her vacation days from work began. Baseer gave Desire the liberty to choose their vacation spot and she chose a weeklong stay at Walt Disney World in Orlando, FL. After talking to Powerful and seeing how much money he was acquiring in the cocaine business, Baseer decided to do likewise upon his return from Walt Disney World. His store was beginning to seem more and more like a failure when compared to the fast money that he could attain illegally – whether via robbery or drug selling. Before he and Desire departed for Orlando on Sunday night, he posted up flyers on the outside of his store announcing the closing of "Seerious Fashion" and a liquidation sale that was to be held in one week. Baseer withdrew $5000 from his stash for their vacation and left the remaining $8500 at home in the same stash.

Instead of driving his Expedition, Baseer drove Desire's Lincoln LS because the gas prices were less expensive. Before they left Fayetteville, Baseer stopped at Bullet's apartment in Mount Sinai and bought a half ounce of sour diesel and 7 grams of purple haze. Baseer then mixed all of the weed into one small bag and gave it to Desire to hold in her navy blue Roc-a-Wear purse. At 9:45 Monday morning, the couple checked into a suite at the All Star Resort where Baseer paid $1700 cash for 6 days and 6 nights. The lawn was decorated with giant-sized sculptures and hedges that were trimmed into the shapes of various Walt Disney Characters. Their suite came with two complimentary bottles of Remy Martin V.S.O.P. The bedroom was decorated with artificial sporting goods like: artificial baseballs for door knobs and a football shaped telephone for instance. Baseer felt like the entire set-up was childish but it was tolerable as long as Desire was satisfied. On the first day, they visited Universal Studios for 3 hours, then they retired back to their suite. Baseer was content with simply relaxing and smoking sour diesel in the hotel room. On the second day, they visited the Epcot Center and on the third day they visited Sea World. After Desire begged Baseer repeatedly; he rode on a few rides with her; such as the Space Mountain roller coaster and the Tower of Terror. Baseer was high for every second of their vacation. Their private time in their room and their last 3 days were mostly spent having sex and eating foods that they ordered through the hotel's room service. They used up two disposable cameras taking pictures; some were tourist–type pictures and the others were more explicit ones that were captured in their hotel room. On Sunday morning at 8:30 they checked out of their suite and drove back to Fayetteville. Baseer drove the entire way back because Desire had to be at work at 8:30 am on the following day.

At 4:18, Sunday afternoon, the couple arrived at their home in Cambridge Arms Apartments. That's when he tapped Desire on her left leg to wake her up. After parking, Baseer walked to the trunk of the car to retrieve their luggage and the two of them entered the apartment together. Baseer told Desire to wait at the door while he inspected the apartment for burglars. When he saw that the boxes of inventory from his store were unmoved, he yelled "You're straight baby" and Desire went into the bedroom to check their caller ID for missed calls. Baseer went into the bathroom to make sure that the $8500 that he had stashed was still there. He had approximately $2500 leftover in his pocket so he stashed that along with the rest of his money – all with the exception of two $20 bills. Desire went to sleep after calling Dana and her parents to inform them that she had enjoyed her vacation and returned home safely. Baseer then went into the kitchen and rolled his last blunt of sour diesel. Next he carried all of his boxes outside and packed them into his Expedition.

He left Desire asleep and drove downtown Fayetteville to his store at 7:30 pm. When he arrived downtown, every establishment was closed with the exception of "Jefferson's Barber College" that was opened 7 days a week. The sun had already set so Baseer was carrying his German Luger .380 in his right pants pocket. He entered his security code to deactivate the store's alarm system and single-handedly carried each box inside of the store. Then he locked the door and covered the windows with black sheets so that he could smoke his blunt and put all of the merchandise out on display for the next day. The smell of sour diesel is very potent. Baseer lit 5 Medina incenses so that the smell would be gone by the next morning when the store opened. It took Baseer almost 2.5 hours to put everything out on display. Then he reset the alarm, locked the door and drove home to Desire. He left the sheets covering the windows and the music playing for the sake of burglars. When he walked into the apartment, Desire was still sleeping so he laid down in the bed beside her and fell asleep also.

On the next morning, Desire left for work at 7:45 and Baseer remained asleep until 9:30. Then he took a hot shower, got dressed and drove downtown to open his store. Baseer suspected that Monday would be a slow day so he decided to do a few things to attract more attention to his store. He took his stereo outside and sat it on top of a blue Coburg Milk crate on the sidewalk to keep the music playing all day. Next, he took 3 racks of jeans outside and spent the majority of the day standing in front of the store inviting by passers inside to buy sneakers and clothing. He also had black market CD's and DVD's for sale. The sale lasted for 5 days and after every item was sold, Baseer had accumulated approximately $7200. He also made an extra $1800 by selling his Bonneville to a guy named Joey Nells. Joey was a Baptist Minister and a barber who had moved to Columbia, SC during the previous year. Before moving, he used to work at Diamond Cuts Barbershop that was located downtown Fayetteville next door to Seerious Fashion. At first Baseer felt guilty about selling the bank heist's getaway vehicle to a man that trusted him as a friend but the guilt only lasted for about twenty-four hours.

Baseer had approximately $20,000 to his name. By then, the bank robbery was no longer making news coverage but he was still extremely cautious about being in the public eye more than necessary. He needed a hustle that would enable him to make money while being stationary at home. He spent the following week relaxing and deciding on what to invest in. He chose to sell coke because Powerful could get him a Kilo for $17,000 and he could profit $19,000 if he sold each ounce for $1000 without having to mix it with any additives. The cocaine from Harlem was almost 50 percent more pure than what was being sold in the Fayetteville area. He could make $44,000 per Kilo by adding 14 grams of Procaine to each ounce. All of that, he could do without his clientele feeling like they were getting ripped off because that quality would've met the status quo in Fayetteville.

In the beginning, Desire didn't agree with Baseer's decision to close down his store and partake in the drug business. She was very materialistic though, so her attitude changed completely when he explained how much money he was expecting to make. On that following Friday night at 9:30, Baseer and Desire left Fayetteville and drove the Lincoln LS to NYC for Baseer to buy the first Kilo. Their stay in NYC was only for about an hour. Powerful had already bought the coke for Baseer and he reimbursed him with $17,000 when they met at the "No Pork on My Fork" restaurant on 7th Avenue in Harlem.

Powerful and Tiffy were waiting inside of the restaurant and having breakfast. Baseer had called Powerful's cellular phone when he was twenty minutes away from the restaurant and explained how he wanted the transaction to happen. When Baseer and Desire walked into the restaurant, Desire had the $17,000 in a sandwich bag that was concealed in her purse. There was nothing else in the purse. Tiffy had the cocaine in a brown Louis Vuitton miniature backpack sitting next to her. The four of them pretended to be perfect strangers. Baseer walked directly to the cashier and ordered two veggie patties and two cups of Tropicana Orange Juice for carry out. Desire walked into the ladies restroom and went into one of the stalls as if she had to use the restroom. Both women entered the restroom 30 seconds apart, Desire being first. There, they quickly exchanged bags and exited the restroom 30 seconds apart.Tiffy returned to their table and she and Powerful finished eating their breakfast. Desire joined Baseer in the serving line until their order was ready. Then the two of them got into the car and Baseer drove them out of New York because Desire was afraid of the traffic. He drove until they reached Richmond, Virginia; then Desire drove for the remainder of the trip. Baseer's pistol was under the hood of the car and he didn't carry along any weed to smoke for the entire ride back to Fayetteville. While driving, they both set the car on cruise control to assure that they never exceeded the speed limit. They returned home safely at 8:30 Saturday night.

When they entered the apartment, Baseer went into the living room and inserted the "Life After Death" cd by The Notorious B.I.G. Then he set the song "I Love the Dough" featuring Jay Z on repeat, and turned the volume up loud enough for him to hear it in the kitchen. He didn't even bother to check his stash in the bathroom; he just took the backpack into the kitchen to inspect the product, because there was no window in the kitchen. He opened the backpack and found a cardboard box that was heavily wrapped in plastic. The box was stamped with the symbol of a bird with it's wings spreaded and it was taped shut with black electrical tape. The contents of the box was two individually wrapped packages of cocaine. They were both triple-bagged with Vaseline between each bag to drown the scent. Baseer pulled a digital scale and a 50-pack of sandwich bags from the cabinets above his oven. When he weighed each package, they both weighed 505 grams. They were compressed into hard blocks and the odor was loud. He put on a dust mask and emptied them into a dry cake-mixing bowl. He used his butterfly knife to break it down into smaller fractions. Then he bagged and tied thirty-six bags; all weighing at twenty-eight grams each.

Baseer decided not to add any procaine to his first package because he wanted to establish his clientele. He stipulated that no one could purchase anything less than an ounce from him. Next, Baseer called four guys that he knew could possibly buy coke from him. Their names were Wise, True, Infinite and Asiatic. They were young smalltime coke dealers who were hustling and saving money together to add on to their recording studio. They were trying to form a rap group called "The Supreme Investigators".

They were also members of the Nation of Gods and Earths but Baseer barely identified with them, because they seemed totally different from the Gods that he grew up around in NYC. He only kept the lines of communication open for business purposes. On the next day, each one of them bought an ounce. Neither one of them was a dollar short. He added that $4000 to the $3000 that was left in his stash. By the following Monday, Baseer had sold the entire kilo by only dealing with those four individuals. He then had approximately $40,000. When he called Powerful and told him that he was ready to re-up, he said that he could get him two kilos for $30,000 or another one for $17,000. Baseer decided to buy two because he realized how fast the turnover would be and he would take no more than three weeks if he only sold ounces. He planned to make the quota of $100,000 and gracefully bow out of the drug business. Then he wanted to invest in something else that was more legitimate, but equally lucrative.

On Friday, Baseer drove alone to Harlem in his Expedition to pick up the next package (two kilos). Baseer arrived in Manhattan at 4:00 am on Saturday and drove directly to his sister Lashawn's apartment near Morningside Park in Harlem to rest. At 10:00 am he drove to the Bronx to visit his oldest sister Carmin who owned a private house on Woodlawn Avenue. At 12:30, he went back to Harlem to meet with Powerful and the transaction was done inside of a fish and chips spot on 126th Street. Baseer didn't waste any time riding around the city. This time, he kept the cocaine concealed in a metal tool box behind the backseat of his truck.

As he was driving across the George Washington Bridge to leave New York City, he called TK's cellular phone and he answered "Peace." Baseer asked "God, what's good?" "You. What's Goody?" "Everything. I'm leaving the town right now." "Damn B, come to Brooklyn." "Dunn, I've got like a million years fed time in the truck with me. I'm almost on the Turnpike." "My nigga. . . you're speedin'. You've gotta be careful, I don't need you going back to the beast." "Yeah, but anyway what's going on with that rap shit?" "Oh yeah. I'm supposed to go to the Marley Marl mansion in Long Island next weekend. My manager wants to give Marley Marl a copy of my new single to play on his Wednesday night show with Pete Rock called "Future Flavas" on Hot 97. The joint is called Talk 2 'Em." " Word? That's big family. You already know that I'm the eyes in the back of you." "Fuck that Ba. You're supposed to be putting it down with me. If we get back in the booth together, it would be curtains for the rap game." "I know God, but it's your time. I'm going hard for this paper right now. But, send a nigga a beat CD and I'll see what I can do." "Bet that. I've got mad beats. I'll drop some in the mail tomorrow on my way to work."

The two of them talked for a few more minutes, then they hung up their phones so that Baseer could focus on the traffic. He started his trip listening to TK's demo cd which was entitled Money on My Mind. While listening, he began thinking about what TK had said about reforming their group. He turned the volume up loud and paid close attention to TK's lyrical content. He wrote songs about the lifestyle that Baseer and Powerful were living; not his own lifestyle. His topics usually surrounded gunplay, drug dealing, and even imprisonment. TK never owned a firearm, he never sold drugs and he was never incarcerated. He didn't drink alcohol and he didn't smoke either. He was an excellent lyricist and he made songs that appealed to the gangsters and the hustlers. He produced his own tracks with the Akai MPC2000 and Korg's Triton keyboard, right in the privacy of his home.

At one time, Baseer simply preferred to be "the unknown guy" waving guns and flashing wads of cash in the background on TK's videos while TK enjoyed the limelight; even though he was equally talented. Baseer began to consider getting back involved with music, especially since he and Powerful were making enough money to pay for the production, the manufacturing, and the marketing promotion. TK was living paycheck to paycheck working at McDonald's on West 4th in Manhattan. In his spare time, he recorded music in his home studio in Crown Heights, Brooklyn. He didn't have much money but he was being watched by a number of A and R's who were scouting new talent for various record labels.

Baseer drove the entire way back to Fayetteville without smoking or drinking alcohol. He also drove at a sensible speed and managed not to get pulled over by the police. He arrived at his apartment just after midnight Saturday night.

CHAPTER FIVE

On Sunday, Baseer initially decided to spend the entire day relaxing. At 9:30 am, he went to Bullet's apartment and bought 2 grams of Mango Pina to smoke, then he returned home. On the previous night, he never opened his package to inspect it. He simply stored the toolbox in the closet and decided not to touch it until Monday. When he returned home from Bullet's apartment he rolled a blunt on the couch and started watching the "King of New York" movie. Then he turned his cellular phone off and fell asleep. Desire left home around 10:00 to shop for groceries and wash their laundry at the "Wash Tub" Laundromat. While Baseer was sleeping, he had a dream that he was in a hotel room and dressed in all black as if he had just committed a robbery. Then he emptied a camouflage duffel bag full of money onto the bed. After he began to tally up the money, he noticed the glow of blue lights flashing through the shades over the window. He hurried over to the peep-hole on the door and saw that the entire parking lot was flooded with police cars, and his room was completely surrounded. He then began to panic because he realized that he had no way to escape. Then he received a loud knock on the door and heard what seemed to be a female police officer calling out his name.

After the knock on the hotel room's door, Baseer awoke from his dream in a cold sweat and his heart was beating rapidly. He paused with a feeling of relief after realizing he was only dreaming. Then, five seconds later, he received a loud knock on the door of his apartment, causing him to panic momentarily. That was until he recognized his mother Catherine's voice on the other side of the door calling out his name. He walked over to the peep hole and saw that his mother was alone, so he opened the door to invite her inside. She seemed to look worried and she asked "Why is your cell phone off? I've been calling you all morning." Baseer replied "my bad Ma, I was trying to get some Z's." "And what took you so long to answer the door? I was knocking for at least five minutes." "I didn't even hear you but what brings you to this side of town this morning?" "Baby, it's your Father. I'm starting to think that he's smoking that stuff again. He isn't helping me around the house at all and I can't see what he does with all of his money. He's always broke and he stays out all night with those lowlife friends of his." "Word? You're probably right. You know that I rarely get the chance to talk to him, but I'll talk to him for you." "Baseer, I know that I'm right because his friend Barry called Friday night and I was listening to their conversation on a telephone in another room. James told him that he was about to get a forty piece. He had just borrowed $40 from me because he said that he needed to pay a debt that he owed." "Alright Ma, I'll see what's up. Don't let that nigga stress you out though. As a matter fact, hold fast. . . ."

Baseer excused himself from the living room and walked into the bathroom. Then he removed $300 from his stash and gave it to his mother. She then returned home while Baseer laid on the couch and attempted to resume sleeping. The dream that he had was starting to trouble him and it was hard for him to go back to sleep. He wondered if the dream signified anything or if he was being over-paranoid. That's when he called Powerful to make sure that he hadn't been arrested. Powerful and his family were having dinner at his grandmother's house in Queens. Next Baseer called Peru and Peru was in a Mexican restaurant eating with Monique. Eventually, Baseer fell asleep and didn't wake up until Desire returned home around 3:30 that afternoon.

Desire walked into the apartment carrying two large Veggie Lover's pizzas from Pizza Hut; just the way that Baseer liked them, whole and un-sliced. Desire went into the bathroom and took a shower while Baseer went outside to grab the two laundry baskets from the backseat of the car, and the groceries that were in the trunk. Baseer put all of the foods where they belonged, then he turned his cellular phone back on. He was eating a couple of slices of pizza when he decided to check his messages on his cell phone. There were seven new voicemail messages. The first four messages were from his mother when she was calling him earlier that morning. The other three messages were from True and Asiatic. They were both calling to let him know that they needed more coke. True wanted to buy two ounces and Asiatic wanted to buy a big eighth (4.5 ounces). Baseer called both of them back and said that he was out of town until the following day.

When the sun set around 7:00 that night, Baseer drove to the Exxon gas station near his apartment and bought a box of sandwich bags and a Palma Dutch Master Cigar to roll his last blunt of Mango Pina with. Then he went back home and began bagging his coke. He bagged two big eighths and 27 individual ounces. That night, he only broke down one kilo and left the second one untouched. He decided not to use any procaine because he saw that the coke was selling fast and his clients never complained about his prices. That's because Baseer had the best coke in town and they knew that they could use additives to stretch the quantity from 40-50% more. He always made his transactions away from his apartment so none of his customers knew exactly where he resided. He made all of his deliveries alone while armed with a fully loaded pistol that was kept in the passenger seat.

When Baseer finished breaking down the first Kilo, he stored each bag in a brand new plastic garbage can that he filled with white rice to keep the coke fresh. On Monday morning, Desire went to work at 7:40. At 10:15, Asiatic called Baseer and woke him up. Baseer agreed to meet him in a Wendy's parking lot that was nearby at 11:00. He grabbed a big eighth out of the garbage can and weighed it on his digital scale to reassure that it weighed only 126 grams. Before leaving the apartment, he decided to call True to see if he still wanted to buy two ounces. True still wanted it so they met at the McDonald's on Raeford Road to make the transaction. When Baseer returned home, he stashed his money. Then he began cleaning his entire apartment and waited on his cellular phone to ring for more sales. As he expected, Wise and Infinite bought two more ounces before Desire came home from work around 6:00 that evening.

Baseer spent the remainder of that week taking and filling coke orders. Business was booming and the law enforcement didn't have a clue as to what he was doing. On Thursday afternoon, he received a package in the mail from TK. It was two separate cds – TK's new single entitled Talk 2 em and an instrumental cd with 19 beats that he had made. By Friday morning, Baseer had almost sold the entire first kilo and stashed away an additional $30,000 to the $10,000 that he already had. He was averaging at least $7000 daily. On Thursday night, Baseer listened to TK's beat CD while he broke down the second kilo into individual ounces. One of the beats captured his attention so he set the track on repeat until he finished bagging up his coke. He was trying to figure out a concept for the song. The beat contained a sample from Stevie Wonder's classic hit "Part-Time Lover". When he finished bagging up his coke, he stashed each bag into the garbage can that he had filled with rice. Then, Baseer went into the bedroom and grabbed an ink pen and notebook to begin writing his verse to the track. He decided to write a hustler's anthem entitled "Part-Time Hustle". For the hook, TK sampled Stevie Wonder's voice scatting to the melody of the song. That's when Baseer decided to write an R&B chorus for a male vocalist to sing during the hook. The chorus read "each and everyday – you know we're on the grind/straight getting paid – that's all that's on my mind. It aint a part time hustle. That's just the way I choose to live my life. Get money all day til I get right – that's how it is – it ain't a part time hustle."

Baseer started writing his first verse but he only completed the first six bars before Asiatic called him to buy another big eighth. The verse started out as such "I hustle five days out of the week/Tuesday-n-Thursday I'm duckin the T-N-T/I take it slow and never get greedy/That's why the cops can't catch a nigga like speedy/Not a rat, but I get that cheese/Don't do no hot shit that'll get back leads. . . ."

Baseer fixed up a big eighth and drove to meet Asiatic at the Chilli's restaurant that was nearby his apartment complex. He carried the beat CD along with him so that he could play the track in his stereo system and make sure that it was properly mixed down and the levels were correct. Before returning home he called Bullet and then stopped by his apartment to buy 1.5 ounces of sour diesel for $600. Then he drove home to smoke and complete the song that he had begun writing. When he walked into the kitchen to grab his notebook, the odor of cocaine was still lingering in the kitchen so he mopped the floor and wiped down the countertops with Pine Sol. Plus he switched on the exhaust fan above the oven. Next, he rolled a blunt to smoke and commenced to writing. He only wrote one verse because he had a vision to make that track into a reunion track. He believed that would be the start of something major. He wanted to reform the "Terrible Three" but change the group's name to "The Rothschilds."

Desire walked into the apartment at 7:00 and Baseer was writing the last bar for his verse. When she noticed how clean the apartment was, she left Baseer to his work and proceeded to the bedroom to prepare for a hot bath. Baseer noticed that Desire looked exhausted so he, surprisingly, took the initiative to run her bath water for her. She got undressed and sat down in the bathtub while Baseer went into the living room to change the cd in the stereo. He inserted an R & B mixed cd called "Thug Passion" and played "The Places I Will Kiss You" by Aaron Hall on repeat.

He went back into the bathroom, sat on the edge of the bathtub and began scrubbing Desire's back with a wash cloth. He used a bar of Medina's Mango and Shea Butter soap and the bathroom started to smell like oranges. Then he proceeded to scrub the rest of her body while she relaxed with her eyes closed, in a reclined position. Baseer continued until he had washed every inch of her body. Next, he removed the stopper to drain out all of the soapy water from the bathtub. Desire stood up and closed the shower curtain so that she could turn on the shower and rinse the soap from her body. The curtain was transparent so Baseer stood up against the sink counter and admired her naked body as he watched her through the curtain. When she was done, Baseer dried her body off with a peach colored beach towel. Then he wrapped the towel around her and carried her in his arms to their bedroom.

Baseer laid Desire across the bed, horizontally, and told her to lay on her stomach and close her eyes. The room's temperature was warm so she didn't complain about being naked. Baseer removed her towel and sat down next to her. That's when he opened a bottle of Johnson and Johnson's Baby Oil and let it drip onto her lower back. She opened her eyes and her body tensed up immediately after the first drop because it was cool and unexpected. After spreading the oil across the entire back side of her body, Baseer asked her to turn over and lie on her back. Then Baseer began to spread the baby oil across her entire front. As he was caressing her, he noticed that her nipples were hard. He could tell by the expressions on her face that she was getting aroused, even though her eyes remained shut. He omitted her vaginal area because he wanted to save that for last. He was getting equally aroused because Desire had a beautiful body. Her pubic area was neatly shaven and she didn't seem to have a single blemish. The baby oil caused her body to shimmer when the light hit it.

When Baseer reached her vagina, he started by spreading baby oil around it and then he started to play with her clitoris with his middle finger. When he saw that she was enjoying it, he slowly put his middle finger inside of her to see how wet she was. She was soaking wet. Baseer then began making a circular motion around her clitoris with his tongue. He had planned to continue until he made her have an orgasm but he couldn't wait any longer to penetrate her. That's when he withdrew his finger and wiped her vaginal juices on his penis just before penetrating her. They made love for an entire hour. During that hour, Baseer's cellular phone rung three different times but he disregarded the calls. When he finished, Desire went to sleep on top of the covers while still completely naked. Baseer carried his cellular phone into the kitchen because the screen read that he had 2 voicemail messages and one text message. The first voice message was from Powerful. The second voice message was from

Infinite who was calling because he wanted to buy a big eighth. Baseer called Infinite back and agreed to meet him in thirty minutes at the "Chili's" restaurant that was a few minutes away from his apartment complex.

Baseer made up a big eighth and drove Desire's car to meet with Infinite. When he arrived at "Chili's" he called Infinite and he said that he was only three minutes away. That's when Baseer decided to read the text message that was sent to his inbox. He didn't recognize the sender's telephone number (404-678-0411), so he opened the message and it read "Hit me back if you're not pissed at me." Moments later, Infinite pulled into the parking lot driving a navy blue Chevy Caprice with 22" chrome rims. Baseer removed his pistol from the passenger seat and placed it in his lap. Then Infinite opened the door and sat in the passenger seat. When the car's interior lights went off, Infinite pulled out $4000 that was held together by a rubber band. Baseer told him to grab his package from under his seat. The two of them went their separate ways after the transaction was made.

As Baseer was driving home, he flipped his cellular phone open once again to call the number that the text message was sent from. When the person answered, the caller was a female. "Hello" "Yea, did someone call Baseer?" "That would be me. How are you doing?" "I'm fine, who is this?" "Dang you got that many girls calling you?" "I don't recognize this voice." "This is Yahnis, the girl from the club." "God damn Ma, I thought that you wasn't feelin me or something." "No, I broke the screen on my cell phone when I dropped it in the club. I was hoping that you would've called because I couldn't read my text messages. Today I bought a new cell phone and luckily your text message was still saved on my sim card. But anyway, are you still in town?" "Oh, nah. I'm back in the Carolinas. I left Atlanta that Friday after we met." "Dang, I'm sorry. I really wanted to chill with you that night. You seem so real. You don't see too many real niggas down here in the "A". Half of these dudes is gay and the rest of them play too many games". "Oh, is that right?" "Yes. So when are you coming back to see me so that we can pick back up where we left off?" "I can't call it right this second but it won't be long. Just keep in touch because right now

I'm trying to take care of some business." "Yea you seem like you're about your business." "Oh word? Well listen. . . I'm gonna have to call you back later because I'm in traffic right now." "Alright Shawty, don't be a stranger." "Alright boo." "Byyee." "Bye."

Baseer hung up his cellular phone because he was parking the car and getting ready to walk into his apartment. When he walked into the bedroom, Desire was lying on top of the covers completely naked and sound asleep. Baseer went into the kitchen to grab a cigar out of the freezer and rolled another blunt of sour diesel. Then he inserted TK's beat cd into his cd-rom and e-mailed a copy of the Part Time Hustler beat to Tiffy's e-mail address (mizztiffy@aol.com) for Powerful. Next, he went into the living room and watched the movie State Property Part 2 while he smoked his blunt on the couch. Thirty minutes into the movie, Baseer decided to call Peru. Peru answered the phone, "Yo" in an intoxicated voice. "Yo Peru what's the science?" "I'm chillin Ba' what's crackin?" "I just spoke to the little wiz that I bagged in the club down there." "Word? What's she talking about?" "Screaming some shit about me comin down there. I'm thinking about coming after I move this last pack." "What, boy or girl?" "Girl. This bitch is fire too. I'm fuckin wit some D.R. Niggas from Wash Heights." "True, I know about them niggas. So are you strong right now? Because I might need to spend some bread with you." "Right now I'm sitting on a lil bird but probably not for long. You might wanna wait until I re-up." "True. Well God, I'm about to call it because I'm tired as fuck. I'll hit you up on the next day." "Peace."

Baseer placed his blunt into an ashtray on the coffee table and fell asleep on the couch while he was still fully dressed. He slept until the following morning when Desire was getting dressed for work. When he reached into his pocket he realized that he had forgotten to stash the money that he picked up from Infinite and Asiatic. It was $7400 because he had spent $600 on sour diesel. Baseer lit the leftover blunt that was on the coffee table and smoked until it was time to walk Desire to her car at 7:45. Then he went into the bathroom and added the money from his pocket to the rest of his stash. At 10:00 am, Baseer took his Expedition to a local detailing shop to be detailed. Then he drove to his parents' house, hoping that his father James was there so that they could talk about his relapse.

When Baseer pulled into their driveway, Catherine was painting the wooden rails on their front porch. Baseer stepped out of his truck and asked "Ma where is your husband at?" Then she answered "Where else would you he be? His lazy ass is in the bed." The front door was unlocked so Baseer entered the house and proceeded to his parent's bedroom. When he walked into their bedroom, he found his father James sitting up on the bed and watching "Sanford and Son" on the television. He was laughing aloud with his feet kicked up, legs crossed, and fingers interlocked behind his head in a very relaxed position. He was surprised to see Baseer enter the room. He greeted him by saying "Hey son, what's up?" Baseer paused for a moment as if he was trying to restrain himself from saying something disrespectful. Then he calmly asked "Pops, why is my mother outside painting while you're in here chillin?" "Son, you know how your mother is. When she wants something done, she wants it done right then. I told her that I would do it later. She couldn't wait so she went ahead and did it herself." "Dad, if you weren't my Pops I would probably smack flames out ya ass right now. You've gotta do better G. You're the man, not her." "I know son but Cathy's crazy, she's always trippin." "I know Pops, but get it together alright."

Baseer gave James $200 then asked him if he would go outside and assist his mother. As he was exiting the bedroom, James said "Oh yeah son, one more thing. I know that you bought some weed with you." Baseer simply replied "next time." He didn't even bother to inquire about his father's relapse because he didn't want to endanger his mother. Baseer went back outside and spoke with his mother for about five minutes until James came outside to help her. Before Baseer drove away, he inserted the "After Taxes" cd by Sheek Louch into his cd player. Then he skipped through the disc to track #14, "Pressure". That's when he turned the volume up high and drove off in route to Cambridge Arms apartments. On his way home, he received a phone call from Peru. Baseer answered "Peace," then Peru responded "Paz Dios (Peace

God)" When Baseer recognized that Peru was speaking in Spanish, he knew that the subject involved something illegal so he responded in Spanish also. "Que Paso! (What's happening?)" "oye, Por cuanto me venderias un kilo de coca?" (listen how much will you sell me a half of kilo of cocaine for?) "No me gustaria vendertelo porque me tendrias que dar $12,000" (I really don't want to sell it to you because I'll have to get $12,000) No hay problema. Porque pues nos ajuntaremos en Sur Carolina este fin de semana?" "(No problem. Why don't you meet me in South Carolina this weekend.) "Puedo verte el domingo" (I can meet you on Sunday) "Esta bien." (Alright) "Peace."

CHAPTER SIX

By nightfall on Friday, Baseer had made another $8000 from True and Asiatic and stashed it along with the rest of his money. He then had 25 ounces left. He set aside 18 ounces for Peru and hoped to sell the other seven before leaving to meet with Peru on Sunday. During the course of that day, Baseer called both TK and Powerful to discuss his idea about "The Rothschilds." In turn, they both began writing their verses for "Part Time Hustle." Powerful delivered $200 to TK so that he could reserve two hours of studio time at a Manhattan recording studio on Broadway. They were scheduled to record the "Part Time Hustle" single four weeks later. Baseer also spoke to Yahnis on Friday for an hour. She didn't have to work on that weekend so she and Baseer decided to meet in South Carolina and spend the day together in a hotel room after he completed his business with Peru. When their secret little rendezvous was confirmed, Baseer told Desire that he had to take another business trip to New York and that he would return on Monday evening. As usual, she began arguing and complaining.

"Baseer, I'm so fucking tired of this shit. Every single week you're leaving me. You must think that my brain is the size of a mustard seed; I know that you're fuckin around on me." Baseer responded, "Baby, what did I tell you about trusting me? I'm out here grinding and trying to secure you a home in heaven. I'm almost where I need to be, just be cool for a little while longer. I promise, it's almost over." "What's almost over?"

Baseer exited the bedroom without answering Desire's question. He went into the bathroom to retrieve his entire savings that was stashed in the light fixture. It was $55,000 in two separate brown paper bags. He went into the bedroom and emptied both bags onto the bed. When Desire saw how much money he had, she grew silent for about ten seconds. Then she softly uttered "Baby where did you get all of that money from?" Baseer then felt as if he had won that argument so he replied sarcastically, "I got it while I was out fuckin around on you." Then he left the money on the bed and asked her to follow him into the storage closet, where the cocaine was. He reached down into the garbage can and began rummaging through the rice until he finally pulled out one ounce of coke and said "Baby, this one bag is $1000." Then he reached down into the garbage can for a second time, removed Peru's package and said "This is $18,000. This is another $1000 and this is another thousand." "Okay, baby, I get the point. Just tell me how much longer do I have to tolerate you being gone all the time." "Desi I promise you after I sell the rest of this shit, it's over. No more trips without you, alright?" "alright" "You love me?" "Yes, I love you." "We're gonna be great alright? I love you too."

The couple kissed and then Baseer went back into the bedroom to put his money back in his stash spot. Desire followed him into the bedroom and sat on the bed while Baseer refilled the paper bags with the money. That's when his cellular phone rang and he noticed that the caller was "Infinite." He knew that it was a business call so he answered the call with the speaker phone on for Desire to hear the conversation. "Inf, what's good?" "Peace Allah. Are you around the way?" "I'm at the kingdom. Why what's good?" "I need three zones." "Where are you at right now?" "I'm leaving the Cross Creek Mall." "Well go to the Olive Garden restaurant across the street and I'll be there in like 600 seconds."

When Baseer hung up the telephone, he asked Desire "Baby will you go into the closet and grab three of those smaller bags that I showed you. I need to put this cash up." Desire did what she was asked to and Baseer stashed his money back in the light fixture. Before leaving to meet with Infinite, he assured Desire that he would be back in fifteen minutes so she didn't complain. While Baseer was on his way, he told her to have two more ounces ready for him when he walked through the door because True wanted them. Then he met with Infinite at the Olive Garden and the deal went smoothly.

When Baseer returned home after his meeting with True, he went into the bedroom and turned his cellular phone off. Next, he placed the $5000 from his pocket on the dresser and rolled a blunt of sour diesel. After only taking six drags from the blunt, he placed it into an ashtray on the dresser and got undressed for bed. Then they both fell asleep until the following morning. On Saturday morning, Baseer and Desire woke up early and drove the Lincoln LS to IHOP to eat breakfast. Then they went to the mall and bought matching Ralph Lauren's polo outfits from the Hecht's store. Peru called Baseer at 12:00, that afternoon and said that he and Monique were already in Florence, South Carolina at the Red Roof Inn. Baseer wrote down the interstate's exit number and told Peru that he would be departing from Fayetteville around 8:30 am because Florence was only one hour away. After that phone call, Baseer set his cellular phone to "silent" ring mode just in case Yahnis decided to call. He spent the remainder of the day smoking weed and relaxing at home with Desire. Around 7:00 pm, he stepped outside of the apartment and called Yahnis, to make sure that her plans had not changed. He gave her the interstate's exit number and the name of the hotel in Florence. She said that she would be departing from Atlanta, around 6:00 am and that she expected to arrive in Florence around 12:00, Sunday afternoon.

When Baseer awoke on Sunday morning, it was 8:00. The first thing that he did was smoke the rest of the blunt that was left in the ashtray from the previous night. Then he went into the storage closet and placed Peru's ½ of a kilo in the brown Louis Vuitton backpack that Desire got from Tiffy at the "No Pork on My Fork" restaurant. He ate a bowl of frosted flakes cereal, just before taking a hot shower. He decided to wear the new Polo outfit that he had bought at Hecht's, plus his gold chain and a pair of black suede construction Timberlands. Desire awoke from her sleep while Baseer was getting dressed. That's when she decides to call Dana and ask her if she wanted to join her for breakfast at IHOP. When Dana accepted her offer, Desire decided to join Baseer in the shower and they ended up having sex in the shower. Then they both got dressed and walked out of the apartment together.

Baseer gave Desire a kiss on her lips and she suggested that he drove carefully, just before she drove away in her Lincoln LS. Instead of concealing his pistol under the hood as he normally would, Baseer decided to put his .380 under the driver's seat, then he placed the Louis Vuitton bag on the floor behind the backseat. Before driving off, Baseer inserted the "Massacre" cd by 50 cent into his cd player. Then he skipped to track #17, "Position of Power". He stopped at a nearby Exxon and filled his gas tank with Super unleaded gas. Plus he bought an air freshener to hang from the rearview mirror. He was on the highway by 9:15. Baseer was driving through Laurinburg, North Carolina when he noticed that there were very few cars on the highway. He flipped open his cellular phone and called Yahnis to find out her location. She said that she was on the highway and that her navigational system said that she was approximately three hours away from the hotel.

The north and south lanes on the interstate were separated by a cluster of pine trees. Baseer didn't see any police behind him or in front of him so he set the cruise control on 70 miles per hour, even though the speed limit was only 65 mph. His intentions were to press the brakes and decelerate at the first sighting of the police. He was wearing his safety belt and the truck didn't smell like marijuana on the interior. While he was talking to Yahnis, he suddenly realized that he had just passed a State Trooper whose car was parked in the midst of the pine trees. His car was completely invisible until Baseer had already passed him, and he never would've noticed him if he didn't coincidentally look back. Baseer pressed the brakes lightly, only enough to disengage the cruise control. When the officer noticed the brake lights, he turned on his blue lights and pursued Baseer. When Baseer noticed the blue lights in his rearview mirror, he told Yahnis "Boo, I've gotta hit you back. This devil's pulling me over."

Then he hung up the phone, turned on his right turn signal, and veered off into the emergency lane. When he parked, he immediately tucked his gold chain beneath his shirt and shut off the truck.

The state trooper remained in his car for a minute and a half before he walked to Baseer's driver's side window. The officer was a Caucasian male who appeared to be at least 40 years old. On his way to Baseer's Expedition, Baseer noticed him spitting chewing tobacco with an unpleasant expression on his face so he automatically assumed that he was a racist. That's when Baseer let down the driver's side window. "Good morning sir." "Yea son, I'm gonna need your license, registration, and proof of insurance." "Just one second. Is there a problem sir?" "There are two problems. In the state of North Carolina, it's against the law to talk on a cellular phone while you're driving, then you were doing 71 in a 65." "I apologize sir, I didn't realize that I was speeding. Here are the things that you asked me for." Baseer handed the officer his license, registration and insurance card. He knew that all of his paperwork was legitimate. The officer returned to his car. When the officer turned his back to walk away, Baseer quickly grabbed his German Luger .380 from beneath his seat. Then he let the window back up and cocked the hammer back to make sure that there was a bullet in the chamber. Seconds later, Baseer became more nervous because he noticed another state trooper car through the pine trees driving on the north lane of the interstate. Baseer had decided that if the officer called back-up and tried to search his vehicle he was going to open fire on the both of them and lead them on a high-speed chase. Baseer placed the gun on his right side, beside the driver's safety-belt buckle. He planned to grab his gun with his right hand as if he was unlocking his safety belt, if the officer was to ask him to step out of the truck.

Three minutes later, the officer stepped out of his car and began to approach Baseer's truck. Baseer grew more and more nervous as the officer came closer to his truck. "Alright son, I had to write you a $150 ticket for talking on the phone while driving. Plus, I wrote you a second ticket for $150 for doing 71 in a 65. If you appear in court, then the judge may modify it. Here's your paperwork. And slow it down, alright." The officer proceeded back to his car. Baseer pulled out into the slow lane and drove at 40 mph until the state trooper drove past him. When the officer was out of sight, he muted his stereo and dialed Yahnis' cell. Then he turned the speakerphone on and placed the phone into his lap so that he could talk and not look so obvious. She answered, "Is everything alright?" "Yea, I'm good. I just got a ticket for talking and driving so I'm not gonna speak for long. How's the traffic?" "Oh, it's straight. I'm just ready to kick it with you." "I'm coming. What are you wearing anyway?" "You'll see when we get there." "Alright, well I should be there in like 45 minutes. I'll call you when I touch down." "Alright."

45 minutes later. . . . Baseer veered off on Interstate 20's exit #114B. That was the first exit into Florence. Then he called Peru's cell phone. "Peace" "Peace G. I just got off on 114B, so I should be there in a few." "Yeah, just get over into the far-right lane and make a right at the first traffic light. You'll see the hotel on your right, right beside the Huddle House." "Alright." "Peace."

Baseer arrived at the Red Roof Inn at 10:33 am. He circled around the parking lot until he found Monique's black Lincoln Navigator parked in the back. Then he parked in an available parking space right next to it. Next, he put his .380 into his right pants pocket and called Peru's cell phone. Peru answered, "Yo" "what's your room number? I'm outside" "116" Baseer carried the Louis Vuitton bag to room 116 and tapped on the door three times. Peru opened the door with a 9mm Ruger in his right hand and his shirt was off. Monique was lying in one of the beds with the bedspread pulled all the way up to her neck as if she was naked beneath the covers. Baseer walked into the room and sat down on the other bed. Then he opened his backpack and withdrew the cocaine. Peru had a digital scale on the table near the window so he plugged it into the wall. Then he dipped his pinky into the Ziploc bag and scooped out a small amount of coke with his fingernail. He placed the coke on the very tip of his tongue and his tongue became numb instantly. Then he set the scale to "grams" mode and placed the entire Ziploc bag on the scale. The numbers on the scale kept fluctuating from 505.3 to 505.1 grams because the table wasn't sturdy. Then Peru passed Baseer a black Jansport backpack.

Baseer unzipped the bag to count the money that was inside. When he opened it, he looked at Peru suspensefully and asked "yo dunn, what the fuck is this?" "That's 12 stacks B." "Man, what's with all these five and ten dollar bills? It's gonna take me all day to count this shit. Whatever happened to fifties and hundreds like normal people?" "C'mon son, all of that shit spends." "Well yo, I'll get wit you later. I'm going to my hut to get situated. Oh yea, did you bring any weed with you? I didn't bring shit." "I brought like 7 grams of Kush, I can give you a blunt or two." "Word. And I know that you bought blunts too." "Yeah, I got you." Peru gave Baseer two grams of Kush and a Dutch Master Cigar. Then he zipped his bag shut and walked to purchase a hotel room, #124. When he entered his room he placed the bag on one of the beds. Then he placed his pistol on top of the television and searched through the channels until he found the edited version of the movie Juice showing on BET.

Baseer decided not to call Yahnis until he was done counting his money. First he rolled his blunt of Kush and began smoking. Then he took off his Timberland boots and emptied the backpack onto the table to begin separating the bills. In the middle of his count, Yahnis called Baseer's cellular phone. He answered "Where you at?" "I'm like 35 minutes away from Florence." "Alright, I'm already here in the hotel room waiting on you." "Okay, did you need anything?" "No, I'm peace." "I brought you a bottle of Patron with me." "Oh word? That's what's up. Look I need to grab the rest of my shit out of my truck so let me call you back." "Well, I'll just see you when I get there. What's the room number?" "124" "Alright, deuces." "Alright Ma".

Baseer hung up the phone and completed his count. He had exactly $12,000. There were 725 $5 bills, 413 $10 bills, 84 $20 bills, 42 $50 bills and 465 $1 bills. When he was done, he placed the money back into the backpack and sat it down in the corner near the lampstand. Then he stashed his pistol in the bottom drawer of the dresser. He hadn't talked to Desire since he kissed her goodbye earlier that morning so he called her and said that he had stopped at a rest area in Virginia to use the restroom. He spoke with her for about eight minutes and then he said that he would call her back later on that night. Almost 20 minutes later, Baseer received a soft knock on the door, then he walked over to the peephole and saw that it was Yahnis. When he opened the door to invite her in, she said "hey baby." Then before Baseer had the opportunity to respond, she wrapped her arms around his neck and started tongue kissing him. The kiss was slow and it lasted for an entire minute.

She looked exceptionally beautiful. Her hair was freshly permed and combed down into a wrap. She was wearing Baby Phat from her earrings to her toes, plus she had the matching purse. Her shirt was a blue and white Baby Phat halter top that exposed her shoulders, down to the upper part of her breasts. On each breast, she had a tattoo of an eye so it appeared as if someone was peeping out of her shirt. Her jeans were stone-washed indigo blue and they fitted tightly against her legs. The color was shaded lighter near the bottom of her butt cheeks to accent her curves. She was wearing a pair of black and gold Baby Phat stiletto heels that exposed her toes, as well as the tattoo of a blue and gray dolphin that she had on the top of her right foot. Her toes were pedicured and she was wearing the rapper Trina's signature "Diamond Princess" perfume. She was also wearing all of the jewelry that she had worn on the night when she met Baseer at the Prime Time nightclub in Atlanta.

Yahnis opened her eyes after the kiss, then she threw her purse onto the bed and began removing her shirt. Baseer removed his shirt also while Yahnis began to loosen his belt. Next, she pulled his pants and his boxers down to his ankles and slowly kneeled down to begin performing oral sex on him. Baseer never even got the chance to sit down. In his opinion, Yahnis didn't seem very experienced in what she was doing but he didn't complain to ruin the mood. One thing that did turn Baseer on was the innocent look that she gave him as she looked up into his eyes while she was down on her knees. Then she closed her eyes and continued for about 3 more minutes before she stood back up and said "I want you inside of me right now." When she removed her heels and her jeans, she was wearing nothing but a white Baby Phat thong with the logo on the front. Baseer removed the bedspread and placed it on the floor. He was so aroused by her that he laid her on the bed and penetrated her without using a condom. Baseer took his time with her and she had three orgasms before he came once. When he finally did, he released inside of her and she held him tightly to assure that she received every drop of his sperm.

Yahnis climbed underneath the sheets. Baseer put on his boxers and his Polo jeans and then he asked "baby, where is that Patron at?" She grunted as if she was restless and then replied "Oh baby, I left it in the trunk of my car." Baseer walked over to the window and asked "Where is your car?" "I'm driving that white Dodge Charger with the rims on it." That's when Baseer looked through the curtains and noticed a white Dodge Charger with 22" chrome Lexani rims, chrome door handles, chrome mirror covers, and a chrome Bentley-style grill on the front. When Yahnis gave Baseer her keys to grab the liquor out of her trunk, she asked him to bring in her luggage also. She had a small-sized suitcase with only 3 outfits, a few articles of lingerie and some cosmetics. When Baseer re-entered the room, Yahnis began taking a shower. Baseer poured himself a shot of Patron into one of the hotel's complimentary plastic cups and resumed smoking the blunt of Kush. By then, the movie "Juice" had ended and he had begun watching a documentary about William H. Bonnie on the History Channel.

When Yahnis finished taking her shower, she walked back into the room wearing nothing but a black laced thong and a matching bra. Then she began to search through her suitcase for an outfit to wear. That's when she asked "Do you wanna go out to eat?" Baseer replied, "Yea we can do that. But first I'm gonna need a favor." "What is it" "Did you see the Magnolia Mall across the street when you came up?" " Yes" "I want to give you some money so that you can go snatch me up an outfit. I don't care what it is – Ed Hardy, Akademiks, LRG or whatever." "Alright baby, I can handle that."

Yahnis put on a lime-green and black Apple bottoms outfit and combed her hair down. When Baseer saw that she was fully dressed, he pulled $400 from his backpack and gave it to her. Then he wrote down his shoes and clothes sizes and gave her the room's keycard, just before reminding her to buy him some new socks and boxer shorts. As Yahnis was leaving she said "Give me a kiss," then Baseer gave her a peck on her lips and she exited the room. Moments later, Baseer picked up the hotel room's phone and dialed "116." After two rings, Monique answered. "Hello Monique, let me speak to Peru for a second." "Hold on . . . . here baby it's your friend." Peru grabbed the telephone and said "Peace." "Ayo, did you and your wiz eat already?" "Nahh. What's good?" "Me and my little shortie are going out in about an hour. You and yours might as well follow us." "That's peace. Just call when you're ready." "Alright."

About ten minutes later, Baseer carried his backpack and his pistol into the bathroom. He placed the backpack on top of the sink counter and he placed the gun on the soap holder in the shower. Then he locked the bathroom door and began taking a shower. Yahnis returned about 45 minutes later as Baseer was just stepping out of the shower. He unlocked the bathroom door and asked Yahnis to bring him a pair of boxer shorts. When he came out of the bathroom, his new outfit was laid out across the bed. She had picked out a black, white and lime green LRG outfit and a pair of black and lime green Nike Huraches sneakers. Baseer told her "Okay, You've got a little taste," then Baseer got dressed and called Peru to let him know that they were ready to leave.

When they walked over to Peru's room, the girls were introduced to each other and they decided to ride together in Monique's Navigator. Baseer and Peru decided to ride together in Yahnis' Dodge Charger. When they got into her car, he noticed she had a loud stereo system so he grabbed the "Heart of the Streets" cd by B.G. out of his Expedition. Baseer carried the backpack with him in the trunk because he didn't trust the housekeepers. He also carried his gun in his right pants-pocket. The girls drove in front and they turned into a nearby, privately owned restaurant called "Percy and Willie's." The parking lot was crowded so they weren't able to park next to each other. When the guys opened their doors, a cloud of smoke ascended from the inside because they were smoking a blunt of Kush. When the girls walked over to the car, they were laughing together as if they were getting along very well, then they all entered the restaurant together. Both couples sat at the same table directly across from each other. Peru, Monique and Yahnis ordered T-Bone steaks with baked potatoes. Baseer ordered a vegetable casserole with a side order of baked potatoes because he was a vegetarian. The girls ordered Sprites to drink and the fellows ordered Hennessey and Coca-Cola.

The women enjoyed their meals as they listened to Baseer and Peru sharing funny stories about growing up in New York City. The laughter from their table began to irritate some of the other customers in the restaurant. Baseer and Peru didn't seem to care because the alcohol was beginning to take it's effect, plus they were high on Kush. There was a Caucasian man, woman and child (boy) sitting directly behind Baseer and Yahnis. Yahnis laughed in a loud outburst after one of Baseer's jokes. Then the man turned around and asked, "Excuse me but could you all keep it down?" Yahnis respectfully said "Oh I'm sorry" and Monique toned down her laughter. Then Baseer told the girls "Yo fuck him. You don't have to keep shit down," in a tone that was loud enough for the man to hear it. Then he told the man "Aye sir – Fuck You!" Peru began laughing and then he told Baseer "Chill out G". The man began speaking to his family in a low voice that wasn't loud enough for Baseer to understand what he was saying. The only words that he heard were "stupid niggers" in the middle of one of his sentences. That's when Baseer placed his porcelain plate flat into the palm of his right hand. The plate was still full of steaming hot vegetable casserole. Yahnis figured that he was about to strike the man with the plate so she said "baby stop." Baseer totally ignored her. Instead, he stood up, turned around and slapped the man on the right side of his face with the plate from behind. The slap was so hard that it cracked the dish into two pieces. The man immediately stood up and began fighting with Baseer. He was much larger than Baseer so Peru began helping him.

Baseer's palm was bleeding because the plate cut his hand when it broke in two. The man's wife began to yell for help and their son was screaming "Stop, please stop."

Yahnis and Monique wanted to break up the fight but they probably would've gotten themselves hurt so they kept their distances. The store manager called the police and 3 Florence County Police cars arrived in less than two minutes. When they entered the restaurant, the man was on the floor and the guys were still beating him. The store was ransacked and there was blood and food all over the floor. The officers broke up the fight and ordered all three of the men to place their hands on the wall and spread their legs to be patted down. Baseer had totally forgotten that his .380 pistol was concealed in his right pants pocket. As they were being searched, Monique and Yahnis began explaining to the officers that the man started the fight and that Baseer and Peru had only retaliated in self defense. When the officer withdrew the pistol from Baseer's pocket, the girls instantly became silent. That's when the officers began to handle Baseer more roughly and placed him into handcuffs. One of them said "You're under arrest for assault and battery, and unlawful possession of a loaded firearm." As Baseer was being escorted to the transport unit, he told Yahnis to stay in town until he called. Peru and the other man were then placed in handcuffs, then they were apprehended and put into separate transport units. They were transported to the Florence County Detention Center, called Effingham.

For the entire ride to jail, Baseer and Peru were both extremely paranoid. Baseer was upset because he had left the backpack full of money in Yahnis' trunk. Therefore he didn't have any bond money. He knew that his only choice would be to call Desire and tell her to bail him out with the money from the light fixture if he couldn't get in contact with Yahnis. He didn't want to do that because she would realize that he had lied about going to New York and possibly get angry enough to disappear with his money. Peru gave the arresting officer an alias name and he was worried that he would not be given a bond since he didn't have an identification card.

When they arrived at Effingham, they were individually searched and everything from their pockets was inventoried and placed into their personal property. One of the female officers granted Baseer the opportunity to write down Yahnis' cell phone number out of his phone.

The Caucasian man remained handcuffed and was told to sit down in a chair directly in front of the "Bookings" desk. Peru and Baseer were released from their handcuffs and placed into a holding tank called Detox until they were called individually to be booked in. When the Caucasian man was called up to the desk, Baseer and Peru walked up to the window in the Detox tank to get a better view and try to read the officer's lips. After he was booked in, a female officer gave him a small piece of paper. Then he walked over to the telephone and began making a call. About 5 minutes later, a different female officer opened the door of the Detox tank and said "Mr. Baseer or Bazzeer Watson," then Baseer stood up and said "That's me." "How do you pronounce that?" "However you want to, that's not important." Baseer answered each question hastily to speed up the process. When he was done getting booked in, the officer gave him a small piece of paper with a pin number on it that would enable him to use the telephone and make a collect phone call. As Baseer walked over to the telephone, he worried that he wouldn't be able to call Yahnis' cell phone collect.

Fortunately, the phone service was a privately-owned service named "Paytell Communications" and he could call cellular phones collect. He dialed Yahnis' phone number and she answered "Hello." Then a recording played, "You have a collect call from Baseer in the Florence County Detention Center. This call may be monitored or recorded. To accept the charges for this call, press zero. If you choose not to accept this call, please hang up now." That's when Baseer heard a number being pressed just before the recording continued – "Thank you for using Paytell Communications, go ahead with your call." "Hello." "Yahnis what's up?" "Oh my God, hey Boo.." "Hey where are you at?" "I'm back at the hotel sitting here with Monique. Are you alright?" "Yeah, I think that I broke my finger and I cut my hand pretty bad but I'm alright. Listen, they say that I'll be going before a judge in the morning for a bond hearing at 8:30. I need for you to stick around until tomorrow so that you can bond me out. I left some money in the trunk of your car and you may have to give Monique some to bail Peru out." "Where are you at?" "It's called Effingham or Florence County Detention Center." "Alright, my navigational system will help me find it. I'll be there. I just have to call my job because I was supposed to be back in Atlanta to work at 12:30 tomorrow afternoon." "Alright Boo, hold me down." "I got you baby." "Alright, and tell Monique that Peru should be calling her in the next 20 to 30 minutes after he gets booked." "ok" "Alright, One."

When the officer noticed that Baseer had completed his phone call, he was told to wait in a holding cell until it was time for him to be fingerprinted. The cell was about 8x10" wide with only one bench that was about 6 feet long. Also, there was one stainless steel toilet with a sink made into it. The floor was filthy with stains all over it. When Baseer walked into the cell, there were three men already in it. Two of them were lying on the floor balled up with their arms and heads tucked also. Baseer didn't say one word. Instead, he stood up at the window on the cell door and watched the "Bookings" desk to see what was about to happen with Peru.

After about ten minutes, Peru was called out of the Detox tank to be booked. The process only lasted for about 8 minutes. Then, Peru proceeded to the telephone and called Monique collect on her cellular phone. He told her the alias name that he had used and urged that she bonded him out before his finger prints came back. He also told her to leave the cocaine in the hotel room when she came to his hearing on the next day. Peru then hung up the telephone and went into the same holding cell that Baseer was in. After about five minutes, Peru woke up the man on the bench and told him to make room for him and Baseer to sit down. The five of them remained in that cell until the following morning. Baseer and Peru stayed up talking all night with no regards to the other men who were in the cell trying to sleep.

On Monday morning, at 6:00, a white female officer opened the holding cell door and asked "Breakfast?". The other three men awoke from their sleep and walked to the door to receive their breakfast trays. Baseer and Peru refused theirs. A few minutes later, Peru decided to rest his head in his lap and sleep until he was called for his bond hearing. Baseer stayed awake. At 8:33, the cell's door opened once more. Then all five of them were called out of the cell and lined up against the wall. Each one of them were handcuffed in the front and chains were placed around their ankles. Then they were, collectively, escorted to a small courtroom in a nearby section of the jail. When they walked into the courtroom, Baseer and Peru were both relieved to see Yahnis and Monique sitting together in the back row of the court room.

CHAPTER SEVEN

Baseer's name was the fourth name to be called by the judge. The three men before him were given P.R. bonds because they were arrested for misdemeanor charges. That gave Baseer and Peru a ray of hope because the judge seemed to be showing leniency. When Baseer's name was called by the judge he arose from his seat and the entire courtroom was silent. Then the judge said "For the charge of Assault and Battery, I'm setting your bond at $20,000 surety. And for unlawful possession of a firearm, your bond is set for $50,000 surety." Baseer was then seated and one of the officers brought him some papers to sign and date. The next name to be called was Carlos Ortiz, Peru's alias. Peru had also given the officers at Bookings a bogus Florence address. The judge set his bond at $20,000 surety for Assault and Battery.

All of the men were then lined up and escorted back to the Bookings area. Baseer and Peru weren't allowed to speak to their girls but they noticed them in the rear of the courtroom speaking with a gentleman who appeared to be a bail bondsman. The other three men were released from their handcuffs and prepared to be released. Peru and Baseer were placed back inside of the holding cell. Peru tried really hard to maintain his composure but his nerves were rattled because he knew that his cocaine was in the hotel room, and check out time was only 2 hours away. He also worried that his true identity might've been disclosed before Monique bonded him out. They sat in the holding cell for an hour before the door opened and a white female officer said "Mr. Watson, you're being released." Peru then asked the officer "Aye Miss, have you heard anything about Carlos Ortiz being released?" She replied "Sorry sir, not yet."

Baseer looked over at Peru and said "No te Precoupes, tu mujer va a estar aqui en unos minutos. Si se dan cuenta de tu nombre verdadero, yo tengo sufficient dinero para pagar tu bon. (Don't worry , your girl should be here in a few minutes. If they find out your real name, I still have enough money to bail you out.)" Peru then looked at the female officer to try and discern whether or not she had comprehended what Baseer said. When Peru saw how confused she looked, he responded "Agarra la coca del cuarto tam bien (Get the coke out of the room too)." Then Baseer went to the bookings desk to receive his personal property and was escorted to the lobby where he found Yahnis and Monique. Yahnis hurried over to him and gave him a hug. He refused to kiss her because he hadn't brushed his teeth since the previous day.

Monique then asked Baseer "Where is Peru?" He replied "He's still inside. You did pay his bond right?" "Yeah, me and Yahnis paid the same bail bondsman." "Well he'll probably be coming out in a second." The three of them waited in the lobby until Peru came walking out, about ten minutes later. Yahnis had driven her car and Monique left her truck parked at the hotel, so they all returned to the hotel in Yahnis' car. Peru and Baseer rode in the backseat. They rushed back to the hotel to remove Peru's cocaine before the housekeepers discovered it. When they arrived back at the room it was 10:45 and the coke was untouched. Peru offered Baseer 2.5 ounces to repay him for the $2000 that Monique borrowed to bond him out. Baseer declined the offer because he didn't want to travel back to Fayetteville with drugs in his truck. He simply said "I ain't worried about that, I charge it to the game since that was my fault."

Baseer and Yahnis walked back to room 124 to gather their belongings and prepare to depart from each other. Check out time was at 11:00 am. They left the bottle of Patron sitting on the table because it was opened, then they carried their things to their vehicles. Peru and Monique did likewise because they were about to travel back to Clarkston, Georgia. After everyone had loaded their luggage, they exchanged their goodbyes and went their separate ways. When Baseer got into his truck to leave, he turned his cell back on and saw that he had 23 new messages in his voicemail. He knew that the majority of them were from Desire. He was already aggravated about the money that he had lost so he didn't even bother to listen to his messages. He used his left hand to drive the entire way back to Fayetteville because of the condition of his right hand.

Baseer went to the emergency room to have his hand examined, as soon as he arrived in Fayetteville. The doctor concluded that his index finger was not broken, it was only sprained. He also said that the laceration didn't require stitches and that it would begin healing in a few days as long as he cleaned it properly with peroxide and kept it covered with gauze pads. When he arrived back at his apartment, it was almost 3:00 pm. Desire wasn't expected to come home from work until 7:00. Once he got settled in, he sent Desire a text message and left her a voice message marked urgent. The text read "HMB ASAP, I just got out of jail." She didn't return his call in the next few minutes so Baseer emptied the backpack onto the coffee table to count the money that he had left. It was approximately $2600 so he added that to the $55,000 that was in the bathroom's light fixture. Then he went into the storage closet to make sure that he still had 2 ounces of coke left.

Desire finally returned Baseer's call while he was in the middle of taking a hot bath. She said that she was on a 15 minute break and asked Baseer to expound on the voice message that he had left her. Baseer couldn't figure out an explanation as to why he was in South Carolina so he told Desire that he was arrested in Maryland on his way back from New York. He told her that he had gotten pulled over and was arrested for having his .380 in his truck. Then he began to explain that he had taken a $9000 loss and that he would soon be spending more money for an attorney to represent him in his case. When Desire sensed how upset he was, she began to speak softly and console him. They talked until the duration of her break, and then she went back to work. That's when Baseer finished listening to the messages that were in his voicemail. Asiatic had called twice and said that he needed to buy a big eighth. True called and said that he needed two ounces, and Infinite had also called for a big eighth. Baseer called True back and delivered his last two ounces to him at the Chili's restaurant. He was on his way back to his apartment when Yahnis called him and said that she had returned home safely to her apartment in East Lake Meadows near downtown Atlanta.

At 7:04 pm Desire walked into the apartment. Baseer was in the living room listening to the "Part Time Hustle" instrumental in the stereo and talking to TK on his cell phone about what had happened at the Percy and Willie's restaurant. Before Desire could realize the topic of their conversation, Baseer told TK that he would call him back later. That's when she asked "Baseer, why is your hand wrapped up?" Then he replied "Oh I cut my shit. It's no big deal." "So why didn't you have your gun under the hood like you usually do?" "Because Baby, I was carrying too much money to be riding around New York City unarmed. When I got back on I-95, I just kept the pistol under the seat." "So what now? Do you have to go to court or something?" "Yeah. I have to go to General Sessions Court. But Desi can we talk about this later? I'm vexed right now." "Okay, well, I'll be in the bedroom." "Aigght." Baseer began rehearsing his verse until he finally memorized it. Then he passed out on the couch and left the "Part Time Hustle" instrumental repeating all night long.

Desire went to work at 7:30 on Tuesday morning. Baseer called Powerful at 10:00 that morning and began explaining, boastfully, how he and Peru had beaten the man in the restaurant and the man at the Prime Time nightclub. Powerful didn't show much enthusiasm and he didn't find it humorous that Baseer had been arrested and taken such a big loss. Powerful had never met Peru but he didn't like what he knew of him from some of Baseer's stories. Powerful was still prospering and he wasn't spending his money frivolously. He had accumulated almost $75,000. When Baseer asked him to pick up another kilo for him, he suggested that Baseer relaxed for a few weeks because he seemed to be living recklessly. Baseer took offense to the comment but, deep down, he knew that it was said out of sheer concern. Baseer knew that Powerful was his only source to buy kilos for such a low price, so he pretended to humbly accept his advice and ended the conversation peacefully. In his mind, he was still trying to figure out illegal means to attain enough money to replace what he had lost and what he was about to spend on an attorney.

Baseer didn't hear from Yahnis for that entire day. He knew that she had to work so he decided not to call her. Asiatic and Infinite continued to call but Baseer disregarded their calls because he knew that he couldn't supply them. He couldn't think of a better profit than the cocaine profit, so he decided to wait on Powerful to change his mind; instead of investing in something different. Baseer found out that the next General Sessions Court term would begin two months later, so he didn't hire a lawyer immediately. He knew that most attorneys would charge him at least $15,000. That was because he had a new gun charge and he was released from his first bid in prison under the Federal Gun Law Act. Baseer spent the remainder of the week relaxing in his apartment writing lyrics to some of the other instrumentals that were on TK's beat cd. After about 5 days, all of his clientele had stopped calling his phone. Baseer and Yahnis spoke frequently, but only during Desire's work hours.

On Friday, Baseer called Powerful once more. He decided not to mention any cocaine business. Instead they discussed some of his new ideas concerning their music group. They still had three weeks remaining before their scheduled recording date in Manhattan. On the following Monday, Baseer and Desire drove to the "Quick Silver Pawn Shop" in Fayetteville to purchase a pistol in Desire's name. Baseer didn't want to seem bitter by asking Powerful to return his .45 Ruger. In turn, they paid $500 for another brand new all-black .45 Ruger with a magazine that held 16 bullets. Desire didn't agree with him buying another gun since he had just recently been arrested for gun possession. She bought it anyway because she knew that Baseer would've bought one with or without her help. Baseer told her to wait until two weeks had passed, and then report the gun stolen to the Fayetteville Police Department.

Peru called Baseer on Tuesday, gloating about how lucky he was to escape before his fingerprints came back. Baseer didn't share the excitement because he had given the police his actual name and was now facing felony criminal charges. They only spoke for a few minutes before the conversation reminded him about his predicament and caused him to become upset. For the remainder of that week, Baseer refrained from calling Peru again. Instead, he chose to stay in contact with TK and Powerful. He wasn't able to reach TK until Friday morning because he wasn't answering his cellular phone. Baseer decided to call him around 8:00 am., just before Desire left home to go to work. TK answered the phone as if he was barely awake. "Peace God." "Peace, get up G. The only thing that comes to a sleeper is a dream." "I'm up. I'm about to burn this CD so that I can take it to that nigga Marley Marl tonite." "Oh word? I'd forgotten all about that shit. Who do you think is gonna be there?" "I don't even know son, probably just him and a few of his people. He's cool with my manager, it's not like an industry party or nothing." "True. What songs are you giving him?" "I'm only giving him the clean version of Talk 2 Em to play on his show." "Word. I like that joint, he should play it ." "I hope so." "Listen, I may be coming to New York this week, if I can get Powerful to cop some work for me." "I don't think that's gonna happen." "Why not?" "I saw Powerful downtown on Wednesday and he said a few things about you." "Like what?" "He just said that you were hot." "Hot?! Hot like how, on some snitch shit? That niggas got me twisted. As a matter of fact, I'm gonna hit you back."

Baseer hung up the telephone immediately and began dialing Powerful's cellular phone number. Powerful didn't answer his phone so Baseer tried again three hours later, but to no avail. Baseer didn't bother to call until the next day and his calls still went unanswered. In the meantime, Baseer was growing more and more upset. He called Powerful once, everyday , and he never answered or returned his calls. Baseer assumed that he was deliberately avoiding his calls and that he had decided to disassociate himself completely. He wasn't even answering the calls that were made on TK's cell phone so they both figured that he had withdrawn himself from their music group. That's when Baseer and TK decided to divide the third verse to "Part Time Hustle" between themselves.

After ten days, Baseer finally received a phone call from Powerful. Instead of answering with his usual greeting, "Peace" Baseer answered "Whattup." Then Powerful responded, "Peace." "What's good?" "I'm maintaining, it's been sorta hectic this week. That's why I haven't been answering your calls." "Oh is that right?" "Why Equality Self (yes)" "Yea, same here. I still need you to cop some work for me son, what's good?" "God, believe me when I tell you – I'm fucked up right now. Some niggas broke in my rest and stole some money and jewels, then I found out who it was so I went to the spot and aired it out by myself, shit was crazy B!" Baseer remained silent as if he didn't believe one single word that was said. Then he said sarcastically, "Yeah, that's real gangster – you know what Power? You're full of shit son. TK told me what you said. I can't believe that you would shit on me. I was your man ever since the days of playing Manhunt and shit. Now you wanna tell me lies and all this fake shit. Fuck you, you soft ass nigga!" (CLICK!)

Baseer hung up the phone and Powerful didn't bother to call back. Baseer then decided that he was gonna have to rob another bank to acquire the amount of money that he needed. Only this time, he didn't have a partner in mind that he had shared experience with. Baseer smoked a lot of weed and drank a lot of Hennessey that week because he was really stressed out. He even called TK and told him that he could use their two hours of studio time to record a solo track. Desire had a first cousin named Maria who was getting married on that following Sunday in Allentown, PA. Desire chose to attend the wedding but Baseer didn't want to go. She had planned to leave Fayetteville on Saturday morning and return on Monday. Desire took seven vacation days from her job on Tuesday because Baseer wanted to spend some quality time with her before she left to go to Pennsylvania. On Tuesday afternoon, they rented a hotel at the Marriott in Fayetteville until Saturday morning. Tuesday began with a bad start because Baseer couldn't remember where he had misplaced his gold chain. It seemed to had mysteriously disappeared. The hotel room was plush and the getaway helped Baseer to ease his mind from all of the things that were troubling him – his differences with Powerful, the perils of his next robbery, his arraignment in court, and etc., Desire did everything within her powers to keep Baseer happy until it was time for her to leave for Allentown.

On Saturday morning. Baseer woke up around 8:30. He decided to omit breakfast and go swimming in the hotel's indoor swimming pool for an hour before they checked out. Then Desire dropped Baseer off at their apartment around 10:45 and continued on her way to Pennsylvania. Baseer entered the apartment and dropped his luggage onto the living room floor. Then he walked into his bedroom to check his caller ID for missed calls. He noticed that the name Linda Clarke and her number had appeared eleven times since Tuesday. That was Powerful's grandmother who lived in Queens, NY. Baseer recognized her name instantly because she was always like a grandmother to him while he and Powerful were growing up as best friends in NYC.

Baseer was still upset with Powerful but he still needed him to buy more cocaine. When he recognized how many times Mrs. Clarke's name appeared on his caller ID, he figured that Powerful was calling to apologize and tell him that he was finally ready to pick up more drugs for him. That's when Baseer decided to call the number back, 7-1-8-9-4-9-6-9-0-2. Powerful's uncle Marcus answered the phone. Marcus was a 10-year old little boy that Powerful's grandmother had adopted, thus making him Powerful's uncle. The little boy answered, "Hello." Baseer said "Hello, may I speak to Kevin?" "Who is this?" "This is Baseer." "Kevin – got shot." When the little boy made that statement, Baseer paused to hear if he had anymore to say. Then he continued "and . . . he's dead." Baseer then began to consider the fact that little Marcus was only ten and that he probably didn't know what he was talking about. That's when Baseer said "let me speak to your mother."

Marcus carried the telephone to Mrs. Clarke and she answered, "Hello" "Hi grandma. This is Baseer." "Hi Baby" "Is Kevin around?" "No that was me calling your phone. I got the number from Kevin's mother. I'm sorry son, but .

. . your buddy is gone." Her confirmation caused Baseer to become silent for almost sixty seconds and he became suddenly confused. Then he slowly asked "What happened Grandma?" "Kevin got shot Tuesday morning by some guys in Harlem. He had just told me last week that some guys had broken into his apartment and robbed him. You see. . . I think that Kevin was dealing drugs or something." Tears began running down Baseer's face and he remained silent as Mrs. Clark explained her understanding of the murder. He became saddened as he realized that Powerful was telling the truth about being robbed and shooting someone. Mrs. Clarke's voice began to crack as she was speaking and she began crying softly. Baseer then said "I'm sorry Grandma, it's gonna be ok. Don't cry" as he was beginning to whimper himself. As her cries began to diminish, Baseer asked "When is the funeral Grandma?" She said "In one hour." That's when Baseer told her that he would call her back later on that evening. He knew that he didn't have enough time to make it to Powerful's funeral so he laid across his bed and tried to get his thoughts together. The argument that he and Powerful had kept replaying in his mind. Then he realized that he had lost his chain on the same day that Powerful got murdered; the same chain and charm that Powerful picked out for him at the Cross Creek mall.

Baseer sat up on his bed and decided to call Desire because he needed someone to talk to. For some odd reason, Desire didn't answer her cellular phone. That's when Baseer called Yahnis. When she answered her telephone, she was still lying in her bed. She answered "Hey Baby" Baseer's voice began to crack as he said "Boo guess what?" "Baby what's wrong?" Then, before Baseer could say a single word, he began to cry aloud like a young baby. Then he began saying "they killed my man. . . . they killed him." Yahnis then began trying to pacify him but there was only so much that she could do from the other end of the telephone line. Baseer then told Yahnis "I'm sorry for calling you like this, I'll talk to you later." Then he hung up the phone as she was saying "wait".

Baseer laid across his bed and resumed crying aloud. His telephone began ringing repeatedly but he ignored every call. He cried so hard that he dehydrated himself

93

and his fingers began to tremble beyond his control, as if he was about to have a seizure. That was because he was swimming that morning and he didn't eat breakfast or drink any fluids. He then fell asleep on his pillow that was drenched from tears and slept for five hours. When he woke up he called Desire and told her the news about Powerful. She was passing through Washington DC at the time. Desire gave her condolences and promised to call him back as soon as she arrived in Allentown. Then, Baseer called TK and conveyed the bad news to him. TK didn't take it as hard as Baseer did because he and Powerful weren't as close. When they were done talking, Baseer went into his living room and inserted the "All Eyez on Me" cd by Tupac into the stereo. Then he set the song "Unconditional Love" on repeat, smoked a blunt of sour diesel and began sifting through childhood memories about his crew. He also began to dwell on other things that had gone wrong in his life. After about an hour, he decided to take a shower and drive around Fayetteville to clear his mind. He drove for about 45 minutes before he decided to visit his mother Catherine.

When Baseer arrived at his parents' house, Catherine was home alone. He had a key to the backdoor, so he walked inside and found her sitting in the computer-room. She had on a pair of reading glasses and she was playing the "Solitary" card game on her computer. Baseer kissed his mother on the cheek and sat down on the daybed. The daybed was unmade as if she had slept there on the previous night; instead of in the bedroom with James. As Baseer was sitting down, Catherine said "Heyyyy. What are you doing here?" She was happy to see him because she seldomly received company, although most of her time was spent at home. Baseer replied "What's up Ma? I just felt like stopping by." "Nothing much just playing a little solitary." "Oh I noticed that you finished painting your rails out front. They look nice." "Thank you." "Yeah ma, today I found out that Kevin got killed." "What?" "Mrs. Clarke called and said that he got shot uptown on Tuesday morning." Catherine then paused her game to give Baseer her undivided attention. Then she asked "Well how are you taking it?" He replied "I dropped a few tears earlier but I'm alright. I just can't figure out why so much stuff is happening to me." "Son, God wouldn't put anything on you that you couldn't bear." "C'mon ma. You already know that I don't believe in that mystery God stuff." "Maybe that's the problem. I know that you have your beliefs and I've respected that since you were a teenager. But baby God is real and it's time for you to get your soul right because I don't think that this world will be around much longer." "I hear you Ma." "Baseer, I'm serious. You keep going around calling yourself God. You don't even realize what you are doing."

Baseer remained silent because he knew that this was an argument that he could not win. Catherine was a firm believer in Jesus Christ and Baseer couldn't convince her to believe otherwise – even if he pointed out a billion discrepancies in her religion. That's when Catherine grabbed a black King James Version Bible from the bookshelf directly across from the daybed. She opened it to Matthew 12:31 and insisted that Baseer read it aloud. To satisfy her he read it: "Therefore I say to you, every sin and blasphemy will be forgiven men but the blasphemy against the spirit will not be forgiven men."

The next day was Sunday, Mother's Day. Catherine asked Baseer to attend church with her. Baseer answered "C'Mon Ma, you know I'm not feeling that." Then she asked "Son – what's one time gonna hurt? Do it for me, that'll be the best Mother's Day present that I could ask for." When Catherine phrased it like that she made it nearly impossible for Baseer to deny her. Then he said "I don't even own a suit, and the mall closes at 9:00." "Oh don't worry about that. My Pastor says come as you are. There are plenty of young guys who attend my church and they all wear jeans and sneakers. Plus there are a lot of single girls your age that will be there." Baseer realized how much his mother wanted him to go with her so he finally agreed. He hadn't been to church in over fourteen years; not even for a funeral. Catherine said that she would pick him up at 8:00 on Sunday morning and they could ride together.

CHAPTER EIGHT

Baseer's alarm clock sounded at 6:00 on Sunday morning. That's when he awoke from his sleep and went directly into the kitchen to eat two bowls of Cinnamon Toast Crunch cereal. When he was done, he rolled a blunt of sour diesel and smoked half of it in the living room until it was almost 7:00. Then he went into his walk-in closet to decide on what he was going to wear to his mother's church. He decided to wear a black and gray Roc-A-Wear outfit because the pockets on his jeans were deep enough to conceal his pistol without it being noticeable. Ever since the incident with Powerful, Baseer became over cautious because he was involved in the same type of business. When his mother arrived at 8:00, Baseer was fresh out of the shower. He didn't smell like weed but his eyes were bloodshot red. When Catherine noticed them, she simply shook her head and said "Son, what am I gonna do with you?" His pistol was in his right pants pocket and the fully loaded clip was in the left pocket. They arrived at the church around 8:20.

The service lasted until 1:30 pm. The sermon wasn't strong enough to convince Baseer to convert, as Catherine intended for it to. The gospel music sounded really somber and caused Baseer to ponder on his problems for the most part of the service. As the worship service was coming to it's closing, the pastor said "I would like for all of the young sons and daughters to come up front and pick up a rose for your mother." As all of the other people began to stand up, Baseer was hesitant because he seemed to be the only man that wasn't wearing a suit. He knew that all eyes would've been on him. Catherine pinched Baseer on his left arm and said "Boy you'd better get me a rose." "Oww Ma!" said Baseer as he snatched his arm away. Then Baseer stood up and walked down the aisle slowly so that his pistol wouldn't sway back and forth in his pocket. As he was walking he scanned the crowd so that he wouldn't appear shy. When he sat back down, he handed Catherine her rose and she smiled proudly because she knew that other church members were watching.

After the service, Baseer paid for their dinner at the Golden Corral Restaurant. While they were eating, Baseer told Catherine about his court situation for the first time. He said that he was considering going on the run because he was probably facing eight to ten years. That's when Catherine said "Son you don't wanna be on the run for the rest of your life. Even if you have to do the whole eight years you will still be young when you get out. You have a long life ahead of you." Baseer replied "I know Ma, but that's easier said than done. I know that I can handle it because I've done it before, I just don't want to." "You just need to pray about it and ask God to help you." "There you go again. All I know is this, if they try to give me more than six years – I'm running."

After they ate dinner, Catherine dropped Baseer back off at his apartment. Then he searched the internet to find a criminal lawyer from South Carolina. He wrote down ten different names and telephone numbers. They were all from the state's capitol, Columbia. He had planned to call them on Monday morning. Then, since he had completed his legal business – he went back to the drawing-boards and got back to his illegal business. He figured out a possible way to pay for a lawyer without having to touch his stash. That's when he called Peru and he answered "Peace" "What's goody?" "Shit, you know me – just trying to hang on like a hubcap in the fast lane." "You're stupid kid. But look, I need for you to holla at your son for me." "Who?" "The Mexican dude. Find out if he ever found anybody to do that job. I need bread for a lawyer." "Alright well give me a minute. I'll get back with you by the end of the day." "Alright Peace." "One"

Baseer also needed to begin preparing for life on the run just incase worst came to worst. He decided to call one of his friends in Harlem named Almighty. That's when he dialed 2-1-2-5-6-4-1-8-8-1 and Almighty answered "Peace". "Peace All, how you?" "All wise and civilized." "True, I need to know if you still have a connect on the I Divines (I.D's)" "Indeed. Plus, I just bagged this little X-chromosome who works at the DMV on 125th Street across from the state building." "Word? I don't really need a New York picture ID, I just need a birth certificate and a social security card." "Well shit, just send me like power add two ($500) and I can get that tomorrow." "Alright well I'm about to go to the Western Union right now, it should be there in the next hour. The password is gonna be "Purple Kush". "You're gonna need my government and my address." "Yeah, let me grab a pen – alright." "The name is David Wilson and the address is 257 W. 118th Street, zip code 10027." "Got it. Nice look too G, just hit me on the hip when you get it – pause." "Peace" "Mercury Mercury." Almighty called Baseer one hour later and said that he had received the money. Peru also called in the same hour and said that Calin's offer still stood. Baseer told Peru to notify Calin that the job would be done in one month.

On Monday, Desire arrived back home around 12:30 pm. She was exhausted from driving so she went directly to bed. Her seven-day vacation had ended and she was scheduled to work on the next day, so Baseer didn't disturb her. He spent the entire day at home, cleaning and then relaxing. He also ironed 5 outfits for Desire to wear for every day of that week. When she finally woke up around 7:00 pm that night, Baseer was lying next to her asleep. She simply placed her head on his chest and returned to sleep with a smile on her face.

On Tuesday morning, Baseer woke up and noticed that the time was 6:15. He hadn't had sex ever since their last morning at the Marriott so he woke Desire up and made love to her. She would've been departing for work at 7:45. After she left, Baseer waited until 8:30 and began calling the lawyers that he pulled up on the internet. He only called five of them before he finally chose one, a 32-year old black female named Karen Ellison. She seemed to be the most sincere and the most experienced after hearing her explain how she had won similar cases in the past. She charged Baseer $15,000 to add him to her caseload and she also agreed to let him pay bi-weekly installments of $2000. Their first meeting was scheduled for the following Friday, when Baseer would make his first payment.

Almighty called Baseer before that afternoon. He said that he had the credentials and that he needed Baseer's address so that he could send them. Then he went to a local post office and paid an additional fee to have them delivered overnight. The name used on the ID's was Maurice Baker. Baseer called his old friend Big Keef. He met Big Keef while incarcerated some years back. Ikeef was a sloppy dark skinned man who weighed about 350 pounds. He was 26 years old.

"Hello" "What's up, big homie? It's Baseer" "Oh what's going on bro?" "Chillin out, man. Listen I need a favor." "What's up?" "I need to use your address to do this little scam that I have in mind. All you have to do is say that you don't know me when the police come by showing you pictures of me. If you can do that for me, I've got $1000 for you right now." "Shit, say no more. When are you coming through?" "I can be there in like 30 minutes." "Alright, now I need a favor too." "What's good?" "Stop by the substation II and pick me up two foot-long #19s and a two liter Pepsi." "God damm Keef, I got you kid." "Oh yeah, tell them to put a lot of cheese on both of them." "Yeah, I'm out."

Baseer went into the light fixture and removed $1000. Then he drove to Laurinburg to meet with Big Keef. He walked up to his door with the Substation II bag in his hand and the soda was tucked under his arm. Ikeef grabbed his food and then he invited Baseer inside. There was no where for Baseer to sit so he decided to keep the visit brief. The couch was covered with smelly blankets as if Big Keef had been sleeping there. There were empty Yoo-Hoo bottles and Debbie Cake wrappers all over the place. The room smelled terrible. Baseer hastily wrote down Keef's address while basically breathing through his mouth to avoid the odor. After doing so, Baseer gave him $1000 and left. His very next stop was the DMV in Laurinburg. When he entered the building, he plucked a number to be placed in line and waited on. Then he grabbed a driver's permit application. Shortly after he filled it out, a woman behind the desk yelled "#43." That was Baseer's number so he stood up and walked over to stand directly in front of her. Then she asked "How may I help you young man?" "Good morning ma'am, I would like to try for my driver's permit" said Baseer as he presented the application that he had filled out. As she was reviewing the application, she said "Mr. Baker, I'm gonna need your birth certificate and social security card." Baseer presented her with both of them and she began typing his information into the computer.

Baseer became nervous at that point but he tried really hard to suppress it. Only seconds later, the woman returned his information to him and asked him to begin an eye examination. After being asked to read a few lines, she concluded that he had 20/20 vision. Then she escorted him to a computer in a nearby room to begin testing for his permit. Baseer knew the correct answers to every question but he answered two questions wrong, intentionally, so that his actual age wouldn't be so obvious. When his results were processed the elderly woman congratulated him and told him to wait until his name was called so that he could take his picture. When he was called, he took his picture with an innocent smile on his face. Moments later, he received his brand new id card. That's when he told the woman "Thank you very much and have a blessed day." She replied "You do the same son."

Baseer returned to his Expedition and drove back to Fayetteville. While he was driving, he called Yahnis in Atlanta. He told her that he was planning to come to Atlanta in one month but he didn't tell her why. She became excited and insisted that he stayed at her apartment instead of Peru's. When they finished talking, Baseer drove home to get $300. Then he bought a money order and mailed in the payment for both of his traffic tickets to the Laurinburg Traffic Court.

It was almost 2:00 when Baseer finished handling all of his business for that day. That's when he went to Bullet's apartment and bought three grams of Mango Pina to smoke. Next he retired to his apartment to smoke and write some lyrics for a "rest in peace" song for Powerful. TK had given Baseer a beat with a sample from "Without Your Love" by Teddy Pendergrass that seemed appropriate for the song. As he began writing, he suddenly caught a severe case of writer's block. That's because he was becoming upset about not knowing who Powerful's assailants were. He wished that he knew so that he could murder them personally. As he was struggling to write, he suddenly remembered TK's appointment with Marley Marl. That's when he decided to call him and he answered loudly "Peace God!" "Damn son, don't bust my eardrum. What's the science?" "My nigga-I'm thinking it's about to go down." "What's that?" "This rapshit. They've been playing my shit on Hot 97 for the past three nights. I checked my Myspace page today and I've got like 800 new fans since they started playing "Talk 2 Em" "Say word?" "Word is bond and bond is life." "That's beautiful God, I'm proud of you." "You already know that if I can get one foot in the door I'm pulling you in with me. Rothschilds baby!" "Yeah for life. Be sure to keep me posted dunn – and let me know if you need anything, studio time, equipment, anything." "I appreciate that son." "Yeah, love is love." "Peace."

When Baseer hung up the phone, he closed his notebook because he realized that he wasn't in the mood to write. That's when he decided to write down a list of questions that he needed to ask Karen Ellison, his lawyer, on the next day. He fell asleep until 6:00 that evening when his cellular phone rang. It was Peru calling to let him know that Calin was willing to wait one month for Baseer to perform the job. Then Baseer ordered two pizzas from Papa John's so that they would be delivered around the same time that Desire returned home from work. After she returned home and they ate dinner, Baseer asked Desire to ride with him to the Cross Creek Mall so that he could buy a casual outfit for his lawyer visit on the next day. That's when they rode to the mall together in Desire's Lincoln LS around 8:00 pm.

Baseer bought a simple Ralph Lauren's Polo button up shirt and a pair of Khaki Polo slacks from Belk's. Then he and Desire walked to the Foot Locker to find him a pair of casual Timberland shoes. As they were looking at the shoes on the wall, in the Timberland section, a girl's voice came from behind them saying "Your name's Baseer right?" They both turned around to see who she was. Desire had an angry expression on her face as if she suspected her to be one of Baseer's undercover friends. Baseer didn't seem to recognize her until she said "Hi my name is Myra." That's when he told Desire "Oh baby, that's Power's girl." Then Myra asked, "Have you talked to him? He hasn't been answering his phone all week." "I'm sorry Ma, but Powerful was murdered last Tuesday." "Say what?" "Yeah Ma, it fucked me up too. That was my heart." "Oh my God! Thank you so much for telling me." Myra's eyes began to water as she turned to walk away. Her reaction caused Baseer to feel sad but he held back his tears. Then he paid for a pair of casual style Timberland shoes and exited the store. That's when they returned home and prepared for the next day.

Friday morning, Baseer drove to Columbia, SC to meet with his lawyer at 8:30. He gave her $2000 and assured her that she could expect another $2000 in exactly two weeks. Their meeting only lasted for about 30 minutes. He presented her with his arrest papers and explained his version of the incident. After hearing it, she said that he could've possibly been facing up to 15 years but she would seek the minimum sentence which would've been 5 years. She said that she was close friends with both the solicitor and the prosecutor of the following court term that would begin in less than two months. Then she gave Baseer a business card with her cell phone number on it and the contact information for her Paralegal, Kevin Henderson. That's when they shook hands and Baseer exited her office. Next Baseer drove to Laurinburg, NC around 10:20 am.

Baseer was dressed casually in his new outfit and his face was neatly shaved. When he arrived in Laurinburg, his first stop was the First National bank. He entered the bank and stood in line until a teller was available. He was called to the desk by a white male teller who looked between the ages of 21 and 25. He asked Baseer "Good morning Sir, how can I help you?" "I would like to open a checking account and I would like to deposit $400 into that account." Then the teller handed him an application and said "If you will be seated in the lobby and fill

this out, our next available staff will be with you shortly."
Baseer completed the application in ten minutes. Then
another young white male invited him into his office that
was down the hallway. As Baseer was being seated, he
handed the application to the man. Then the man asked
"Okay Mr. Baker, do you have your social security card
and your picture ID?" "Yes, Just a moment." Baseer retrieved all three identifications from his wallet including
the birth certificate, along with $400.

After noticing the issue date on Baseer's driving permit, the man said "So I see that you just got your driver's
permit on yesterday." "Yes, I just moved into town from
NYC about two weeks ago. I needed a NC ID so that I could
start this new job." "Okay well there's a $25 fee to open a
checking account and if you ever decide to withdraw that
$25 then your account will be closed." "I understand. I
would like to open my account with $400." Baseer hand-
ed the money to the man and he held each bill towards
the light as if he suspected that they were counterfeit.
Then he slid a sheet of paper over to Baseer and said
"OK, Mr. Baker, just sign here by the "X". As Baseer was
signing his alias name, the man said "Your check books
will be mailed to you and the process usually takes about
two weeks." "That's fine," said Baseer as he returned the
paper to him. "And is there anything else that I can assist you with sir?" "No sir, that will be all, thank you."
"Alright Mr. Baker, have a nice day and thanks for doing
business with First National." As Baseer exited the office,
he mumbled under his breath, "sucker". Then he drove
home to change into a t-shirt and some jeans.

Baseer spent the next two weeks patiently waiting
for his checkbooks to arrive at Big Keef's house. They
finally arrived on that Wednesday, before Baseer's second lawyer visit. When Big Keef called Baseer to inform
him that his package was there, he drove to Laurinburg
to pick them up immediately. Then he returned home
and called around for the cheapest storage rental. The
next morning, Thursday, Baseer paid $80 to rent a
storage lot for one month. The clerk gave him a key
to the lock on his storage room and a pass code that
would get him through the entrance gate 24 hours a day,
7 days a week.

On that Friday morning, Baseer visited his lawyer wearing the same casual Polo outfit that he had worn on his last visit. He made a payment of $2000 and the visit only lasted for 15 minutes. Then he returned to his apartment and waited until the First National Bank closed at 6 pm. Around 6:30 Baseer began his shopping spree with his checks. He knew that the bank would be closed until that following Monday morning at 8:00. His plans were to write bad checks all weekend long, without sleeping, because the bank wouldn't realize that his checks bounced until they reopened on Monday. By that time, he would've bought everything that he needed to sustain him for a long while if he had to go on the run.

Baseer spent the entire weekend spending checks in Laurinburg and all of it's neighboring small towns. Most of his shopping was done in shopping malls, outlets, Wal-Marts, liquor stores or grocery stores. He had to make numerous trips back and forth to his storage room and he stored everything in cardboard boxes. When he was done writing his last check, he destroyed all 3 of his ID's with a pair of scissors. He had bought over 20 new outfits (all top named brands), 5 winter coats, ten pairs of Timberlands boots (all colors), almost $1000 worth of hygiene, boxers, t-shirts, socks, 2 televisions, a stereo system, 20 cases of Dutch Master's Cigars, 20 gallons of Hennessey, cooking and eating utensils, bullets, and some sneakers and clothes for Desire. He bought all of these things to restrict being in the public eye once he relocated on the run.

When Baseer returned home, the only things that he took with him were the items that he had bought for Desire. When he walked into the apartment Monday morning, he placed Desire's bags in their walk in closet and went to sleep on his bed. He was happy that Desire was at work that morning because he had intended to sleep all day long. He slept for 10 hours until Desire turned on the bedroom light at 7:05 pm., when she returned home. She wasn't very upset because they had spoken frequently over the phone that weekend. She understood that he was local and handling important business. She just didn't know what the business was. When Desire walked over to the closet to put away her purse, she found several bags of clothes and female Timberland boots to match Baseer's. He figured that would prevent her from complaining when he left for Atlanta in the next two weeks. Desire was very excited about her gifts and she didn't even bother to ask how he had bought them. She simply assumed that he had used a portion of the money that was stashed in the light fixture.

On the next morning, Baseer called Almighty and told him that he would be needing another birth certificate and a social security card under a different name. They were to be used to lease himself a house when it was time to relocate on the run. When Almighty agreed to help him once again, he wired him another $525. The ID's arrived in Baseer's mailbox on Saturday because Almighty had sent them by regular delivery. The name on the ID's was Walter Edwards Jr. Baseer stashed the envelope in a Timberland shoe box in his closet. That same box was where he often kept his pistol at. Baseer spent the remainder of that week relaxing indoors and building up the nerve to commit the murder that he had promised Calin.

On Friday, Desire returned home around 7:15 pm. When she walked in the door, Baseer was asleep on the couch. That's when Desire tapped him on his leg and said "Baby, wake up. I need to tell you something." Baseer opened his eyes and sat uprightly to offer his undivided attention. Then he said "I'm listening. What's on your mind?" "Baseer, my menstrual cycle was over 2 months late so I called my job this morning and told my boss that I would be a few hours late. Then I drove to the hospital and the doctor said that I was two months pregnant." Baseer's eyes instantly began to beam because he had always wanted a child of his own. That's when he rose to his feet and asked "Word boo?" When she nodded her head, "yes", Baseer kneeled down, placed his head on her stomach, and wrapped his arms around her waist. For that moment, Baseer had forgotten all of his troubles. He envisioned himself carrying a baby boy or a baby girl, while saying "I'm so happy right now." Desire looked down upon him and a tear fell from her left eye. She became emotional when she saw how happy the news had made Baseer because she knew that he was going through a lot of tribulations at that time. When Baseer looked up and noticed that Desire was distilling tears, he stood up and wiped her tears away with the side of his thumb. They sat on the couch together and held a conversation where Baseer promised to be the best father and provider that he could be. Desire asked him what he was planning to do about his court situation and he simply answered "I'll figure something out."

CHAPTER NINE

Two weeks passed and the time had arrived for Baseer to drive to Atlanta and meet with Calin. Peru arranged for them to meet at the "La Pantera" Mexican restaurant on Jimmy Carter Boulevard in Atlanta on Wednesday afternoon. Baseer arrived in Clarkston on Wednesday morning. He decided not to notify Yahnis that he was in town until he had completed his business with Calin. Peru and Baseer went to the "La Pantera" restaurant at 12:30, Wednesday afternoon. Calin was the owner of the restaurant. When they entered, they were seated by a Mexican female greeter. That's when Peru told her, "Mr. Calin nos espera (Mr. Calin is expecting us)" She then went to Calin's office to verify that Peru was telling the truth. Two minutes later, she returned to their table and said "sigume por favor (follow me please)" Next she escorted Baseer and Peru to Calin's office that was located upstairs. When they entered the office, Calin was sitting behind his desk and talking on the telephone in Spanish. He gestured with his hands that Baseer and Peru should seat themselves.

Calin was a 25 year old Mexican man who stood 5'9" and weighed about 200 pounds. He had a demeanor about himself that was very serious. When he was done speaking on the phone he began speaking to Baseer in Spanish because he didn't speak English at all. "Ungusto Conocerte (nice to meet you)" As Baseer extended his arm to shake his hand, Calin then said "Yo he oido cosas buenas de ti (I've heard some good things about you)" Baseer then asked him "como que (like what?)" "He oido que te gusta hacer dinero (I've heard that you like to make money)" "No todos? (Doesn't everybody)" replied Baseer. Calin recognized that Baseer seemed to be very serious about his business, so he got straight to the point and said "Estoy seguro que Peru y ate dijo cuanto yo pagaria por ti verdad? (I'm sure that Peru already told you how much I'm willing to pay you right)" Baseer, while maintaining his poker face answered, "si, veintemil (Yes $20,000)." Then Calin said "correcto (correct)" and began opening a brown clasp envelope. Next he pulled out two photos and handed them to Baseer as he said "Esta es una foto de su casa y carro (This is a picture of his house and his car)." He placed the pictures on the desk before Baseer. Then he said "Esta es una foto de ei. Talves ei se vea diferente porque yo oi que ua tiene una cortada en su cara" (This is a picture of him. He might look a little different now because I heard that he has a cut on his face.)

When Baseer received the picture from Calin, he immediately recognized the man. He was the same guy that Baseer and Peru had fought in the restroom at the Prime Time nightclub. Calin noticed that Baseer seemed surprised so he asked "Conoses a ei? (Do you know him?)" Baseer simply shook his head "no." That's when Calin went on to explain who the guy was. "El le puso el dedo a mi hermano y el Jues le dio 30 anos en prison (He snitched on my brother and the judge gave him 30 years in prison)" Then Baseer asked "Porque no lo mataste tu mismo? (Why didn't you kill him yourself?)" "El Policia me sospechara. Necesito estar en un hoter fuera del pueblo cuando lo mates (The police will suspect me. I need to be in a hotel out of town when you murder him)"

After Calin finished expressing his hatred for the man, Baseer told him to evacuate the town that night and that he would have the job done by Saturday. Calin then placed the pictures back into the envelope along with the address to the man's apartment. He also gave him a prepaid cellular phone to call him on once the job was completed. He told Baseer to get rid of the phone immediately after the call. The phone number that Calin gave Baseer was also to a disposable phone that he had bought strictly for that purpose. At the end of their meeting, Calin presented Baseer with a black briefcase. The contents of the briefcase was $10,000 cash; half of the agreed amount. Calin assured him that he would receive the other half when the job was done. After the meeting, Baseer and Peru returned to Peru's apartment in Clarkston.

When Baseer and Peru arrived back at the apartment, it was almost 3:00 pm. Baseer placed the briefcase beneath his bed in Peru's guest bedroom. Then he sat on the bed and reopened the envelope to study all of the information. The man's name was Bamboo. He lived in an apartment on Lawrenceville Highway in Tucker, GA. Peru recognized the address because Monique lived in that same town, so they drove to Tucker around 8:30 that night. Their first stop was at Monique's apartment. Peru told Monique that they needed to borrow her Lincoln Navigator for a couple of hours. Then they drove to Bamboo's apartment complex to learn of his nightly routine. Just before they got there, they pulled into a Checker's restaurant's parking lot and removed Monique's license tags. Bamboos apartment was right around the corner.

Baseer didn't see the car from the pictures in the parking lot but he did see the apartment. All of the lights in the apartment seemed to be turned off. Baseer parked beside a garbage dumpster, facing Bamboo's door and shut off the truck. Bamboo lived on the first floor. Monique's windows had dark limo tints all around, except for the front windshield. Baseer and Peru began smoking a blunt of Kush and waited for Bamboo to return home. After waiting for almost an hour, two cars turned into the parking lot; one following the other. They parked next to each other, directly in front of Bamboo's door. That's when Baseer and Peru sunk down into their seats so that they wouldn't be seen. Bamboo stepped out of the first car which was a 1986 Bonneville with a "Skittles" paint job and 22 inch chrome rims, then a female stepped out of the second car which was a white Honda Civic. They both entered the apartment together, without even looking in the direction of the Navigator. Seconds later, lights turned on in the apartment and Baseer and Peru began to watch them through the window shades. The female turned on the television and sat on the couch directly in front of the window. Then Bamboo closed the shades and

Baseer could no longer see what they were doing. After about 20 minutes, the lights went out in the room but Baseer could still see the glow from the TV through the shades.

Baseer was uncertain about whether or not Bamboo had that female living with him. That's when he decided to leave and return one hour later. When they returned they noticed that the Honda Civic was gone but the Bonneville was still parked in the same space. The glow from the television still shone through the window shades but Baseer didn't know if anyone was in the apartment. After about ten minutes, Baseer noticed the silhouette of Bamboo talking on the phone in front of the window. When Bamboo walked away from the window, Baseer and Peru left and went back to Monique's apartment to return her truck. They placed the license tags back on her truck in a nearby parking lot, after they left Bamboo's apartment complex. When they entered Monique's apartment, it was 12:10 am and she was asleep in her bedroom. Baseer and Peru decided to watch television and smoke in her living room until another two hours had passed. Then they left in Baseer's Expedition to make one final trip to Bamboo's apartment complex. This time, Baseer didn't turn into the apartment complex. He continued down Lawrenceville Highway and examined the parking lot as he was passing by. He noticed that the Honda Civic had not returned so he concluded that Bamboo lived alone. That's when Baseer and Peru returned to Clarkston around 2:30 am.

On the next morning at 9:15, Baseer called Calin on his prepaid mobile phone. When he answered, Baseer asked "Ya estas afuera del Pueble? (Are you already out of town?)" Calin responded "Si, estoy en el cuarto en un hoter ahorita (Yes I'm in my hotel room right now.)" When Baseer ended his conversation with Calin, then he called Desire. He basically called to see how she was feeling and to remind her to buy some fruits. He also told her to get into the habit of drinking at least eight cups of water every day. He began to explain how important it was for her to discipline herself to eat the right foods during her pregnancy. Desire was at work so she had to cut the conversation short. Overall, she was happy to have received the call.

Throughout the day, Baseer had recurring thoughts about his unborn child. He also kept having thoughts about his upcoming arraignment in court. He was nervous about committing the homicide but also determined because he really wanted the cash. When he thought about what happened to Powerful, he began to imagine Bamboo as his assassin. That seemed to give him the extra push that he needed, in order to kill him. Baseer spent the remainder of the day in Clarkston, smoking Kush and drinking Heineken beers with Peru. He wanted to get drunk when it was time for him to kill Bamboo. At 8:00 pm Baseer emptied the clip to his .45 ruger and replaced the bullets with brand new ones. He reloaded the clip with a black handkerchief covering his fingertips, so that his fingerprints wouldn't be on the shells. When he was done, he went outside and placed the pistol under the hood of his Expedition.

On the previous night, Bamboo arrived at home around 9:45 pm. Baseer memorized the route to Bamboo's apartment so he drove to Tucker, alone around 9:15. Just before he reached Bamboo's apartment complex, he pulled into an ABC store's parking lot and removed his license tags. Next he drove into the apartment complex and parked in an empty space that was directly beside the space where Bamboo had parked on Wednesday night. Bamboo's car was not in the parking lot. For the next 15 minutes, Baseer sat in his truck and drunk two straight shots of Hennessey as he listened to "Somebody's Gotta Die" by the Notorious BIG. At 9:30, Baseer popped the hood of his truck open. Then he stepped out of his truck and opened the hood as if he was having problems getting the truck started. He left the key in the ignition. Shortly afterwards, a Caucasian man and his son exited their apartment and began walking towards the man's car. The man asked Baseer if he needed any assistance but he calmly replied "No I'm fine. My truck does this all the time." That's when they got into the man's car and drove away.

Almost ten minutes later, Baseer began to hear bass pounding from a nearby car stereo. That's when he noticed two headlights on a car that was about to turn into the complex. When the car came into view, Baseer noticed the "skittles" paint job immediately. This time, the Honda Civic wasn't following the Bonneville. Baseers' adrenaline then began to rush. His hood was raised and he was standing in front of it. The Bonneville pulled around the rear of the Expedition and parked directly next to it. As the driver was parking, Baseer grabbed his pistol from under his hood and cocked the hammer back. Then he began speeding towards Bamboo's driver's-side door. Before Baseer even had enough time to see who was driving the vehicle, he fired three rounds through the driver's side window. After the first shot, blood splattered across the front windshield. The second and third shots shattered the window and the majority of the glass fell into the car. That's when he noticed Bamboo slumped over the arm rest; fighting for his life. He was bleeding from a shot to his neck and one to his face. Then Baseer shot him in his temple and said "Coup De Grace muthafucka!"

Baseer closed the hood of his truck with his pistol still in his right hand. He didn't bother to look for the bullet shells because he knew that his fingerprints were not on them. That's when he hopped back into his Expedition and sped off. His adrenaline was still pumping as he drove with his pistol in his passenger seat. In less than two minutes, he passed by two speeding police cars with their blue lights flashing; headed in the direction of Bamboo's apartment. Baseer began to panic because he was driving without a license tag. Fortunately, for him, he was being followed by another SUV so the police never noticed it. They continued towards the apartment. A few seconds later, Baseer saw an ambulance truck speeding in the exact same direction as the police cars. That confirmed that they were responding to a call that was received from the crime scene. Baseer drove the entire way back to Clarkston without stopping to place the tags back on the truck. When he arrived back at Peru's apartment, he backed into a parking space directly in front of Peru's building. Then he concealed his pistol in his right pants pocket and retrieved the license tags from under the driver's seat. There was no one outside in the parking lot so Baseer placed the license plate back on the truck.

When he walked into the apartment, it was 10:17pm. Peru and Monique were sitting on the couch and watching television with the lights off. Baseer went directly to his bedroom and called Calin. After only one ring, Calin answered "Hola (Hello)" Then Baseer said "Esta echo. (It's done)" "Estas seguro? (Are you sure?)" "Si, yo lo dispare en el cuello, su cara y su cabesa (Yes, I shot him in his neck, his face and his head)" Calin remained silent, so Baseer continued, "Manana va ha estar en las noticia (It should be all over the news tomorrow)" Calin had planned to remain out of town for three more days, so he said "Mis compass van a estar viendo las noticias manana (My partners will be watching the news tomorrow), Si ei esta muerto, pues manana puedes ir a recojer el dinero de mi restaurante (If he is dead, then you can pick up your money tomorrow from my restaurant)" "A que hora (At what time?)" "Manana en el tarde (Tomorrow afternoon)."

Baseer was almost certain that Bamboo was dead so he was confident that he would be receiving his money on the following day. He placed his pistol in his briefcase with his money and pushed the briefcase back under the bed. Then he took a hot shower and changed into a pair of black sweat shorts and a solid black t-shirt. When he stepped out of the bathroom, it was almost 11:00. That's when he turned on the television in his bedroom and found a local news channel. As he was waiting to see if the news reporters were gonna mention the homicide, Peru knocked on his door and he said "Come in God". Peru was smoking a blunt of Kush so he sat on the bed beside Baseer and passed it to him. Then he asked "So what happened?" "You already know. . . it's about to be a lot of slow singing and flower bringing." "You returned that nigga?" "Yea man, I think I sent him back to the essence. I'm waiting to see what the news is talking about." "Word? Well yo. . "you can dead that blunt or whatever, me and Monique are about to take it down." "Alright son of man. We'll build."

Thirty minutes passed and the news reporters didn't mention any developing stories about a homicide in Tucker, Georgia. Baseer didn't get discouraged, he simply called Yahnis and she answered "Hey Boo." Baseer replied "Sexy, what's good?" "Nothing I'm just chillin at home." "Yeah, I just touched down in Atlanta like 20 minutes ago." "For real?" "Yeah." "Where are you now?" "I'm at my niggas crib in Clarkston." "Well, can we meet somewhere or something?" Baseer didn't think that it would've been wise to drive his truck anymore that night so he said "Actually, I'm sort of tired right now from all of that driving. Why don't you just come and pick me up?" "That's fine. Exactly where are you?" "I'm in some apartments directly across from The Georgia Perimeter College." "Just give me the address and my navigational system will tell me how to find it." Baseer placed Yahnis on hold and went to Peru's bedroom to ask him what his address was. Then he retrieved the call and said "It's 3948 Memorial College Avenue, Apt #19." "Alright baby, I'll be there in about 35 minutes."

While Baseer was waiting for Yahnis to arrive, the news reporter finally gave a report on the incident. She said that a man named Daniel Porter (Bamboo) was pronounced dead at the scene as a result of multiple gunshots. She also said that there were no suspects, but four bullet shells were discovered and taken to the laboratory to be examined. The crime scene investigators didn't seem to have any leads on what the shooter was driving. Baseer picked out an Akademiks outfit and a pair of wheat color construction Timberlands to take with him to Yahnis' apartment for the next day. When Yahnis arrived, Baseer walked outside while still dressed in a T-shirt, sweat shorts and bedroom shoes. His outfit and his boots were in two leftover shopping bags. When Baseer got into Yahnis' car, she was listening to the "Heart of the Streets" cd by B.G. Coincidentally, she too was dressed in her relaxed wear – a spongebob pajama set and a blue headwrap. Baseer placed his bags in her backseat and then he leaned towards her to give her a peck on the lips. That's when Yahnis backed out of her parking space and began driving to her apartment in East Lake Meadows. Baseer didn't take his pistol or his money with him. He only carried $40 with him. When he recognized what cd she was listening to, he said "Hold up boo. What the fuck do you know about B.G.?" She replied "What? I like this song. You left this cd in my car and I've been listening to it ever since." "Look at my baby trying to get on some gangsta shit." Baseer had about a quarter of his blunt left so he turned the music up and began smoking as Yahnis drove to her apartment.

Baseer had fallen asleep by the time that they arrived

at Yahnis' apartment. When they went inside, Baseer was impressed by the way that her apartment was decorated. The color scheme in her living room was navy blue and burgundy. The leather couches were burgundy with small navy blue pillows on them, and the curtains were navy blue with burgundy streaks. The color scheme for her bedroom was white and brown. She had a cherrywood bedroom set with a brown comforter on the bed. The carpet was all white with a rug that was made out of bear fur. Yahnis recognized how tense Baseer seemed so she asked "Baby, are you good?" He answered "Yeah Ma, I'm straight." "You look like you have a million thoughts racing through your brain right now." "Damn, is it that obvious?" "Yeah, it is. Let me see if I can help you to relax."

Yahnis removed two pillows from her bed and placed them on the bear rug. Then she said "Boo, take your shirt off and lay down right here on this rug." Baseer removed his shirt and laid flat on his stomach. The rug was very soft. Baseer figured that a back massage was next so he closed his eyes and waited. That's when Yahnis removed her bedroom shoes and placed her right foot on his lower back. Next, she placed her left foot on his back and applied her full body weight. She was a petite girl so she wasn't heavy at all. Baseer's eyes remained shut as Yahnis began taking soft steps all across his back. When she found the spots where he was the most stiff, she placed her left foot on the floor and began massaging them with the ball of her right foot. Baseer became so relaxed that he drifted off to sleep for a half-hour. That's when Yahnis woke him up and told him to join her in bed.

When Baseer woke up, Yahnis had already dimmed the lights and the song "The Softest Place on Earth" by Xscape was playing in the stereo. Plus she had two vanilla scented candles lit on her dresser. Baseer climbed into the bed next to her and laid flat on his back. Yahnis was completely naked beneath the covers. She climbed on top of him immediately and began sucking on his neck. Baseer didn't want her to leave a hickey on his neck so he traded positions and began kissing and sucking on her breasts. Then he removed his shorts and penetrated her missionary style, without protection. The sex was slow and every stroke was to the rhythm of the music that was playing. During the course of them having sex, Yahnis whispered "I love you" into his ear. The sex was so good that he responded, "I love you too." Then she sunk her fingertips into his upper back and began moaning and calling his name. After about 45 minutes, Baseer released inside of her for the second time. They both fell asleep shortly afterwards.

Baseer woke up around 4:15 am while Yahnis was still sleeping. He began to stare up at the ceiling and meditate about his life. He thought about Powerful's death, Desire's pregnancy, his father's addiction, his court situation, the murder that he had committed and a number of other things. He also thought about how it would be virtually impossible to be an active father figure in his child's life from prison or on the run. Then he began to wonder if any of his other crimes would ever catch up to him. When he looked over at Yahnis, she was asleep with the most-innocent look on her face. That's when he realized that he was starting to develop love for her. He was going through a downtime and he was becoming overwhelmed by the way that she was treating him. At that moment, he began feeling bad because he realized that his feelings for Yahnis didn't supersede his love for Desire. Therefore, his dealings with Yahnis had to come to an end really soon. He meditated to himself for almost an hour while Yahnis remained asleep. Then he closed his eyes and went back to sleep also.

Around 8:30 am., Yahnis stepped out of the bed and went into the kitchen to prepare breakfast. That's when Baseer decided to call Calin. The phone only rung once before Calin answered "Hola (hello)" Baseer then asked "Que Paso? (What's happening?)" "Mi compa me able en la manona y me dijo que vio a Bamboo en las noticia. (My partner called me this morning and told me that he saw Bamboo on the news.)" "Esta bien (Alright)" "Yo te agradesco por nacereso (I really appreciate you doing that)" "No problema (No problem)." "Tu pueded reguntar tu dinero despues de la un a hoy (You can pick up your money after 1:00 today)" "Solo ves a mi restaurante y preguntale a mi hermana Maria ella teva ha estar esperando (Just go to my restaurant and ask for my sister Maria. She will be waiting for you.)" Just before the call ended,

Calin reminded Baseer "Destrulle este telefono (destroy this telephone)."

After the call ended, Baseer removed his sim card and flushed it down the toilet in Yahnis' bathroom. Then he walked into the kitchen to see what Yahnis was cooking. She remembered that he was a vegetarian so she cooked grits with cheese, buttered biscuits, hash browns with red and green peppers, and waffles. They ate breakfast together at the kitchen table. While they were eating, Baseer asked "What time do you have to work today?" She answered "I'm supposed to go in at 12:30 pm this afternoon but I'm about to call in sick." "Word. Because I need for you to take me to pick this money up." "From where" "Do you know where Jimmy Carter Boulevard is?" "Yeah I know exactly where it is." "I want you to take me there around 1:00." Baseer was planning to return to Fayetteville later on that night.

CHAPTER TEN

Affter they ate breakfast, Yahnis washed the dishes and they returned to the bedroom to have sex one final time. It was around 11:00 when they finished. That's when they took individual showers and got dressed. Baseer and Yahnis left her apartment at exactly 1:00 pm. They stopped by a local gas station and Baseer spent his $40 on gas for Yahnis' car. They arrived at the "La Pantera" restaurant about 20 minutes later. Baseer told Yahnis to remain in the car while he went inside. When he entered, he was greeted by the same female greeter that seated him and Peru on Wednesday. He responded "Necesito hablar con Maria porfavor (I need to speak with Maria please)." "Yo soy Maria (I am Maria)" "Tu hermano me dijo que tenias algo para mi (Your brother told me that you had something for me)." "Si Ahorita regresa (I'll be right back)." Maria walked into the back and Baseer noticed her going upstairs towards Calin's office. Almost two minutes later, she returned with a small black briefcase that was identical to the one that he had received from Calin. Then she told him "Aqui esta, Calin me dijo que te disera que todo esta aqui (Here it is, and Calin told me to tell you that it's all there)" "Esta bien, gracias y que diete bonita (Alright, thank you and stay beautiful)" "No gracias (No, thank you)."

Yahnis still had the car started when Baseer got back inside. He placed the briefcase in his lap and told Yahnis that she could drive off. When they turned onto the boulevard, Baseer closed every window and opened the briefcase in his lap. That's when he found ten separate stacks of $50 bills. He removed one stack and saw that it had twenty $50 bills in it. Then he placed the money back into the briefcase and placed it on the floor behind the driver's seat. Their next stop was Peru's apartment. When they went inside, Monique and Yahnis began talking in the living room. Baseer carried the briefcase into the bedroom and Peru followed him. As soon as they closed the bedroom door, Peru said "I saw the news at 6:00 this morning. They said that the cops don't know shit. All that the witnesses know is that they heard shots." "Oh word?" "Keep your eyes peeled for me son because I'm leaving tonight." "No question, I got you."

Baseer opened the briefcase on the bed and removed a stack of $50 bills. Then he hooped it over to Peru, and said "that's a stack son . . that's off the arms." Peru caught it and said "My G you don't owe me nothing." "I know but that's the least that I can do for you putting the whole shit together." Peru placed the money in his pocket and asked "Do you feel like rolling up?" Baseer replied "Hell yeah fam. I haven't smoked all day." Then he placed the briefcase under the bed and they returned to the living room to smoke and hang out with their girls. Baseer and Yahnis stayed at Peru's apartment until 7:00 pm, then it was time for Baseer to return back to Fayetteville. That's when he went outside and stashed his pistol under the hood of his Expedition. He removed $100 from one of the briefcases to pay for gas. Then he departed from Yahnis and drove back to North Carolina. The entire trip went smooth and he returned home around 1:00 Saturday morning. He entered his apartment carrying one briefcase in each hand. When he walked into his bedroom, Desire was sitting up on the bed and watching TV. He placed the briefcases on the floor next to the bed, and walked over to Desire to kiss her. She kissed him but she didn't seem very happy to see him.

Baseer emptied both briefcases onto the bed and began counting the money right in front of her. In the middle of his count, Desire walked over to their nightstand and pulled an opened envelope from the drawer. Then she asked Baseer "Could you please explain this?" Baseer received the envelope and saw that it was a letter that was sent from the Florence County General Sessions Court. It was sent to notify him of the next court term that was to begin in exactly 28 days. Baseer then told Desire "Apparently you already read it." She argued "Yes I read it and it said that you have to go to court in South Carolina." "So what?" "You told me that you got arrested in Maryland. South Carolina is in the opposite direction so what the fuck is going on?" Baseer paused for a moment as she stared angrily at him. Then he said "Alright Desi, I'm about to tell you the truth. That Sunday morning when I said that I was driving to New York . . . I really went to Atlanta to meet with Peru." "So why would you lie about some simple shit like that Baseer?" "Because I didn't wanna hear you riffin about how you think I've got another bitch in Atlanta. You know how you can get sometimes." "So who were you fighting in South Carolina?" "Some devil in this restaurant that I stopped at on my way back." "Baseer, I can tell that you are lying. You can't even look me in my eyes." "Desi, that's the truth- hate it or love it. You can argue with yourself if you want to but I'm about to jump in the shower."

Baseer carried the $18,900 into the bathroom and stashed it in the light fixture along with the $50,975 that was already there. Then he took a shower and returned to his bed about 30 minutes later. Desire was still upset so she didn't speak to him for the remainder of the night. On Saturday morning, Baseer woke up around 9:00. Desire didn't have to go to work so Baseer asked her to ride with him to South Carolina for his lawyer's visit. Before they left, he withdrew $4000 from his stash to pay her with. They drove Desire's Lincoln LS instead of his Expedition. On their way to South Carolina, Baseer said "Desire, I've been doing a lot of thinking about what I'm gonna do about my court situation. On one hand, I wanna get this shit behind me. But another side of me is telling me to go O.T on the run." Then Desire said "Baby, I think that you should just get it out of the way so that we can be a family and live a normal life." "I feel you too but I wanna be around when the baby comes. Plus, I want to be there and provide for it." "Well Baseer, how are you gonna be there and provide if you're running from the law?" Baseer paused in deep thought, then he finally uttered "I just

need to hear what this lawyer bitch is talking about."
That's when he turned the music back up.

Baseer and Desire entered Karen Ellison's office together. The first thing that Baseer did was present her
with $4000 and she began writing out a receipt for him.
Then she began to explain what his current status was.
She said that she had spoken to the solicitor that week,
and that he said that he could get Baseer five years if he
agreed to plea guilty during the first week of the court
term. She then went on to explain that if he chose to pro-
long or have a trial, that he could face up to 20 years
if he was found guilty. Then, Baseer began to explain
that Desire was 2 months pregnant with his child and
asked if she could get the plea bargain extended for 7
more months; until after the birth of his child. She said
that she seriously doubted that to be possible. She also
warned him that the plea offer would be a negotiated
sentencing and that it would have a two-week expiration
date. Baseer knew that 5-years was a good deal because
he had signed the Federal Gun Law act when he was last
released from prison. The federal Gun Law Act stated that
if he was ever charged with possession of another firearm,
he would receive five years for the gun and an additional
year for every bullet. Baseer's .380 was fully loaded with
16 bullets.

Baseer was stressed out when they left the lawyer's office. He drove and remained silent for the first 30 minutes
of the drive. When he did begin speaking, he expressed
that he was leaning more towards the idea of going on the
run. Desire said that the idea was foolish and that she
preferred not to continue listening to him talk about it.
When they arrived back in Fayetteville, Baseer drove to
Mt. Sinai Apartments to buy some sour diesel from Bullet. Then they returned to their apartment. Baseer spent
the remainder of the day smoking and dwelling on his
problems. When he and Desire went to bed that night,
they had a long and deep conversation. Desire said "Baseer, I understand your plight and I don't want you to go
to jail just as much as you don't want to go. Your lawyer
said that you will only have to do 85 percent of your sentence right?" "Yeah, but " "Well, that's only four years and
three months. That's not really that long. When I do have

the baby, we'll come to visit you every chance that I get."

Baseer gazed deeply into her eyes for a few seconds just before he said "Desi, another major reason why I don't wanna do that bid is because I'm afraid of losing you." "You're not gonna lose me." "You say that now because I'm here and everything is peaches. When I go back to the beast I can't fuck you, I can't spend time with you and I can't really be there when you need me. Eventually you're gonna say fuck Baseer." "Baby where is all of this coming from?" "This is real spit. I've been to prison before and I've seen the shit a million times. Bitches get lonely after awhile and move on. Most times they start throwing old bullshit up in a nigga's face. That's just an easy way to cop out." "Well baby, I'm not one of those quote unquote bitches that you're speaking about. You're always telling me to trust you but you don't even trust in me." The conversation carried on for another 20 minutes before Baseer finally agreed to go to court and plea guilty. That's when he said "I'll do the time – only for the sake of you and my child." "Our child." "Yeah. And Desi don't turn your fuckin back on me when my back's against the wall and my dick is in the dirt." "Stop saying shit like that. I couldn't turn my back even if I wanted to. I'm in love with you Baseer." The couple then went into their bedroom to have sex. Baseer performed well even though his thoughts were elsewhere. In the back of his mind, he imagined the day when Desire would find someone else. That was probably his biggest fear even though he'd cheated on her many times. He wanted to believe in Desire but he had trouble doing so. He believed that Desire was in love with him but, naturally her love would begin to die if he was to leave for a long period of time.

The next morning at breakfast, Baseer suggested that Desire stopped eating meat. Her response was "Look, I left the pork alone for you but now you're going too far." Baseer argued, "All vegetables serve a purpose in your diet. Eating meat is a habit that we picked up from white people. They started eating dead animals when they used to live in caves. What exactly do you expect to get from eating meat?" Desire remained quiet as Baseer answered himself, "nothing but an early grave." Then Desire said "But Baseer I know people who have eaten meat for their entire lives and still lived to be 100 years old." "100 years? Baby that's young. If you read the Bible you'll see people like Methuselah who lived 969 years." "Well Baseer, I see your point. I can't say that I'll quit cold turkey but I'll try for you." "Don't try for me, do it for yourself and do it for that baby in your stomach that you poison every time that you swallow that shit." "Alright already damn!"

After breakfast, Baseer asked Desire to take a ride with him. Then they got dressed and got into Baseer's Expedition. Baseer drove them to his storage room. When he drove through the entrance gate, he parked directly in front of his storage lot. When they stepped out of the truck, Baseer opened the master lock and raised the garage door. That's when Desire asked "What's in all of these boxes?" Baseer answered "Open one and look for yourself." She opened one box and saw over 100 canned vegetables. Then she opened a second box and found hundreds of bars of soap and tubes of toothpaste. That's when she smirked at Baseer and said sarcastically, "Now baby, I've heard of being a good consumer. But what the hell is this? A bomb shelter?" "Got jokes?" "This was some stuff that I bought just in case I had to go O.T on the run." "So this is what you did with all of that money?' "No this stuff was free." "Free?" "Yeah. Now before you start asking a million questions – can you open the back door on my truck so that I can load up a few of these boxes?"

Desire went back to the truck to open both back doors. Then Baseer placed a few boxes in the backseat and behind the backseat. He took a few of the boxes that contained food and hygiene items to their apartment. Plus he grabbed a case of cigars and a gallon of Hennessey to carry home. He figured that it would be best for Desire to have the vegetables so that she could practice eating right without having an excuse not to. The hygiene items were enough to sustain her long after he went off to prison. When they returned home, Baseer single-handedly put everything where it belonged. He filled the kitchen's cabinets with canned vegetables and dry beans. The hygiene products were placed in the bathroom cabinet beneath the sink and in the linen closet in the hallway.

On Sunday morning, Desire and Baseer drove to Baseer's parents' house. It was only 10:00 when they arrived and James was already out running the streets. Catherine was outside watering her flower garden. As they were walking towards her, Desire asked "How are you doing Mrs. Watson?" Then Catherine gave her a hug and replied "I'm fine baby, how are you doing?" "I'm fine." Catherine always liked Desire and she wanted Baseer to marry her but marriage through the government was forbidden in Baseer's belief system. Desire was telling Catherine how beautiful her flowers looked when Baseer interrupted, "Ma, we have a surprise for you." She asked "What is it?" "You have another grand-baby on the way." Catherine smiled and said "Well it's about time." Then she looked at Desire and asked "How many months?" "A little over 2". Catherine was very happy to hear the news but there was also something troubling her.

Catherine began to speak, "At least, I received some good news today. I was talking to Sadie this morning and she just had her biopsy. The doctor diagnosed her with breast cancer." Then Baseer said "No Ma, are you serious?" "I wouldn't joke about that." Desire seemed confused and that's when she asked Baseer "Who is Sadie?" He answered, "She practically raised me. That's my mother's older sister, plus she's my god mother." Then Catherine continued "I'm driving up to NY this week to pick her up. She's gonna stay with us for a while." Since Catherine was already upset about Sadie being sick, Baseer decided not to tell her that he was going to prison in 4-6 weeks. She was already suffering from hypertension and high blood pressure. More stress at that point could've been detrimental.

Baseer spent the next few days deciding on what he was going to do with all of his money. He wanted to have something to come home to upon his release from prison. On Wednesday morning, he removed his money from the light fixture to recount it. The count came up to $65,875. He still owed Karen Ellison $7000 but he realized that he would only have given her another $4000 by the time that he got sentenced. He didn't plan to pay her the remaining $3000. Then he considered the fact that Desire was going to need some extra money and that he also needed money to take care of his basic needs in prison. He decided to set aside $20,875. He placed the other $45,000 into a metal tool box along with the false ID's that he had stashed in the Timberland shoe box.

After Baseer decided on what he was gonna do with the $45,000, he drove to a "Lowe's" department store. Then he went inside to the Lawn and Gardening department to buy a shovel and grass seeds. When he returned home, he left them in the backseat of his truck. It began to drizzle around 7:00; just as it was becoming dark outside. Desire had not made it home from work yet. Baseer grabbed his pistol and the metal tool box, and got into his Expedition. As he was leaving Cambridge Arms, he met Desire going in. They both stopped and let down their windows. Then Desire asked "Where are you going?" "I'm going to get some weed. I'll be back in less than an hour." "Alright well, hurry back because I'm about to cook." "I won't be long." They both let their windows up and Baseer drove off. He then went to Peaceful Lane, a rocky road on the rural outskirts of Fayetteville. Peaceful Lane was where Baseer's grandfather, Julius was buried.

When Baseer arrived there, no one was in sight and the rain had ceased. Baseer turned off his lights and placed his pistol into his pocket. Then he carried the shovel over to his grandfather's grave and began digging a hole directly above his casket. After almost 4 minutes he had dug a hole that was 2x3 feet wide and 3 feet deep. Then he ran to the truck to retrieve the tool box. Next he lowered the tool box into the ground and began replacing the dirt on top of it. When the dirt had almost reached the level of the ground's surface, he sprinkled grass seeds into the hole. Then he added more dirt until the spot was leveled with the ground. Baseer used the back part of the shovel to level it out. There wasn't very much grass around the grave site, so the spot was barely noticeable. Baseer drove back to the grave site everyday for the next two weeks. By then, he began noticing blades of grass beginning to sprout and the gravesite looked perfectly untampered with.

For the first four days of court, Baseer only had to answer to the roll call and then he was allowed to leave. Each day he was accompanied by his mother Catherine, his Aunt Sadie and Desire. On the fifth day, they arrived at the courthouse around 8:30 am. When they entered the courtroom, Mrs. Ellison was speaking to the solicitor and the prosecutor. When she spotted Baseer, she called him into an office behind the Judge's booth. That's where Mrs. Ellison told him "Today is the day. Are you still going to go through with your plea?" Baseer asked to be excused without answering her question, then he returned to the courtroom where his family was seated.

Baseer sat next to Desire and began telling them what Mrs. Ellison had just told him. He started to strongly consider leaving the courtroom that very moment and absconding. Instead, he looked at Desire and asked if he should plead or not. After almost ten seconds, Desire looked into Baseer's eyes and nodded "yes" as a tear fell down her face. The couple then excused themselves from the courtroom and went into the hallway to talk and be alone. Baseer remained strong while Desire became more emotional and continued crying. After about seven minutes, they returned to the courtroom and Baseer walked over to his attorney to inform her that he was ready to plead.

The judge was in his booth and Mrs. Ellison was seated at a desk in front of the judge. The solicitor, the prosecutor and the stenographer were all sitting in a section next to the judge. Mrs. Ellison asked Baseer to be seated in a chair next to her and asked him to sign a paper that stated that he was admitting his guilt. When it was time to proceed with the hearing, his family was allowed to stand before the judge with him for moral support. Desire held his hand on the right of him while Catherine and Sadie stood on his left. That's when he entered his guilty plea and the judge sentenced him to five years in the SC Department of Correction. Baseer didn't display any emotions at that time. First, he hugged Catherine and Sadie and gave them both a kiss on their cheeks. Then he hugged Desire and kissed her lips. Seconds later, one of the court officers approached Baseer with a pair of handcuffs in his hands. A second officer escorted Baseer's family out of the courtroom as he was handcuffed. Then he was placed into a holding cell where he was to wait for the next available transportation unit to transport him to the county jail. He remained in the holding cell for about 30 minutes. He was silent for the entire time. Then he was transported to Effingham, the Florence County Detention Center.

CHAPTER ELEVEN

Baseer had $1400 in his pocket when he went to Eff-
ingham. His money was put into his personal property
until it was time for him to be shipped to SCDC. Then
his money would be transferred to his SCDC inmate account. After he got booked-in and fingerprinted, he was
given a shower and was dressed out in a green jumpsuit with "FCDC" on the back. Then he was escorted to
a pod where he was assigned to a two-man cell. When
he walked into his cell, he saw that his roommate was
a white guy who looked to be about 25 years old. He
looked like the hippy type, having long hair and tattoos
covering both sleeves. Baseer threw his things on the top
bunk and placed his hygiene items on his shelf. As he
was getting unpacked, his roommate asked "What's your
name bro?" Baseer simply turned around and said "Dog
I ain't friendly." Then the guy became quiet and continued reading his Bible. Baseer made his bed and laid on
it without saying a single word. When the officer came
around with their lunch and dinner trays, Baseer told the
officer that he didn't want them. Then he asked when he
could make a collect phone call and when the visitation
hours were. The officer answered, 'You'll be able to come
out for "Rec" tonight from 8:00 to 9:00. You can make a
phone call then. Visitation is Monday trough Friday and
visitors are only allowed to stay for 15 minutes."
    When Baseer came out for rec at 8:00 he spent the

entire hour talking on the phone. There were only four phones in the entire pod and there were other men waiting to use the phones. Baseer didn't care. The first person that he called was his mother Catherine. After she accepted the collect call, she answered, "Hey son, how are you feeling?" He replied "I'm peace. Who's there with you?" "Just me and Sadie. Desire came over for a few hours but she went home." "oh yeah? How is she taking it?" "I think that she will be alright. We all want to come and visit you. How does that work?" "Honestly that would be a waste of gas because visitation only lasts for 15 minutes down here. I should only be here for 2 or 3 days, then I'll get shipped to my next institution. You can visit me there." "Alright, well did you call Desire?" "I'm about to in a second." "Ok, son, we love you and keep your head up." "All the time – love you too" "Bye"

The next day was Saturday. When Baseer came out of his cell, he remained anti-social and kept to himself. He only spoke on the phone for 30 minutes and the last 30 minutes were spent taking a shower. Most of his time in his cell was spent sleeping. Sunday played out the exact same way. On Monday morning, Baseer was told to pack up his things around 6:30 am because he was about to be shipped to SCDC. He left the cell without saying a word to his roommate. He never even learned his name. Around 8:30, Baseer was handcuffed and ankle chains were placed on him. Then he and three other inmates were placed into the back of a white van with dark tinted windows. There were two police officers in the front seats and they were separated from the inmates by a metal partition. When they left Effingham, they were taken to Columbia, SC. The ride was one hour long and they traveled on rural back roads for the entire way. They were taken to an institution called "Kirkland Reception and Evaluation Center." That was where new inmates and revocators were processed and evaluated. They were also classified by their sentences, which would determine their permanent institution.

When they first arrived at Kirkland, the four of them were searched and then placed into a room with about 30 other men from different areas in SC. One by one, they were all processed. Then they were sent to a barber to have their heads shaved completely bald. They also had to shave off their beards and mustaches. Next, they were all given 3 minute showers and then dressed out in a white jumpsuit with white bobos on their feet. After they were dressed out, they each had to take a picture for their inmate identification card. Baseer had an angry facial expression when he took his mug shot. Then he was sent to a nurse to be evaluated for any diseases. She extracted 2 tubes of blood from his arm and injected him with a vaccine for tuberculosis.

The reception and evaluation process took almost five hours. Then Baseer was given his dorm and room assignment. He was assigned to a dorm called B-2 and room 205. When he walked into his cell, he realized that it was a 3-man cell. Baseer placed his mattress on the top bunk because there were two guys on the other beds. Baseer remained silent with a serious facial expression as he began to unpack. As he was making his bed, one of the guys said "Peace, my name's All-wise." The man seemed to be speaking the language of the God's so Baseer returned the greeting, "Peace. Baseer Allah." Their other roommate was a black Christian guy from SC. He remained silent as if he was trying to decipher the language that they were speaking. All-wise told Baseer that they were allowed to make two phone calls per week, once on Tuesday and once on Thursday. Unfortunately, the times that he was permitted to call conflicted with Desire's work hours. They were to be locked in their cells for the entire day except for feeding time. They were only allowed to take showers three times a week. As long as they didn't have any diseases, they would've only been at Kirkland for about 30 days. Then they would be shipped to their permanent institutions.

Baseer was given four stamped envelopes so he wrote a letter to Desire that night. He also sent her a visitation form for her to fill out so that she could be placed on his visitation list. It would've taken at least 30 days for her to be approved so he couldn't see her until he reached the next institution. As soon as Desire received Baseer's letter, she sent him a response along with some pictures. They were all pictures that they had taken together at Walt Disney World in Florida. In Baseer's first week, he decided to start working out inside of his cell; only on the days when they were given showers. He chose not to do much socializing with his roommates. He also thought about his marijuana habit and decided to refrain from smoking while he was incarcerated. His child was his inspiration for those decisions. Since he only had four envelopes, he decided to write Desire one letter per week. He wasn't allowed to buy anymore envelopes during his first 30 days. Desire wrote him at least twice a week. In her second letter, she said that she had Xeroxed a few copies of the visitation form and given them to his mother Catherine.

On Tuesday of Baseer's third week, he received a strange letter from Desire. It was only three sentences long. It read "I really need to talk to you. I'm going to stay home from work on Thursday so please call me. It's really important." Baseer spent that night tossing and turning in his bed. He expected that she wanted to tell him that she was moving on with her life, especially when he noticed that the words "I love you" didn't appear on the letter. On Wednesday morning, Baseer did an intense work-out for two hours, then he was given a shower around 10:30 am. The remainder of the day was spent being silent on his bed. When night fell, Baseer was having trouble falling asleep. That's when he began reciting the 120 Lessons in his mind. The 120 Lessons consists of 120 questions and answers that Baseer had memorized verbatim when he was a teenager attending Allah Youth Center in Mecca. Baseer fell asleep before he reached the final degree.

On Thursday morning, the officer opened Baseer's cell so that he could make a 15-minute collect phone call. Baseer hurried to the telephone and began dialing Desire's telephone number. She answered after only one ring. After she accepted the call, she said "Baby?" Baseer answered "Yes, this is me. What's up?" "Baseer I need to see you so bad right now. I've been crying all week." "Well what's wrong?" Desire paused for 15 seconds before Baseer reminded her "Baby you have to talk because we only have 15 minutes." Then she said "Promise me that you won't get upset." Baseer automatically assumed that she had already began cheating on him but he said "I promise." Then Desire began whimpering just before she

said "Baby I lost it." "Lost what? The money?" "No boo.
. . . the baby." Desire's cry became louder and Baseer
grew silent for about ten seconds. Then Baseer said "Desi
– stop crying. It's alright." "You're not mad at me?" "No
it's not like you went out and had an abortion. It was a
miscarriage right?" "Yeah baby, I'm so sorry." "We'll have
another chance to try again." They spoke for another ten
minutes before their conversation was interrupted by a
recording stating that he had only 15 seconds left to talk.
Desire wanted Baseer to call her again but he wasn't able
to because the officer was watching him to assure that he
only talked for 15 minutes. When the call ended, Baseer
returned to his cell.

On the following Monday night, a black female officer
came around to pass out mail around 8:00. That's when
she informed Baseer that he would be getting shipped to
another institution on the following morning. She wasn't
allowed to tell him the name of the prison. On the next
morning, Baseer was released from his cell and sent to be
prepared for his next institution. As he was leaving his
cell, he told All Wise "Peace Allah – hold it up." All Wise replied "Peace," then Baseer went to the commissary where
he received four new tan colored SCDC uniforms. He and
about 30 other guys were then given a briefing by one of
the Captains just before they were placed on a white bus
with dark tinted windows. Each inmate was handcuffed
and chained to another inmate by their ankles. There
were two correctional officers on the bus and they were
both armed. The driver was carrying a fully-loaded .38 revolver in a holster on his side. The second officer was also
carrying a .38 revolver, plus a 12 gauge pump.

Their first stop was in Bishopville, South Carolina at
a prison called Lee Correctional Institution. When the bus
entered the gate, one of the officers began reading out a
list of names. That's when Baseer found out that he was
at his assigned institution. There were a few inmates on
the bus that had served time at that prison before and
they started making comments about how violent it was.
Baseer remained quiet, just as he did for the entire ride.
He and four other inmates got off of the bus and were released from their handcuffs and ankle chains. Then they
were escorted inside and placed in a small holding cell

until they received their dorm and room assignments. After waiting for almost two hours, Baseer was assigned to a dorm called Darlington in room 1262. Then he was given a mattress and proceeded to his yard. The institution was divided into two yards; the East Yard and the West Yard.

Darlington was one of three dorms on the East Yard. The dorm was divided into two pods; the north side and the south side. Each pod had 64 two-man cells, housing 128 inmates. When Baseer walked into the north side, he was carrying his mattress. The officer was sitting in a small station called "the bubble" located in the center of the pod. Before Baseer walked into his cell, he noticed what appeared to be a fight from a distance. One of the guys involved was black and the other one was white. Baseer became curious when he noticed the white guy hitting the black guy on his shoulder with the side of his fist. That's when he whispered to himself "What the fuck was that?" When the white guy drew back his hand, Baseer realized that he was holding a knife and he had just stabbed the black guy. One of the inmates who was standing nearby passed an improvised ice pick to the black guy and the white guy began running towards the "bubble" to alarm the officer. The black guy began to chase him and they began circling around the officer's station. The officer was a young black male who looked to be around 22 years old. The white guy was yelling "C.O. – help me" and both of their knives were clearly visible. The officer simply said "You two get away from my desk playing around." When the white guy saw that the officer wasn't going to help him, they both ran into the dayroom and resumed fighting. Baseer simply handed the officer his room assignment slip and asked him to open his cell.

When Baseer walked into his cell, there were 5 guys in his room. They seemed to be having a gang meeting. Baseer entered the room with a calm, yet serious, expression on his face. He didn't say anything to the guys except for "pardon myself" as he was trying to get to his bed. The guys made way for him to pass through and he placed his mattress on the top bunk. Then the other four guys told his roommate that they would speak to him later and they exited the room. That's when his roommate introduced himself, "What's poppin homey, the name's Busta but everybody calls me Bloody Bust." Baseer simply said "Baseer" as he continued making his bed. He then realized that Busta was a Bloodmember. Baseer began to clean out his locker so that he could put away his things. The room was in terrible condition. There were holes in the corners of the walls and the corners of the floor. It was an 8x10 foot cell with 2 lockers, 1 sink, 1 toilet, 1 desk and steel beds that were bolted to the floor.

After Baseer put away his things, he waited for the officer to open his door so that he could make a telephone call. The officer only opened doors once every hour. When he finally came around, Baseer walked into the phone room to call Desire and his mother. They both asked when they could visit him but he hadn't received a notice stating that they were approved yet. He stayed in the phone room for almost 45 minutes. When he was done with his calls, he went to his cell and stood by his door until the officer made his next round. He observed everything that was going on around him. There were guys working out, watching television, rapping, playing cards or chess, and others were in groups talking about something that appeared to be gang-related. When Baseer went back into his cell, Bloody Bust was not in the room. Baseer climbed up on his bed and laid down with his coat covering his face. Almost two hours later, Baseer heard keys outside of his door, so he pulled the coat down from his face. He noticed that the officer was only letting Busta in the room so he covered back up.

Baseer didn't say one single word to Busta that night. On the next morning around 7:00, Busta asked Baseer "Are you going to chow?" Baseer understood that he must've meant breakfast so he raised up without answering him. Then he walked over to his locker and grabbed his face cloth, toothbrush and toothpaste. When Busta walked away from the sink, Baseer freshened up and got prepared for breakfast. When the officer opened his door, he posted up right next to his cell. Everybody else formed up into different groups or sat in front of the four televisions that were in the center of the pod. When Baseer walked into the mess hall (cafeteria), he kept his back against the wall for the entire time that he was in line waiting to receive his tray. He noticed different guys watching him, suspensefully, as if they wondered if he belonged to any type of organization. When he received his tray he sat down at the last table by himself. From there, he had a clear view of the entire mess hall and there was no one sitting behind him.

For breakfast, Baseer had yellow grits, 2 boiled eggs and 2 biscuits. The grits had small black specks which appeared to be insect remains. He ate his breakfast in less than three minutes and hurried back to his dorm to call Desire before she went to work. After they talked for about 10 minutes, he walked over to a nearby bulletin board to find out what type of programs were available. He noticed that there were no programs posted except for "education" and "religious services". Baseer already had his diploma which meant that he had to remain in the dorm all day until he received a job. He also saw the canteen and commissary schedule posted up on the bulletin board, along with a price list of the canteen items. Darlington's canteen day was on the following Thursday. Baseer spent the weekly spending limit of $100 on food from the canteen to prevent having to eat the food that was served in the mess hall. On the following Monday, he received the notice of Desire and Catherine's visitation privileges being approved. They visited him, together on the following Saturday. They were both happy to see him and they complimented him on how good he looked. Desire was looking beautiful even though she was wearing loose fitted clothes due to SCDC policy.

They all sat and talked for 3.5 hours before visitation was over. Catherine left five minutes before Desire did so that they could have a little privacy to kiss each other goodbye. Baseer escorted Desire to the exit door, then he gave her a long kiss goodbye until one of the female officers yelled "Ok, you two, that's enough." Then Desire pulled away and said "Boo. . . we'd better stop before they take my visits. I'll be back next weekend." They both said "I Love you" and Desire exited the visitation room. As Baseer was going to get in line to be strip searched, he noticed one of the female officers staring and sizing him up from head to toe. She was cute and she appeared to be interested in him but Baseer didn't approach her because he didn't know if he was reading her wrong. He simply waited in line to be strip searched, and exited the visitation room without giving her a second look.

Seeing Desire and Catherine helped Baseer to cheer up a little bit, even though he still refused to smile around the other inmates. He spent the following week working-out and anticipating his next visit. He remained anti-social; even with his roommate. They spoke sporadically but never about anything personal. On that Thursday afternoon, a stabbing occurred in Darlington North and the entire dorm was locked down until further notice. For that reason, Baseer's visit was canceled for that weekend and they were locked in their cells 24 hours a day. They were fed 2 cold biscuits and a slice of bologna, 3 times a day. Baseer always gave them to Bloody Bust because he refused to eat them. The dorm remained on lockdown for almost 3 weeks. After almost two weeks of complete silence in the cell, Busta asked Baseer "If you don't mind me asking, where are you from?" Baseer paused from writing his letter to Desire and answered "BX" "Damn how did you get trapped off down here?" "On some bullshit."

Baseer resumed writing his letter until Busta interrupted him again by asking "Did they give you a lot of time?" Baseer replied "They gave me a little stretch." "Word? They gave me life plus thirty." "God Damn. Who'd you murk, the president?" "Nah, some nigga around my way." "Damn dunn" "Shit – almost 85% of this dorm have life sentences." "Shit I only caught 5 joints." "5 years? Why did they bring you to a Level three prison?" "What do you mean?" "With 5 years, you were supposed to go to a Level two yard. Level three yards are for inmates with ten years or better. You need to talk to your caseworker." Busta gave Baseer a "Request to Staff" form to fill out so that he could meet with his caseworker. Baseer also applied for a job in the kitchen so that he could go to the West Yard where the inmates had more privileges. Darlington was considered to be a disciplinary dorm and they had lost most of their privileges. They didn't even get recreation outside. They only received about twelve minutes of sunlight daily. That was when they walked to and from the mess hall three times a day. Each walk was approximately two minutes long. Even when they weren't on lock down, they were locked in their cells by 6:00 every evening.

When Darlington came off of lock down, Baseer still hadn't received a response from the caseworker or the kitchen supervisor. When he came out, he posted up beside his cell as he usually did. As he was standing there, he noticed a group of guys observing him and talking amongst each other. Baseer maintained his composure and stared back at them until they eventually looked away. A few moments later, Bloody Bust was walking by so Baseer said "Ayo son" to get his attention. Busta walked over to him, then Baseer covered his mouth and asked "Who's selling bangers?" Busta replied "I think that I know somebody with a few." Baseer noticed that the officer was making his hourly round so he said "Well I'm about to lock in. Just come back and holla at me." Busta walked away and Baseer went into his cell when the officer made it to his door. When Busta entered the room one hour later, he removed two shanks from the sleeve of his coat. Then he said "One of my niggas is selling both of these. One is an ice pick and one is a flat blade." Baseer received them and inspected their points with his index finger. They were both sharp and they pricked his finger. That's when he asked "How much for both of them?" Busta answered "He wants $10 in food, no hygiene." Baseer opened his locker and gave him ten jumbo honey buns. Then Busta left the room when the C.O. made the next round while Baseer remained in the cell to make a stash spot for his knives.

Later on that afternoon, Baseer received a letter in the mail from his mother Catherine. She seemed depressed. She was explaining that her sister Sadie was getting worse and that her head had become completely bald as a result of the Chemo-therapy. She also wrote that Baseer's father James' crack addiction had gotten worse. He had resorted to pan-handling and selling things out of their house. She also mentioned that she was stressed out over the fact that Baseer was incarcerated and Desire had a miscarriage. Baseer was refraining from calling her excessively because the telephone rates were expensive. When he read that letter, he decided to call her and console her. Over the phone, she said that she was going to visit him on Friday alone since Desire was planning to visit him on Saturday. He reminded Catherine to relax and not to over-exert herself. He also reminded her to try and refrain from eating salt and red meats because of her high blood pressure.

On Saturday afternoon, Desire came to visit him at 1:30. She was wearing a Coogi outfit and a pair of Timberland boots that Baseer had bought for her. Every inmate in the visitation room kept looking at her, even though most of them were there with their own girls. Before Baseer sat down, he gave her a kiss and said "C'mon, let's walk to the snack machine so that I can show you off." Desire blushed and said "you're so crazy." They walked to the snack machine to buy a few snacks and returned to their table. As they were walking back to their table, Baseer looked over at the security booth. That's when he noticed the female studying the way that he and Desire were interacting with each other. Desire wasn't watching Baseer so he winked at the female officer in the booth and she smiled. When they sat down, Baseer reminded her to make another payment on his storage rental. They shared a few laughs but Baseer was beginning to resent not going on the run. When the visit was over, Baseer held Desire in his arms for a minute and then kissed her goodbye.

As Desire exited the visitation room, Baseer began walking to the strip-search line. That's when the female officer in the booth said "Hey You." Baseer looked back at her and she told him to come to the booth. Baseer walked up to her and asked "What's good?" "What's your name?" she asked as she zoomed in on his identification card that was clipped to the lapel of his shirt. Baseer answered "Watson." He noticed that her name tag read "Ms. K. Williams". Ms. Williams looked him up and down, and then she excused him by saying "Okay you can get in line now. I just wanted to see who you were." As Baseer was walking away, he looked back to see if she was still watching him. That's when she waved at him. Baseer then realized that his first assumption was correct; she was interested in him. At that moment, he began trying to figure out how he was going to attack the situation because she could've been helpful to him.

After being strip searched, Baseer walked back to his dorm with Ms. Williams on his mind. He wanted to have sex with her. When he entered his dorm, he walked directly to his cell and noticed that there was a towel covering the window on the door. Baseer assumed that Busta was inside using the toilet so he walked over to the phone room. That's when he called Catherine and spoke with her for about ten minutes. Then he walked back to his cell and noticed that the window was still covered. Baseer also noticed that the officer was making his hourly round and he wanted to go inside of the cell. He decided to tap on the cell door and he said "Ayo Bust. The C.O. is doing a round, how much longer do you need?" Busta walked up to the door and answered "You can come in. Just let me know when the C.O. gets close by." When the officer was four doors away, Baseer tapped on the door and Busta removed the towel, then the officer opened their door and Baseer went inside. Busta remained inside also.

When the officer locked the door and walked away, Busta placed the towel back over the window. Then he pulled a cellular phone from under his pillow and began talking. Baseer remained silent on his bed as he wondered where the cell phone had come from. Busta continued talking for almost 30 minutes, then he asked "Do you need to call anybody before I give my man back his jack?' Baseer replied "No I'm good." Busta removed the towel and knocked on the door to get the attention of one of the guys who were walking around in the pod. When the guy walked to their door he looked in every direction to see if anyone was watching. Then he said "C'mon" and Busta slid the phone under the door to him. He placed it into his back-pocket. It was a Motorola Razor phone that fitted perfectly under the door. Baseer was curious so he asked "You got niggas in here selling jacks?" Busta replied "Yeah there are a few floating around." "So are you plugged in?" "Yeah, I know a nigga that's selling a Nokia joint for $600." "Well what's up? I've got half, let's cop that joint." "To be honest with you, my people stopped sending me money years ago." "Word? I could probably come up with the whole six but we'll have to make a stash spot just in case they ever decide to do a random search." Busta walked over to his bed and said "a stash spot isn't a problem." He kneeled down and lifted up one of the floor tiles beneath his bed. Someone had chiseled a hole into the concrete that was big enough for a cell phone as well as a phone charger. When the tile was in it's place it appeared to be glued down just like the other tiles on the floor. That's when Baseer told Busta to find out if his friend still wanted to sell his phone. Busta replied, "He probably will. If he does, you will have to get someone to go to Walgreen's and pick up a Green Dot prepaid reload card. Get the pin number from them and pay him with that."

CHAPTER TWELVE

On Sunday night, the officer brought Baseer an order to report to his caseworker's office at 9:15 on Monday Morning. The caseworker's name was Mrs. Caudles. She was a white woman who looked to be between the ages of 35 and 40. When Baseer walked into her office, she asked him "What can I assist you with Mr. Watson?" He answered "I was told that this was a level 3 prison but I'm incarcerated for a Level 2 offense. I'm trying to find out why I was brought here." "Well do you have any escapes on your record?" "No." "Do you have any pending charges?" "No" "Well have you ever been incarcerated for a Level 3 offense before?" "No, I haven't." "That's strange. Let me pull up your file on my computer."

Mrs. Caudles asked Baseer to hand her his identification card and she began typing his information into the computer. After reviewing his file for almost two minutes, she said "oh, I see." Baseer asked "What do you see?" "It seems that you do have pending charges in NC." "For what?" "It says that you were charged with an armed robbery that occurred in Hamlet County." "That's gotta be a mistake." "Well that's what the computer says. You will need to talk with your lawyer about that because I can't do anything about it." Baseer remained silent for a few moments, then Mrs. Caudles asked "Can I help you with anything else?" "No, I'm fine" "Alright have a nice day Mr. Watson."

Baseer spent the remainder of the night thinking

about his pending charges. He knew that armed robbery carried 10-30 years in prison. Plus the two strike law was effective in NC which sanctioned that having two violent felonies could get Baseer a life sentence. After brainstorming for hours, Baseer finally fell asleep. The next morning, he woke up around 7:00 and went directly to the phone room to call Desire. He explained what he needed her to do concerning the Green Dot reload card and she said that she would have it when she returned home from work around 7 that night. Darlington dorm was locked down every night by 6 pm so he had to wait until Wednesday morning. When he called on Wednesday morning, she gave him 2 19-digit pin numbers from two separate reload cards that were worth $300 each. He decided not to tell her what he had learned from his caseworker. When he saw Busta walking around in the pod, he pulled him to the side and gave him both pin numbers. Then he went into his cell and waited on Busta to return with the merchandise. When Baseer walked into the cell, he placed the towel over the window and retrieved his ice pick from his stash spot; just in case Busta came back without a phone. Then he began sharpening it in a groove on the floor as he whispered to himself, "I'm gonna put some iron in this nigga's diet if he comes back empty-handed."

In the next hour, Busta entered the room carrying a Doritos bag. When the officer locked him in, he placed the towel over the window and emptied the bag onto Baseer's bed. It was a black Nokia cell phone and charger. The sim card was prepaid so he called Desire and told her to buy him a $50 pre paid phone card. Desire's cell phone contract was with the same company, AT&T, so they had free mobile to mobile minutes. After Baseer got his phone, most of his days were spent in his cell. He only came out to take showers and to use the microwave that was in the dayroom. He also allowed Busta to use his phone as much as he needed to.

Baseer's phone remained on silent ring mode at all times. There was a team of Contraband officers that usually made random room searches around 3:00 in the morning, so he always made sure that his phone was stashed away by midnight. During the day, the contraband officers couldn't sneak up on Baseer because the inmates always announced them aloud to warn the other inmates. On Saturday morning, Baseer woke up around 9. That's when he pulled out his cell and listened to the new messages in his voicemail. There was a message from his mother Catherine that was received at 3:43 am. She urged him to return her call as soon as possible. He called her immediately at home, but no one answered. Then he dialed her cell phone number and she answered "Hello". Baseer then asked "Hey ma, what's going on?" "I'm up here at the hospital with your father" "What happened to him?" "He got shot last night." "Is he alright?" "Yeah, he's doped up on medication right now so he's sleeping. Some young boy shot him in his leg last night around 2:00" "Who did it?" "James didn't know his name but he did tell the police their address. If you ask me. . . I think that it was probably over some drugs." Baseer told Catherine not to allow that incident to stress her out and he reminded her to stay strong. He still hadn't told her about what he had learned from his caseworker. Just before ending their conversation, he asked "When do you expect for him to wake up so that I can call him back?" Catherine said "Try to call back around 12:30 or 1:00 this afternoon." "Alright Ma, I love you." "I love you too Baseer."

The fact that James got shot really disturbed Baseer. Even though their relationship wasn't perfect, he didn't want to lose his father. When he called back around 1:00 that afternoon, Catherine passed her cellular phone to James. His words were barely audible because the medication caused his speech to slur. He answered "Hello" "Pops how do you feel?" "I'm OK, I got shot. I'm on this medicine right now." "Why did they shoot you?" "Those young boys tried to rob me. You know those wild little boys at that yellow house right next door to Barry's house." "Mommy said that you told the police." "Yeah. I didn't know their names but I knew the address." "Pops you shouldn't have done that. What if they find out where you live?" "I ain't worrying about that." "Well get well soon G." "Alright son, I love you." "Yeah, I love you too." James passed the cell phone back to Catherine and they spoke for another few minutes. Then Baseer stashed his phone away and began cleaning his cell. He didn't believe that his father was robbed because his appearance would've clearly showed that he didn't have any money. Baseer knew of the guys at the yellow house and they were drug dealers. He believed that his father tried to swindle one of the guys out of their drugs. He also knew that the guys at that house were known to carry guns. He had to clear his mind so he worked out for almost an hour and then took a shower.

James was released from the hospital on Monday morning. The doctor said that he would probably never be able to use his left leg again. He was shot with a .357 Python and the shot disconnected the nerves in his leg. On Wednesday, Baseer received an order to report to the mailroom to pick up some legal mail. When he went there, he received a letter that was sent from the General Sessions Court in Hamlet, NC. The letter was to notify him that he was formally charged with the bank robbery and he was appointed a Public Defender to represent him. The public Defender's name was Karen Patterson. That very same night, Baseer wrote a letter to Mrs. Patterson and requested to have a copy of his "Rule 5 Brady Trial Motion" (commonly called The Motion of Discovery). The Motion of Discovery is all of the physical evidence that they had against him to include all investigative reports, witness statements, still photos and etc,. It took almost two weeks for Baseer to receive a response to his request. When he finally did, he learned that he had made a very careless mistake when he committed the robbery. When he parked in the parking lot behind the bank, he stepped out of his car with his face exposed. His Motion of Discovery contained two clearly visible still photos of his face as well as Powerful's. The pictures were captured by a store video camera near the parking lot where he had parked.

As the months passed, Baseer became more discontent with his situation. Desire had slacked up on writing letters and visiting him, and Baseer was starting to suspect that she had found another guy. It was during a time when Sadie was becoming very sick. James was back to his regular routine; smoking crack in the streets. His leg never healed and he was permanently on crutches. The dorm that Baseer was in was constantly getting locked down because of the gang violence. A riot took place in the dorm and caused the dorm to be locked down for two months. During those months, Darlington inmates were deprived of their visitation, telephone, and canteen privileges. One Sunday night, Baseer decided to call Desire around 8:00. He hadn't called her in four days because she seemed irritable when they last spoke. He felt like she would begin to pull away even more if he called excessively.

When Desire answered her phone, she didn't sound very pleased to hear Baseer's voice. She answered "Hello" then Baseer greeted her "Hey Boo. What are you doing?" "Nothing" "How are you feeling?" Desire grew silent for a few seconds, then she said "Baseer, I have something that I want to say." From her tone, Baseer knew that it was going to be something disappointing. That's when he responded "Speak your mind." "Alright – I think that we should just be friends." Baseer tried to remain as cool as possible, so he said "I can dig it. Now do you mind if I ask why?" "I just feel like I need some oxygen right now, that's all." "True" Baseer predicted that very moment before he went to prison, but he wasn't ready to lose her. He tried to pretend that her decision wasn't affecting him so he switched subjects. He was hoping that maybe he could change her mind if she came to visit him that weekend. That's when he asked "So what are you doing this weekend?" She replied "I'll be in Lumberton this weekend." "What's in Lumberton?" "My homeboy" "Oh so that's how it's going down?" Desire remained silent. Then Baseer asked "So are you fuckin him?" "Yeah, I fucked him." "Word? Well I hope that you have fun this weekend." "I hope so too." "Yeah, Peace." Baseer hung up the phone and told Busta that he could use it.

After talking to Desire, Baseer stopped calling and she had completely stopped writing him. He told her that she could have his Expedition but TK went down to Fayetteville and picked up his storage room key from her. Then he rented a u-haul truck and took all of Baseer's things back to Brooklyn with him. TK was doing good for himself, musically. He had began doing shows around the Tri-state area and he was working on an album. He had just finished a song which he dedicated to Baseer and Powerful entitled "On My Grind with You in Mind." He had moved from Crown Heights to a 2-bedroom apartment in Canarsie, Brooklyn. Peru was also making a lot of money; still in Atlanta. He had found another Cocaine supplier and that became his permanent hustle. Baseer called both of them regularly and they both agreed to help him with whatever he needed, monetarily. He decided not to ask them for anything until he really needed them.

After going for almost three months without hearing a word from Desire, Baseer was almost over her. He wanted to call Yahnis but he had forgotten her telephone number. One Thursday night, Baseer decided to call his mother to see how she was doing. He was slightly worried because on the previous night, he had a peculiar dream. In the dream, Catherine was walking through a shopping mall and carrying a baby boy. Baseer walked up to her and said "Ma, who's baby is that?" She answered "This is you when you were a little boy." Baseer looked at the baby and he looked exactly how he looked on his baby pictures. Then he asked Catherine, "Can I hold him?" Catherine passed the baby to him and they began talking to each other. The baby seemed really smart and he answered every question with a complete sentence.

When Baseer was growing up, Catherine use to talk about how she believed in certain superstitions. Baseer's dream bothered him because he remembered his mother telling him, "If you dream about a baby, that's usually a sign of death." When he dialed his parents' house phone number, nobody answered. Then he dialed Catherine's cell phone number and she still didn't answer. He called five more times and she still didn't answer. That's when Baseer decided to call his sisters in NY to see if they had heard anything from her. He dialed his sister Lashawn's cell phone number and she answered "hello?" "Sis what's up? Did you talk to mommy today?" "Yeah she's upstairs." "I didn't know that she was in NY." "She's not, I'm down here in Fayetteville at the hospital. You've heard about Aunt Sadie right?" "Nah, what happened?" "She passed today." "Damn how is Mommy taking it?" "She's taking it pretty hard. Did you wanna talk to her?" "Yeah, put her on the phone." "You'll have to call back in about three minutes because I 'm about to get on the elevator to go back up there." "Alright."

Baseer called Lashawn back and she answered "Hold

On". Then she passed the phone to Catherine. Baseer had never seen or heard Catherine cry in his entire life. When she said "Hello" Baseer noticed that her voice was already beginning to crack. That's when Baseer asked "Are you alright Ma?" Catherine began to cry softly as she tried to explain how she was feeling. She said that she was in a lot of pain. Baseer knew how she felt because they were like best friends. He thought about how he felt when he found out that Powerful had died. He tried his best to console her but he also knew that she was a strong woman and that she would be alright. He reminded her that he loved her very much and then they ended their conversation.

That night, Baseer turned off his lights early, then he laid on his bed and pulled his coat over his face to meditate and try to ease his mind. Hearing his mother cry really bothered him. That's when he started thinking about everything that had gone wrong and all of the losses that he had taken in the recent past. He even shed a few tears under his coat. In the middle of the night, he began thinking about the time that he was facing with his pending charges. He knew that he would be found guilty so he concluded that he had no choice but to escape. Then he started to think about the other inmates that were around him and he became appalled by the fact that they seemed so content. They had a lot more time than Baseer, and they didn't seem to wanna leave. Baseer became so stressed out that he climbed out of his bed and grabbed his ink pen and his notebook to write a song. He left the lights turned off because Busta was still sleeping. His bed was near the window and a little bit of light shined into his room from the outside. That's when he sat up on his bed and began writing a song called "I Can't Stay." He wrote:

You ain't tired of the pain you'd rather adjust to it

And you wouldn't escape if the judge gave you 30 years
you would just do it

But I'm the opposite, I'd rather risk crossing the gun line

Resort to crime and live my life runnin from one time

Before I let these crackers take away my prime

I've just gotta stay on my grind and stay wit a nine at all
times

That's just a chance I've gotta take

I can't sit up in a cage without attempting to escape

This for them goons locked up behind the fence
who can relate

And that's because we all refuse to give a penny
to the state

I've gotta see another day

Cause my mom needs help and my lady can't wait

If I did my whole sentence it would be too late

But if I got away there's a chance I might be straight

I need some real niggas on the other side of the gate

And I don't really know how much time it will take

But I'm never giving up and I'm plottin everyday

Cause really I don't give a fuck man –
I've gotta make a way.

It took Baseer almost ten minutes to write this verse. Then he placed his writing materials beneath his mattress and went to sleep. From that moment on, he was determined to liberate himself from prison. On the next morning, he woke up early enough to go to breakfast. On his way to the mess hall, he walked slowly as he studied the compound to discern whether or not an escape would be possible. He noticed that there were three fences that he would have to get passed. Just outside of the third fence, was a paved road that went completely around the entire institution. There was a small white Security truck that circled around the perimeter non-stop. All of the fences were the same height, approximately 12 feet high. The first two fences had razor wires across the top of them to prevent anyone from climbing over. The second fence had a motion sensor that would alarm the officers in the 4 security booths on each corner of the outside perimeter. Darlington was the center dorm on the East Yard. There were only cameras monitoring the other two dorms. The last fence was covered in razor wire from the ground to the top of the fence.

When Baseer returned to his cell, he looked out of his window to see if he had a view of the paved road that surrounded the institution. He wanted to learn exactly how often the security truck overlapped. Unfortunately, his room was in a bad location where he could only see the neighboring dorm. At 10:00, that morning, the officer in the dorm made a call for "Pill Line." Pill Line was for the inmates who received special medication. They were allowed to walk up to the Medical Building which was at least 5 minutes away. Baseer exited the building with the Pill Line patients so that he could see the truck and estimate how long it took to overlap. After doing so, he realized that it took approximately 3.5 minutes to come back around. There was only one officer in the truck and it appeared to be a female.

Around 5:30 that evening, Baseer called TK while Busta was outside of the cell. TK answered "Peace God." Baseer greeted him. "True King, what's the science?" "I'm on my way to the studio to mix down this track that I recorded last night." "Word? Listen, I just found out that I have some new charges for an armed robbery. They sent me copies of evidence sheets and they've got me red-handed. I could be facing life, kid. I'm breaking out." TK remained silent for a second because he knew Baseer very well and he could tell that he wasn't joking. Then he said "Baseer, we definitely can't have you doing life. But escaping – do you think it's possible?" "Yeah. It's just that my plans are in the baby stages right now. Most of the officers are all old and washed up, so they're not a threat. Plus they wouldn't expect for anybody to try to leave because these other niggas act so content. These dumb ass niggas laugh and joke with the CO's." "Well how are you gonna get over the wall?" "They don't have walls down here, they have fences. But like I said, I'm still putting this shit together so it won't be this week or anything like that. I'm just giving you a heads-up because I'm gonna need your help." "Well you already know that's not a question. Just be careful and keep me posted dunn." "True indeed." "Peace"

Next Baseer called Peru and explained his plans to him. Peru was also willing to help him. He said that he didn't want to risk going back to SC but he could assist him monetarily. He said that he could provide him with a vehicle, some money and two loaded guns inside of it. Baseer would just have to tell him when and where to have the car waiting for him once he crossed the third fence. That night, Baseer began formulating ideas about how he was going to provide for himself as a prison escapist on the run. He knew that working a legal job was completely ruled out and that he only had $45,000 to his name. Plus, the things that TK had taken back to Brooklyn with him. He concluded that he would need to do one more bank robbery which would enable him to be comfortably incognito for at least one year in a new city or small town. For that entire year, he would have to remain indoors and refrain from contacting his relatives. His residence was going to be leased in TK's name and all future payments would be mailed in. He assumed that his SCDC mug shot would be posted all over the local news and maybe even America's Most Wanted. That's when he decided that he would have to grow some dreads and grow his facial hair so that he would look totally different. He planned to spend his first year making music while indoors and he could network on an underground level through TK. He then began writing a future tense album where the theme was living on the run, "Moving Target."

On the next Saturday, Baseer received a visit from his mother Catherine at 1:00 pm. He decided not to tell her about his pending charges because he knew that she was still upset about the loss of her sister. He simply pretended that everything was fine and that he was in good spirits. During the visit, Baseer noticed that Ms. Williams was working in the security booth. She was observing him as usual. Catherine excused herself from the table because she needed to use the visitor's restroom. That's when Baseer walked over to the camera man and asked him to borrow his ink pen and a small sheet of paper. Next, he wrote his cell phone number on the small sheet of paper and placed it in his ID clip; behind his identification card.

After the visit was over, Baseer escorted his mother to the exit door and kissed her on her cheek. Then she exited the visitation room. The room was filled with other inmates and visitors who were preparing to leave. In the midst of the commotion, Baseer decided to walk up to the security booth and talk to Ms. Williams. He knew that if he didn't say the right things, he could've been charged with soliciting, sexual assault or fraternizing with a staff member. He felt confident so he said "Hey Ms. Williams, can I ask you something off the books?" "Sure," she replied as if she had been waiting for that moment. That's when Baseer continued "Can I call you?' She looked around to see if anyone was watching her. Then she said "I don't know about that. Besides, I couldn't give you my number anyway because you have to get strip searched before you return to your dorm." Baseer removed his ID clip and passed it to her. When she received it he said "My cell number is behind my ID. Just put it in your pocket and call me around 9:00" The security booth sat up higher than the floor so no one could see the ID clip in her hand. That's when she removed the small piece of paper and placed it into her pocket. Then she handed Baseer's ID back to him and said "I got you. 9:00." That's when Baseer got in line and waited to be strip searched.

CHAPTER THIRTEEN

W hen 9:00 came around, Baseer had his cell phone stashed away just incase Ms. Williams had tried to deceive him and send the contraband officers to his cell at that hour. He left the phone turned on so that her number would be saved in his call log after she called. Baseer waited until 11:00 to pull his phone from his stash. When he checked his missed calls, he saw an unknown telephone number with an 803 area code. Then he checked his voicemail messages because he had two messages. The first message was a female voice saying "This is KeKe. How are you gonna tell me to call you and not pick up? Call me back." The second message was the same voice saying "I'm about to go to sleep in a little while."

After listening to that message, Baseer dialed her number back and she answered after the third ring. "Hello". Then Baseer greeted her "Hey Sexy, what's good?" "nothing, I'm just lying in bed watching Law and Order. Where is your roommate?" Busta was still awake so Baseer said "That's all under control. So where are you from ma?" "I'm from Columbia, what about you?" "The Bronx, New York." "Some how I guessed that ever since I saw you with that Puerto Rican girl. Is that your wife?" "No that's my ex. She bounced on a nigga." "Dang, she couldn't wait 5 years for you?" "How did you know that I had 5 years?" "Because I looked you up on the computer a long time ago." "Well damn, what else do you know?" "That's about it – the computer doesn't say too much." "So what's your story?" "Well I'm single, no kids, I'm independent and I have the 5 C's." "What's that?" "Cash, credit, crib, a car and a career." "I like that. So are you working on the next day?" "Yes, but I'll be in that boring ass perimeter truck tomorrow." "What time do you knock off?" "At 7" "Well listen, I'm about to stash this jack because you know how these officers can get sometimes. I'll just call you tomorrow." "Alright cutie, just be sure to call after 8:00" "Got you." "Byeee" "Bye"

Baseer stashed his cell phone and laid in his bed with a smile on his face. He felt like he had her in the palm of his hand. Plus, she was more useful than he had expected; being that she sometimes drove the security truck that always circled around the perimeter. He then realized that he had to do everything in his powers to make her fall in love with him, so that he could manipulate her into helping him escape. He knew that the easiest way for him to do that would be through sex. He hadn't had sex in a long time and he didn't masturbate, so he knew that he would perform like a champion. Until that opportunity presented itself, he had to keep their relationship interesting. He did that by selling her dreams of them being a couple when he got released. He even introduced Keke to his mother Catherine on visitation day about a month later. They began speaking on the telephone for hours every night, and she sometimes sent him letters with bogus return addresses. She started sending him money to his inmate account after only knowing him for two months. All of this, Baseer had accomplished without even having sex with her.

On one Thursday night, Keke called Baseer around 10:30 and Busta answered because he was talking to his girlfriend on the other line. When Busta answered "Hello" Keke thought he was Baseer so she said "Hey baby." Busta knew that the call had to be for Baseer so he told her "This isn't Baseer, hold on for a minute," then he switched over to end his conversation with his girlfriend. When Baseer retrieved the call, Keke was still waiting on the line. He answered "Hey Boo-what's good?" "I'm chillin. Was that your roommate?" "Yeah, I was sleeping so I let him rock for a while." "Well baby, guess what." "What's up?" "I'm gonna give you some this weekend. You just need to get somebody to visit you." "That won't be a problem. I can get my mother to come up here. How are we supposed to get away with that?" "I just found out that the Lieutenant on my shift went on vacation yesterday. He won't be back until next week so I'll be in the visitation room alone this weekend. You will just have to fall to the back of the line. When everybody else gets strip searched you can go and wait for me in the staff restroom. I'll have the door unlocked for you." "That's a bet. I'll tell my mother to come up here on Sunday after church." "I can't wait" "Me either. Well Keke it's getting late and I need to put this phone up." "I know. I just wanted to put that little bug in your ear before you went to sleep" "Alright love." "Goodnight."

On the next morning, Baseer called Catherine and she agreed to visit him on Sunday evening. He spent the remainder of the weekend relaxing in his cell, as he normally did. On Saturday, Desire called his cell phone 4 times but he ignored her calls. She left voice messages each time but Baseer deleted them without even listening to them. Catherine came to visit Baseer at 3:30 on Sunday afternoon. She was still wearing the dress that she had worn to church, that morning. She seemed to be doing fine and she didn't do much complaining. She told Baseer that she had seen Desire in the Super Wal Mart shopping center on Friday evening. Desire was wearing dark sunglasses and she seemed to be deliberately avoiding Catherine. Therefore, Catherine didn't bother to speak to her.

Baseer didn't care to hear anything about Desire so he switched subjects. He noticed that Keke was the only officer that was working in the visitation room. On that particular day, she was wearing more make up than she usually wore. Plus her hair was done in a new style. When the visit was over, Baseer escorted Catherine to the exit door. Then he proceeded to the line where the other guys were waiting to be searched. He made sure that he was the last person that was standing in the line. After the 13th guy went into the "shakedown" room to be strip searched, Baseer hurried over to the "staff restroom." The door was unlocked and the light was turned off.

When Baseer turned on the light, he noticed that there was a magnum condom sitting on the sink counter. The restroom was small; only consisting of a toilet, a sink and a garbage can. When the shakedown officer was done strip searching the last man, he walked into the visitation room to assure that there were no more inmates that needed to be searched. Then he asked Keke "Is that everybody?" "Yeah, that's it." Then she pretended to be busy filling out some paperwork so that he would leave her alone. That's when the officer said "Well, I'm going home. See you tomorrow." "Alright Mr. Wilson, see ya." As soon as Officer Wilson left the building, two inmate visitation workers entered the room to clean up. Their job was to collect all of the trash from the tables, sweep the floor and empty the garbage cans. Keke told them "You guys are okay, you can take the night off. I have to leave early so I'll leave a note for first shift to take care of it." Then the two guys proceeded back to their dorms, relieved that they didn't have to work.

Keke walked into the restroom and locked it from the inside as Baseer began taking off his shirt. Then Keke began unbuttoning her shirt and they both began kissing. Baseer began caressing her breasts and she reached down into his boxers to grab his penis. Then she kneeled down and began performing oral sex on him. After 60 seconds she stood back up and began unbuckling her pants. As she was taking them off, Baseer put the condom on. That's when they began having sex in doggy style. He took his time and penetrated her as deep as he could to assure that she felt sexual gratification. He caused her to have 2 orgasms in seven minutes. Then Baseer lifted her up and penetrated her in a carrier (carry her) position. In that position, she got really passionate and began kissing Baseer on his lips. Baseer kissed her also because he wanted her to believe that he felt love for her. Next, she had another orgasm and Baseer finally released into his condom. When they were done Baseer flushed his condom down the toilet.

After about 15 minutes of sex, they began getting dressed and speaking to each other softly because of the acoustics in the restroom. Keke then began to fall more in love with Baseer because of his sex. She told him, "You need to come home. I want that every night." Baseer agreed, "I know, I hate this place. I'm ready to come home and live that life with you." When they finished dressing, Keke walked back into the visitation room to assure that there were no other officers around. By that time, it was 6:00 and her shift ended at 7:00. Keke saw that they were alone so she returned to the restroom and told Baseer that he could come out. Baseer proceeded back to his dorm without any complications from the other officers.

Baseer slept peacefully that night because he had accomplished one of the main things that he had set out to do. He started out the next day speaking to KeKe over the phone from 10:00 am until 12:00 that afternoon. Baseer stashed his phone and then left to take a shower. As he was getting prepared to get into the shower, he noticed everybody crowding around the bubble where the officer was standing and passing out the daily mail. Baseer didn't expect to receive any mail so he continued to the shower. Then, about 20 seconds later, he heard the officer say "Watson". Baseer walked over to the officer and received his letter. He immediately cuffed the envelope and didn't look at the return address. As he was stepping into the shower, he realized that Desire had sent the letter.

Baseer continued with his shower and read the letter when he returned to his cell. In the letter, she began by saying that she wanted to apologize for hurting him. She said that she realized that she had made a mistake and that she wanted to reconcile with him. Further into the letter, she mentioned that she had left her guy friend and that he was fighting her on the past Thursday. She said that she was currently wearing sunglasses everyday to conceal her black eye. The last words in the letter were "I love you and I need to hear from you." When Baseer finished the letter he ripped it into pieces and flushed them down the toilet. He didn't want to become involved with Desire again. Keke had become his tunnel focus. She was becoming very attached to him and he noticed it. Then he began figuring out a way to introduce the idea of helping him escape to her. Three months had passed since they had become involved with each other.

On the next afternoon, Baseer called Keke when Busta left out of the cell. He pretended to have just received some bad news. When she asked what it was, he made her promise not to abandon him after he revealed it to her. After she promised him, Baseer said "I just received a letter in the mail from The General Sessions court in New York. I just found out that I have a pending charge for armed robbery. The nigga that I did it with got bagged and he snitched on me." "Well what did you rob?" "A bank in Manhattan." "So now what?" "They just offered me 20 years to plea guilty, but I can't do that much time. Plus, it would be ran consecutively with the 5 years that I already have." "Don't tell me that baby. I have so many plans for us" "Keke listen, I need to ask you a very serious question." "What?" "Don't freak out but I want you to help me to get out of here." "And how am I supposed to do that?" "I don't know. You know this place better than I do." "Are you talking about escaping?" "Yeah, all I need is a way out. I buried $200,000 of the bank robbery money so I'm good. You could quit your job and come with me to the west coast – start a new life."

Keke said that she would think about it but she didn't agree immediately. When she hung up the telephone, she began to strongly consider helping him. She really liked Baseer and she believed in him. When they spoke on the following day, she explained how complicated it would be for him to escape. She mentioned the motion sensor on the second fence. She said that he would definitely need wire cutters to get through the third fence because it was completely covered in razor wire. She suggested that he made his attempt during the night because the cameras didn't pick up very well in the dark. Then Baseer asked her if she could possibly cut the third fence for him from the outside; since there was no camera directly behind his dorm. She said that she was afraid to do it. She said that if he could get someone else to do it, she would continue driving in the perimeter truck and pretend not to see them. She also said that she could possibly turn off the motion sensor if she knew the exact time and date that he wanted to make his attempt.

That was almost everything that Baseer needed to hear. When their conversation ended, Baseer called Peru and he answered "Peace G". "Peace God. Yo, do you remember what we spoke about?" "What, you pulling a whodini?" "Yeah. I snagged this little wisdom body who works here. I just fucked her brains out, then I gassed her up to help me bounce. I just need to borrow some current and like two god you nows (guns)." Baseer waited until that night to call TK. He told him that he was gonna need him to lease him an apartment in Glen Burnie, Maryland. Glen Burnie was a small suburban town, just outside of Baltimore City. The cost of living there wasn't very expensive and it was only four hours away from NY City. That would make it convenient for him to work with TK on his music. His uncle Gerald also owned a studio in that town and Baseer was debating on collaborating with him on a few songs. He played the guitar. At that particular time, Baseer was skeptical about even contacting Gerald after he escaped. He decided that he couldn't tell him where he was living at if he did contact him. TK said that he still had all of Baseer's things from the storage and that he would lease the apartment for him in Maryland, free of charge.

Baseer spent the remainder of the night drawing out the blueprint to his plan in his mind. He was faced with the dilemma of not knowing how he was going to get outside of the dorm at night. His dorm was always locked down at 6:00, while the sun still shined. The sun usually would set around 6:40, just 20 minutes before Keke's shift ended. He believed that he could scale the first two fences without injuring himself badly. He planned to tape magazines around his arms, legs, and all vital areas to prevent being pierced by the points on the razor wire. He also needed to figure out a nearby place for Peru to leave the getaway car at.

During the following week, Baseer began working out more intensely. He wanted to condition his body for what he was planning to do. He knew that there would be a lot of running and also climbing involved. Whenever Busta was outside of their cell, Baseer would jog in place for as long as he could endure it. That was to build up his wind and to strengthen his legs. Then he would do 200 pull-ups, in sets of 25. Each workout was strenuous and time consuming. As the days passed, he remained focused and his plan was coming together. Peru had purchased him a used 1991 Pontiac Grand Prix, and he was waiting for Baseer to say that he was ready. Every night, Baseer worked on songs for his Moving Target album.

He envisioned the Moving Target project to be more

of a movement than an album. He realized that he would be on the run for the remainder of his life. He felt like his cause was justified by the amount of losses and disappointments that he had encountered in the past 5 years. It took three weeks for Baseer to decide that he was prepared to leave. Instead of paying a fiend to cut the third fence, he called a group of Gods out of Boston, Massachusetts. They wanted to be involved and assure that he was successful. Their names were True Born, Now Born, and Knowledge Me. They were equipped with lots of guns and ammunition. Keke had arranged for the motion sensor to be turned off at the time of his escape. She was also going to be driving the perimeter truck until 7:00 that night.

Keke told Baseer to get Peru to have the getaway car sent to a wooden barn that wasn't very far from the institution. She said that if Baseer ran in that direction after scaling the third fence, no security truck could follow him through the swamp that he had to run through. He would have enough time to reach the vehicle before the security truck could drive to it. Then he would only be a half mile away from the nearest entrance ramp onto Interstate 95. Peru was going to have two fully loaded guns under the driver's seat with the keys already in the ignition. Baseer only wanted him to leave $1000 in the ashtray. The gas tank would be full and there would be a new outfit for him to switch into in the backseat. Now Born and True Born were both going to run up to the third fence to help Baseer to make his way out. There was a patch of woods on the other side of the swamp where they could camouflage themselves as well as see Baseer when he began making his escape. Plus they would've been talking to each other on their cellular phones.

Three weeks was also how long it took for Baseer to finish writing the Moving Target album. He had written 17 full length songs and mailed them to TK under another inmates' name and identification number. That particular inmate never knew that he had used them. Baseer found his name and number on an inmate roster that happened to be on the floor one day. He began to feel stressed out every time that he spoke to his mother. He always pretended that he was fine and he never told her about his pending armed robbery charge. Catherine always sensed that something was wrong because she would inquire about it. She just didn't know exactly what was troubling him. She simply assumed that he was upset over Desire. He was actually upset because after his escape he wouldn't be able to see her for a very long time. She would be under surveillance by the Feds.

Baseer wrote a letter to Catherine and dropped it into the prison's outgoing mailbox two days before he tried to make his getaway. The letter would arrive at her address on the day after he left. It was actually in the form of a rap song and it read:

Sorry mommy I had to set sail, needed to exhale

I wanna call but it's taps on your Nextel

I wanna write you but I can't leave a paper trail

You know I'm fine, I'm just walking on eggshells

Right now you're being watched by the feds

So nevermind what they say to try to get in your head

When they stop by threatening to kill me dead

I'm low key, OT and I'm growing some dreads

I'mma see you real soon and we'll get to speak

I'll let you know what's going on then I'll kiss your cheek

I'll send word by my nigga every couple of weeks

I can't say much cause I don't want nothing to leak

You're the woman that brought me into this world

And can't nothing keep me from my favorite girl

I'mma always be strong because you raised me thorough

I love you Mommy.

The night of the escape was on a Thursday. On the day before, Baseer flushed every letter that he had received down the toilet. The only thing that he kept was his address/telephone book which contained all of his important contact numbers. The book was small enough to fit inside of his boot beneath his foot. Baseer stayed in his cell the entire day and used his cell phone to make sure that the other Gods were positioning themselves. Baseer began taping magazines around his arms and legs before the officer made a round for dinner. The magazines were concealed beneath his coat and his pants. When the officer released the dorm to go to dinner, Baseer didn't walk to the mess hall with everyone else. Instead he went to the North Pod of Darlington. A man named Officer Wilkes was working on the north side and he would often look out for Baseer. He liked how Baseer carried himself and he didn't worry about Baseer getting him into trouble for permitting him to be out of place. When it was time for Officer Wilkes to begin locking down the North Pod, he opened the wing door so that Baseer could return to his correct pod. Instead of going back, Baseer remained in the Sallyport where he had a view of the entire East Yard.

Baseer had told the Gods from Boston to be parked at the wooden barn at 6:45. Then they were supposed to watch his dorm from the edge of the woods. When Baseer saw that there were no officers on the yard, he hurried over to a blind spot on the corner of the building. Next he put on his gloves and climbed up the first fence in that very same corner. When he reached the top of the fence, he was met by 24 inch wide loops of razor wire. He hooked the open master lock from his pocket onto one loop and attached it to another loop. Then he closed the lock to hold them together. That created a gap that was wide enough for him to get through. Next, he climbed over and jumped to the ground from the top of the fence. After making it over, he ran to another dark blind spot on the side of the building. From that spot, he could see the patch of trees where the Gods were supposed to be waiting for him. Baseer sat still for a few seconds hoping that he had scaled the first fence undetected. There were intercoms all around the yard and Baseer would've heard the "emergency first response" call if it was made.

After about 15 seconds of silence, Baseer realized that he wasn't seen by anyone. That's when he kneeled down in his corner and dialed True Born's cellular phone number.

True Born answered quickly. "Peace, I'm outside right now on the side of the center dorm." "When that white truck passes by one more time, me and Now Born are gonna run up there and cut the last fence for you. He'll throw you a set of cutters across the fence to get you through the second one." Keke drove pass one more time, then True Born and Now Born began speeding towards the direction of the center dorm. They were both armed with guns. True Born had a .45 ruger with an extended clip, plus another .45 that only held 16 bullets. Now Born was carrying an AK47 with a shoulder strap, plus two pairs of wire cutters. Baseer remained hidden in the shadow of the building until he spotted both of them cutting a doggy door type of opening at the bottom of the third fence.

Baseer began running towards the second fence. Now Born noticed him so he threw his set of wire cutters over the fence to him. Baseer picked them up when they landed, and immediately began cutting a similar opening at the bottom of the fence with the motion sensor. The sensor was not on. Baseer was directly in front of True Born and Now Born. It took almost two minutes for Baseer to get through both fences. As he was crawling through the last fence, the other Gods held the gap open so that Baseer could crawl through it without cutting himself on the razor wire that covered the entire fence. When Baseer arose to his feet, True Born passed him the pistol with the extended clip. The three of them hurried into the swamp which was almost knee deep with water, weeds, and Lilly pads. Baseer looked back at the perimeter truck as it overlapped and he continued to run towards the car. They were all clearly visible so they were hoping that Keke was still in the truck. Keke continued to drive at the same slow speed and they proceeded to the wooden barn. They arrived there in less than two minutes. Knowledge Me was waiting there in a green Ford Explorer without a license tag on it. Baseer jumped into the Grand Prix and the other Gods jumped into the Explorer. Then they followed Baseer as he sped towards the interstate. He turned onto the interstate in 1.5 minutes and Knowledge Me remained behind him the entire time.

After driving south on Interstate 95 for almost twenty minutes, True Born called Baseer and said "Yo God, turn off on this next exit." That's where Knowledge Me replaced his license tags on his Explorer. When they got back on I-95, Baseer's getaway became easier because the rain began. It was 8:00. He called Peru's cellular phone number and he answered "Peace" Baseer said "Peace, I'm on the way down there." "Say word." That's when Baseer turned the music back up so that Peru could hear the song that was playing. He was listening to Black Clouds by Noriega, on a cd that Peru had left in the cd player of the getaway car. Peru began laughing and said "Yo Baseer you're the illest nigga. My niggas home. We're about to get this money fam." "Yeah straight up and down. God have me some piff or some Kush to smoke when I get there." "I left you a "L" in the ashtray, I figured that your nerves might be fucked up." Baseer opened the ashtray and found a blunt of sour diesel, plus $1000 in cash. Baseer began smoking and continued driving in route to Clarkston, Georgia.

CHAPTER FOURTEEN

The Gods from Boston followed Baseer as far as Georgia, but they separated before he reached Clarkston. He didn't want them to know where Peru lived. Baseer drove the entire way there with 3 fully loaded pistols in the car. True Born gave him a .45 and Peru had left a .380 and a 9 mm under the driver's seat. He arrived at Peru's apartment around 2:00 am Friday morning. He remained indoors for seven days. Then he returned to North Carolina to dig up the cash that he had buried. He drove to Fayetteville on the following Friday night around 1:30 am, driving a small red Kia truck that Monique had rented for him. He placed the $45,000 into a backpack that he had gotten from Peru. He drove as far as Richmond, Virginia. There, he parked near the Greyhound Terminal and boarded the next bus headed to NYC. He called Peru from the bus, and told him to tell Monique to report the Kia truck in as stolen.

Baseer stayed in Brooklyn with TK for exactly one month. During that time, he used TK's equipment to produce the beats for every song that he had written for the Moving Target Album. During the final week, he recorded every track at a studio in Manhattan. TK still had everything that he had kept for him out of his storage. After that month, TK leased Baseer a 3-bedroom brick house in Glen Burnie, Maryland for six months. Three months later, they both landed a distribution deal with the help of TK's manager. Both of their solo albums were pressed and distributed to 15 major cities. All of their checks were made payable to Tramal "TK" Kennedy.

Six months passed and Baseer had managed not to get caught by the police. TK was the only person that knew where he resided and he never contacted any of his family members. TK would often drive to Maryland to deliver Baseer's portion of the money generated from his album sales. He had recorded a song called Money Money for his album and that single was receiving radio airplay in those 15 cities. By the time that his lease expired, he had accumulated $70,000 from his album sales. That's when he decided to migrate south to Georgia.

Baseer had approximately $110,000 when he went to Georgia. His dreadlocks had grown to almost 7 inches long. He had grown a full beard and looked totally different from the picture that he had taken for his inmate ID. At Peru's apartment, Baseer searched for a house to rent in the classifieds section of the local newspaper. He found a white house in Morrow, Georgia. It had 2 bedrooms, 1 ½ bathrooms, a spacious backyard and it was fenced in. When Baseer called the owner of the house, he turned out to be an elderly Caucasian man named Mr. Barr. Mr. Barr told Baseer that he would have to pay an $1800 security deposit and that his rent would cost $500 a month. The house also had a small storage house in the backyard. That same day, Baseer went to the DMV in Morrow and got a picture ID; he used the name on his false birth certificate, Walter Edwards Jr. On the following morning, Monique and Peru took Baseer to meet with Mr. Barr at the house that he was about to rent. He gave him $3800 to secure him for the following four months rent.

As soon as Baseer began getting settled in, he began trying to figure out a way to generate more money. He was determined to become rich, whether via music or crime. Peru began explaining to him that he was doing really good in the cocaine business. He had found a new supplier whose quality was just as good as the Dominicans in Washington Heights, Harlem. The only difference was that Peru was being charged $22,000 for a Kilo. Peru was stretching his coke with lactose and turning every kilo into 44 ounces. Then he sold every ounce for $1000; this way he doubled his money that he invested every time. Peru said that he could introduce Baseer to some of his customers, just like his cousin "Stax" did for him.

Before investing in any drugs, Baseer went to a local Circuit City and bought two small surveillance cameras to monitor his home at all times. They were both small and barely noticeable. One camera captured the entire front yard and the other one was directly above the front door. He had them installed where the footage would appear on the TV's in his living room and his bedroom. He also placed lights in his front lawn that only came on when they sensed motion in their proximity. Next he went out and bought two pit bulls to put in his backyard. He named the male pit-bull Heroin and the female Cocaine. Peru had an extra police scanner in his apartment so he gave it to Baseer, free of charge. With that, he could hear all police radios in the vicinity of his house. He still had enough food and hygiene to sustain him for another year. He chose not to buy a car because he didn't plan to spend much time away from his house. He preferred taking public transportation in the case of any emergencies, because they seldomly had problems with roadblocks.

After almost two weeks, Baseer called Peru and he answered "Peace" "Peace. I think that I'm gonna have to fuck with you on some work." "How much? I've got a connect on the coke and the pills." "What are the numbers on the pills?" "All that he has right now are Blue Dolphins, Supermans, and Sour Apples but if you buy 5000 then you can get them for one dollar each. You can sell em for $15 each all day long or just sell weight and still flip your bread. It's up to you." "And what about the snow?" "22 a brick" "I'm gonna need like four niggas that buy weight. Like a big eighth at a time." "I got you. Plus you can step on that shit because I add 14 grams of lactose to every ounce and they still move like hotcakes." "Well swing by my crib and pick up this current. I want a brick and 5000 pills. Mix them all up. I've got a stack for you plus I'll throw you 500 pills." "Alright I'm about to call Monique to pick me up and bring me out there. I need like 2 hours." "That's peace. One!"

Monique's Lincoln Navigator pulled up around 5:00 pm. Baseer had his gate opened so that they could enter his driveway. Baseer heard his dogs barking so he looked at his TV screen and saw that Peru was walking up to his front door. After inviting him inside, he handed Peru a backpack containing $27,000, then he pulled an additional $1000 from his pocket and gave it to him. Baseer walked with Peru to the truck while Peru told him about a robbery that he had in mind. That's when Monique let down the passenger's side window and said "Hey Baseer." Baseer responded "Oh Peace, sis what's up?" "Nothing much, when was the last time that you talked to Yahnis?" "I haven't talked to her in over a year. I lost her number." "Well we exchanged numbers when you and Peru were in jail but we never called each other. As a matter of fact, I bought a new phone and changed my number." "Do you still have your old phone?" "I think so." "If you find it, see if you have Yahnis' old telephone number saved into your contacts." "I'll look for it when I get home tonight." "Good looking." That's when Monique and Peru left and picked up the drugs for Baseer.

Peru returned with Baseer's product around 7:15 that night. Baseer spent the remainder of the night bagging his coke up into individual ounces. He didn't add any procaine to it because he wanted to establish his clientele. He only planned to profit $14,000 from the cocaine. He also had 4500 ecstasy pills that he planned to sell his coke customers at wholesale for $3 each. On the next morning, Peru called Baseer and said that he had given his cell phone number to three big spenders. Then Baseer told him to remind Monique to look for Yahnis' old telephone number. That's when Peru said "Oh I forgot. . . . she gave it to me last night." Peru retrieved the telephone number from his pocket and continued "It's 404-678-0411."

When Baseer dialed Yahnis' telephone number, surprisingly, she answered "Hello." When Yahnis recognized Baseer's voice she instantly became excited. She said "Oh my God! Baby I thought that I would never hear from you again. I wanted to look you up on the internet but I couldn't remember your last name." "Why didn't you just look on your bail bonds receipt?" "Because I lost it." "So how have you been doing?" "I'm fine but you should see your . . . " "See my what?" "Hold on, I have someone here that wants to speak to you." Baseer had no clue about who that person could've been because they knew no people in common besides Peru and Monique.

A few seconds passed, then the voice of a small child spoke into the phone. The child said "Hello." Then, Baseer overheard Yahnis telling the child to say "Hi daddy." That's when the child repeated the phrase and Baseer couldn't believe his ears. Yahnis grabbed the telephone from the child and said "That was your son. . . and he's a splitting image of you." Baseer still stunned, asked "Are you sure that he's my son?" "Baseer yes, this is our baby. I wasn't fucking anybody else baby. As a matter of fact – can your phone receive pictures?" "Yeah" "Well give me a second and I'll call you right back after I send it." When Baseer received the picture, he noticed that the child was identical to the child in his dream. When Yahnis called him back, she made him even happier when she told him the name that she had given the child. She said "I remember you crying to me about your boy who got killed and you said that he named his son Baseer, after you. That's when I decided to name your son "Powerful", after him."

Baseer had intended to destroy his cell phone immediately after their conversation ended but he decided not to. That was because Yahnis explained that her phone was pre-paid and that it wasn't registered under her name. Baseer was eager to see his son but he was also paranoid about going to Yahnis' apartment or inviting her to his house. Even though he had been a fugitive for almost 7 ½ months, he knew that it was likely for her to still be under surveillance by the FBI. That's when he began figuring out a way to meet with Yahnis without disclosing his whereabouts to the Feds. In the meantime, Baseer began getting his drug business up and running. He received phone calls from two of the guys that were referred by Peru. One of them was a young black guy named Yozie and he wanted to buy two ounces. Baseer allowed him to come to his home and served him in the kitchen as soon as he entered the house. Baseer didn't have on a shirt. His .45 was in his pocket and the handle was exposed. Yozie also noticed the .380 and the 9mm sitting on the Kitchen table.

The second call came from an older black guy named L.B. He wanted to buy a big eighth. Baseer invited him to his home and served him as well. L.B. agreed to buy some pills when he returned for his second purchase. Both deals went smooth and Baseer relaxed in his house, for the remainder of the day. Peru took a half ounce of Kush to Baseer's house for him to smoke. The visit only lasted for about 30 minutes, then Peru returned home. While Baseer was smoking, he decided to listen to his Moving Target cd. When he thought about the money that he had earned from his album sales, he figured that it would be a good idea to record a follow-up album. That's when he grabbed a pen and a pad, and began writing a song called "Like I Want You."

In that song, Baseer taunted the police by writing –

No matter where I go man I know how to network

Big Chrome 45 under my sweatshirt

So nobody moves, nobody gets hurt

When it comes to this trap shit, I'm an expert

Pits outside, cameras on the entrance

Never slipping, I've got a scanner in the kitchen

So step into my booby trap, I'll let the toolie clap

*Wit more guns than Busta Rhymes
in the movie Strapped*

I never was one to fear cops

And I never was afraid to earn a couple of tear drops

So keep snitch niggas out of my way

Cause I'mma get money 24 hours a day

Like my last breath is 24 hours away

Before I go out like a bitch all you cowards will pay

Cause I'm a G so is everybody running with me

I give a fuck about a cop, try to come and get me.

When Baseer woke up on the next morning, he had realized a way to see his child without attracting any heat from the police. He arranged for Yahnis and Powerful to meet Monique at the Lenox Mall in Atlanta. Once inside, they were going to meet up and go to Baseer's house in Monique's Lincoln Navigator. Baseer figured that, if Yahnis was being followed by the Feds, they wouldn't be seen leaving with her. If the girls met up in the morning, then Baseer could spend the entire day with his son; and Yahnis could take a taxicab to pick up her car when the mall closed at 10:00 pm. Monique agreed to take Yahnis to Baseer's house on the following Saturday morning.

Baseer was nervous about meeting his son for the first time. Plus he was anticipating having sex with Yahnis because he knew that was going to happen. He placed all of his drugs and guns in the top of his wardrobe closet so that they would be out of young Powerful's reach. Monique, Yahnis and Powerful arrived at Baseer's house at 9:30 Saturday morning. When Yahnis stepped out of the truck, she walked to the back door to remove Powerful from his car seat. Baseer remained inside and watched Yahnis on his TV screen. Yahnis approached his door carrying Powerful in her arms and he was asleep with his head resting on her left shoulder. She was carrying his diaper bag in her left hand. When Baseer opened the door to welcome them inside, he immediately extended his arms to embrace his son. That's when a nondescript feeling of happiness befell him. The baby was still asleep, so Baseer continued staring at him in awe; because he looked so much like him. Powerful was wearing an all blue Roc-A-Wear outfit and a pair of wheat-colored baby construction Timberlands. He also had a thick afro, just like the one that Baseer had as a child.

Baseer laid the baby down on his bed because he didn't seem to wanna wake up. Yahnis followed Baseer into his bedroom, then she began trying to seduce him. She said "Baby you look so sexy with your dreads. Plus, you look all toned up now; you must be working out." Baseer replied "Maybe a little bit." Then they quietly made their way to the nearest bathroom and closed the door. Yahnis was wearing a short blue jean skirt and a tight Baby Phat shirt. On her feet, were a pair of crispy white

Nike Air Force Ones. She placed both of her hands on the toilet and Baseer came up behind her. He then raised her skirt and saw that she wasn't wearing any panties. That's when he pulled his shorts down and penetrated her doggy style. Baseer released inside of her twice and she had multiple orgasms. She was aiming for another orgasm until she heard their baby crying in Baseer's bedroom. Then she pulled down her skirt and walked into the bedroom to pick him up. Baseer remained in the bathroom so that he could freshen up.

When Baseer exited the bathroom, Yahnis was sitting on the couch in the living room. Powerful was on the floor playing with a Transformers toy that was in his diaper bag. When Baseer entered the living room, the baby stopped what he was doing and began staring at Baseer with a blank expression on his face. Then Powerful looked at Yahnis and she said "That's Pop Pop." As Baseer moved towards him, Powerful extended his arms for him to pick him up. As Baseer lifted him up, Yahnis said "Awwwe," then she walked over to them and kissed both of them on their cheeks. Baseer began talking to his son, causing Powerful to smile. He even repeated the word "Peace" for him. Their bond seemed to begin instantly, as if they had already known each other. In that small amount of time, Baseer became very attached to his child.

When Yahnis and Powerful left with Monique, Baseer smoked a blunt of Kush and relaxed on his couch. He thought deeply about his life, as well as Yahnis and his son's. He wondered how they could be a happy family while he was still a fugitive of the law. He hadn't spoken to his mother Catherine since he was in prison and thoughts of her were starting to weigh heavily on his mind. She didn't even know that she had a grandson. He was tempted to pay her a visit but he knew that the time was too soon. He finally figured out a way to inform her of the birth of his son. Yahnis gave Baseer an 8x10 photo of Powerful. On the back of the picture, Baseer simply wrote "This is your grandson. His name is Powerful." Baseer knew that Catherine would recognize the resemblance and know that was his son. Baseer mailed the picture to TK along with a letter. He told TK to mail the picture to Catherine from a post office in the Bronx. That way, the picture would seem to have been sent from New York City if the feds were to intercept it.

Over the next two weeks, Baseer sold his entire kilo and the majority of his pills. He had made a total of $39,000 and he still had 1500 pills to sell. He decided not to re-up because he was considering committing the robbery that Peru had in mind. He had presented him with a well thought-out plan to rob his cocaine supplier, and the plan sounded full-proof. He expected that they would get at least 20 kilos from the robbery plus cash. They mutually concluded that it would be best to leave the country after the robbery, because it would involve homicide. Baseer didn't want to take the risk but he realized that was his opportunity to be with Yahnis and Powerful forever. Since Baseer and Peru were both on the run, they decided that Cuba would be the best destination. That was because Cuba didn't extradite fugitives to the USA.

When Baseer explained his plan to Yahnis he never told her exactly what he had to do to get the money. He simply said that he would have at least $500,000 when they departed for Cuba. He could've also earned extra money in the future by recording music and leaving TK in control of the distribution in America. He told Yahnis that she wouldn't have to work another day in her life. Plus, he would fund annual trips to America for her to visit her family. Yahnis was in full support of him; not because she was sluggish or greedy, but because she knew Baseer's situation and how much he wanted to be a part of his son's life. Plus she was very much in love with him. The robbery was scheduled for the first week of the following month. That was only 3 weeks after Baseer proposed his plan to Yahnis.

It took Baseer six more days to sell the rest of his pills. On the seventh day, Monique met with Yahnis at the Lenox Mall and drove her to Morrow to visit him. That time, she took enough clothes for Powerful to stay with Baseer for an entire week. Powerful became upset when Monique left him that night. That's when he cried for an entire hour until he fell asleep on the couch. Then Baseer called Yahnis and she answered "Is he acting up?" "Man, this little nigga spazzed on me as soon as you left." "Let me speak to him." "He's resting right now. Let him get all of his cries out because he's gonna have to get used to me." "Well, when he wakes up, let him watch his Spiderman 3 dvd or let him listen to his TI cd. I left them in his diaper bag." "True. What's his favorite food?" "Pizza" "Let me call Pizza Hut and order two pizzas for him" "Ok baby, just call me back if he starts acting up again." "I got 'em" "Love you." "Love you too."

Baseer ordered two hand tossed Veggie Lover's pizzas and they were delivered before Powerful woke up. When the pizzas arrived, Baseer placed both boxes on top of the coffee table in front of the couch. Then he inserted the TI vs. TIP cd and played the song Big Shit Poppin. Baseer went into the bathroom and turned on the exhaust fan because he wanted to take a few drags from his blunt. When Baseer walked back into the living room, one of the pizza boxes was opened and two slices were missing. Powerful was nowhere in sight. Baseer walked down his hallway and into his bedroom. That's where he found little Powerful with dry tears on his face and tomato sauce all over his hands. He had a slice of pizza sitting on Baseer's beige carpet and there were a few tomato sauce stains right next to it.

Baseer wasn't upset about the mess that he had made. The sight was actually quite comical to him. He picked up his son as he continued eating his pizza, then he looked into his little brown eyes and asked "Do you want juice?" Powerful nodded his head yes. Baseer carried the baby into the kitchen and poured him a small cup of apple juice. Powerful drank his juice and they went into the living room to watch the Spiderman 3 dvd. His eyes were glued to the TV screen and he seemed to know every word of the movie. Baseer couldn't restrain himself from laughing aloud as he watched Powerful trying to emulate the fighting scenes. By the time that the movie ended, the baby was sound asleep on a beanbag directly in front of the television set. Powerful started getting used to his father and he didn't cry anymore. Yahnis called Baseer's cell phone and talked to Powerful at least 3 times each day.

On the following Sunday morning, Monique dropped Yahnis off at Baseer's house. When she walked inside, Powerful ran to her and jumped into her arms. Then she said "Hey Little Man" and kissed him on his cheek. Yahnis went into the kitchen and began preparing breakfast for everyone while the baby played in front of the television set. When breakfast was ready, the three of them ate in the living room. While Powerful focused on the Spiderman 3 movie, Baseer and Yahnis began talking to each other. Baseer said "Baby that little nigga is funny as hell. He had me beaming earlier when I caught him dancing to that TI shit." "Yeah, he loves T.I." "I wish that my mother could see him before we bounce." The both of them became silent, then Baseer got an idea. He said "I just thought about something. We have two weeks before we leave. I want to let my mother keep Powerful for a whole week before we leave." "How are we gonna do that? You said that the feds were watching her." "You can meet her inside of the Cross Creek Mall in Fayetteville, the same way that you always meet Monique. Just call her from a payphone. Tell her that you're Powerful's mother and ask her to meet with you.'

Yahnis took Powerful home with her around 9:30, that night. He had become so attached to his father that he wanted him to leave with them. That's when Baseer told Yahnis to bring him back on Friday so that he could keep him until that Sunday. Then Yahnis would pick him up and take him to NC to meet with Catherine. Yahnis worked everyday until Friday, then she drove to the Lenox Mall with Powerful. With her, she had his diaper bag and a carrier bag with 10 outfits for Powerful. Instead of inconveniencing Monique, Yahnis called a taxi cab to carry them to Baseer's house. She left her car parked in the mall parking lot. When Yahnis and Powerful arrived in their cab, Baseer was in his backyard feeding his dogs. Yahnis carried the baby into the house and they waited inside.

Yahnis and Baseer spent the entire day enjoying each other's company and watching their son play around inside of the house. Powerful didn't want to play outside because he was afraid of the dogs. It was obvious that Powerful was excited about having both of his parents around. When the time came for Yahnis to leave in her taxicab, Powerful didn't even cry. He enjoyed being at Baseer's house because he allowed him to run wild. Baseer felt like he owed him that much for being absent during the first year of his life. That weekend, Powerful did just that, run wild. He even slept wild. On Saturday night, Baseer woke up because he felt something on his face. That's when he realized that it was his son's bare foot. Then he said to himself, "This is gonna take some getting used to."

On the next morning, Baseer woke up at 8:15 and noticed that Powerful wasn't in the bed with him. That's when he went to search the house for him. He found Powerful in the living room, and he was pressing buttons on the stereo. Baseer remained silent and watched him to see if he would ever figure out how to turn the music on. After about 20 seconds, he pressed the "On" button and the music blasted into his ears. The music was so loud that it scared him. He started to run to his father's bedroom but he noticed him standing behind him. Then he extended his arms for Baseer to pick him up and pretended to be crying. He thought that Baseer was about to punish him. When Baseer picked him up, he started laughing and walked over to the stereo to turn the volume down. When Powerful realized that his father wasn't upset, he began giggling also. Then, Baseer fixed him a bowl of cereal and let him eat it in front of the television set.

Yahnis was expected to pick the child up around 10:00 am., so that she could take him to meet his grandmother. While Powerful was eating his breakfast, Baseer went into his closet to retrieve a NY Giants gym bag. That's where all of his money was stashed, almost $128,000. He counted out $50,000 and set it aside from the rest of the money. As he was counting the cash, little Powerful walked into the room. He began staring at the money so Baseer asked "You like that God?" Powerful didn't answer him. Instead he reached out his hand for Baseer to give him some money. Baseer began laughing, then told him "Yeah you've gotta be my son. You like money too huh?" Then Baseer handed him a 100 dollar bill and told him to go back into the living room. Powerful obeyed him and exited the room. That's when Baseer emptied Powerful's carrier bag onto the floor and refilled it with $50,000 in cash. He wanted Catherine to have it because he knew that she didn't have anybody helping her with her bills. He placed

Powerful's outfits on top of the money and zipped the carrier bag shut. Then he put the remainder of his money in his closet.

CHAPTER FIFTEEN

Baseer carried the baby's bags outside and placed them in Monique's backseat while Yahnis strapped Powerful down in his car seat. Then the three of them departed for North Carolina. Baseer went back inside of his house and smoked a blunt of Kush. After about 30 minutes, he called Peru and discussed the robbery in Spanish. Peru still insisted that the robbery wouldn't be difficult. The robbery was scheduled for Friday night. Peru and Baseer only spoke on the telephone for ten minutes, then Baseer fell asleep on his couch.

The Cross Creek Mall closed at 6:00 pm on Sundays, so Monique and Yahnis made sure that they were on the highway by 11:00 am. Monique's navigational system estimated that the Cross Creek Mall was six hours away. Yahnis and Monique laughed and talked for the entire trip, while Powerful slept in his car seat most of the way. When they arrived in Fayetteville and found the mall, it was 5:15 pm. As Monique was parking the truck, Yahnis dug into her pocket to retrieve her cell phone. When she found Catherine's cell phone number in her phone book, she pressed "call" and Catherine's phone began ringing. Yahnis told her where she was and asked that she meet her in the food court, after telling her that she was the mother of the baby from the picture.

Catherine got dressed immediately and hurried to the mall in her Toyota Camry. Yahnis carried one bag on each shoulder and she carried the baby's car seat in her hands when they entered the mall. Monique carried Powerful. Powerful kept trying to kiss Monique and touch her breasts. That's when she laughed and told him 'You're a fresh little boy." Yahnis slapped him on the back of his hand, and told him to stop. He cried for about 5 seconds, then he began looking around at the other children that were with their parents in the mall. When they found the food court, Monique took Powerful with her to find an available table. Yahnis sat the bags and the car seat down, beside their table, and walked to the pizza restaurant to order cheese pizza for all of them. She ordered five slices; 1 for Powerful, 2 for Monique and 2 for her along with 3 peach papaya flavored Fruitopia drinks.

Yahnis paid for the order and returned to their table with their drinks. The cashier said that the pizzas would be delivered to their table momentarily. When the waitress finally brought their food they all began eating. Yahnis had no idea what Catherine looked like so she looked around the food court for any elderly women who resembled Baseer. She saw 3 women that resembled him, slightly, but they all walked pass the food court. Then a short brown skinned woman walked into the food court and she seemed to be looking for someone. When she spotted Yahnis and Powerful she walked over to their table and said "Excuse me, but is his name Powerful?" Yahnis stood up and answered "Yes, that's your bad grandson." They hugged as Catherine responded "Oh my God, he looks just like Baseer did when he was his age."

Catherine pulled a seat from the table and sat next to Powerful while he continued eating his pizza. That's when Yahnis told Catherine "Baseer wanted me to bring Powerful up here so that he could stay with you for a week. He figured that you would want to spend some time with him." "Of course I would." Catherine softly pinched Powerful's cheek and said "Hey cutie – are you ready to come with grandma?" Powerful gave her a blank stare and continued eating his food. That's when Yahnis said "He's just being mean because he doesn't know you. He'll get use to you." "Ok, well How is Baseer doing? I don't want to know where he is, just tell me how he's doing." "Baseer's great. He told me to tell you that he loves you very much and that he misses you." "Tell him that I love him too and to please be careful. Those detectives still keep coming by my house trying to pressure me to tell them where he is. When I say I don't know, they say that they're going to shoot him on sight." "Well Mrs. Watson they'll never find him. Your son is really smart." "Does he need anything?" "No he's fine." Just then, the mall announcement came on stating the mall was closing in ten minutes. Yahnis and Monique walked Catherine out to her car to help her put Powerful and his bag into the car.

Yahnis drove the entire way back to Georgia. They arrived there at 1:00 am and Yahnis went inside to lay in bed with Baseer. They slept until the morning. Monique returned to her apartment in Tucker. When the sun rose around 6:15, Baseer woke Yahnis up and they had sex. When they were done, Yahnis walked into the kitchen and prepared breakfast. That's when Baseer called Peru because on the day passed, Peru said that he was about to pay for their traveling expenses. When Peru answered, Baseer said "Peace did you handle that on the day passed?" "Yeah. I had to give my Cuban homie $20,000 last night but it will be worth it. The nigga owns a private jet, plus his people own a private airstrip where we can land at. We can bring our guns, coke and everything." "That's peace, I'll just give you back 10 stacks on that." "That's what it is. My nigga has a pro bono pilot and everything. His people even have a spot for us to rest at for a day or two until we find our cribs." "Son, I'm real thirsty right now – I need these bricks. That would be my meal ticket. I'm leaving my old earth with a little 50 grand. Plus I'm about to drop another album and let TK handle the distribution. That's royalty money for the rest of my life. All of that's going to my mother. I'm buzzing in like 15 cities right now, that's paper." "I know Baseer, that's why we've gotta put this work in. I know that you're about to cop some fly shit. I want like 6 bedrooms, kid with the grand piano and the whole shit." "Yeah, I know, on some real Last Don shit." Baseer ended the phone call and walked into the kitchen to eat breakfast with Yahnis.

Yahnis and Baseer spent most of the day in bed. Yahnis decided to quit her job that day since they were scheduled to leave before she would've been able to receive her paycheck. Baseer only walked outside twice to feed his dogs. Around 2:30 pm, Yahnis received a phone call from her mother. When she answered, her mother said "Hey Ya Ya. Why does your phone sound like that?" "Sound like what?" "Your voice keeps echoing like you're saying everything twice." "I don't know what's wrong with my crazy phone. It probably needs to be charged up." "Well, I was calling to see what you're doing." Their conversation only lasted for a few minutes. Baseer had been in the living room, eating at the bar. Yahnis had baked him a family size Stouffer's vegetable lasagna. Around 7:30 that night, Baseer heard his dogs barking in the backyard.

When Baseer walked outside to see what they were barking for, he concluded that the dogs were barking at each other because he didn't see any trespassers. When he returned inside, he turned on the television in his bedroom and monitored his surveillance cameras for 20 minutes. Then he pulled his .45 from the closet and placed it beneath his bed on the side that he was sleeping on. Throughout that night, he frequently walked into the bathroom to get a view of the backyard through the window. The dogs didn't bark anymore that night and Baseer didn't hear anything suspicious over the police scanner. Therefore, he eventually fell asleep.

On the next morning, Baseer walked outside to feed his dogs. As he was putting water into their bowls, he noticed a UPS truck parked in front of a house that was 3 houses down the street from him. Seeing the truck made Baseer become slightly paranoid, so he began questioning Yahnis when she entered the house. He asked her "Baby, are you positive that nobody followed you?" "Yes I'm sure. I can remember times when there wasn't another vehicle in sight on the interstate. Stop being so paranoid." "I'm just being cautious because I didn't make it this far to start slipping." Yahnis walked into the kitchen to prepare breakfast. While she was cooking, Baseer smoked a blunt of Kush and began writing his second verse for "Like I Want You". When he completed the verse, he placed the sheet of paper under his ashtray on the bar. He had planned to add a third verse to it later on that night.

Baseer got stimulated for the entire day and had Yahnis to massage him for almost 2 hours. He used that time to meditate and to build up the nerve to rob and kill Peru's coke supplier. Around 8:15 pm, Heroin and Cocaine began barking again as if something was wrong. When Baseer walked outside, his dogs were still barking and staring into a patch of trees directly behind his house. He walked around his entire house with his .45 drawn. That time he noticed an electric company's business van parked down the block. There were two men in white hard hats who appeared to be operating on the power lines.

Baseer realized that there was nothing wrong with the electricity in his house, so he became even more paranoid. That's when he walked back inside and began questioning Yahnis. "Aye baby, did you give my mother your number or anything?" Then she answered "She could've gotten my number when I called her from the mall." "How could she do that when you called her from a payphone?" "I didn't call her from a payphone. I called from my cell." "What the fuck baby? You're playing right?" "No why?" "Because I told you to call from a payphone in the mall." "Baseer I had the baby and his bags. Plus his car seat. I totally forgot what you said about the payphone." "Hold up. Where is your phone at right now?" "It's in my purse why?" "Because if you called my mother, your jack might be tapped. They have satellites called GPS that can pinpoint where your phone is within a ten foot radius. We have to throw it away." "Slow down baby, don't just throw my phone away, it isn't wired, you're paranoid." "When was the last time that you spoke on it?" "Yesterday when my mother called" "Did it sound strange like someone was listening to you?" "No." "Did you hear your voice echo or anything?"

Yahnis paused for a few moments as if she was trying to remember, then she answered "My mom did say something about my voice echoing." Baseer removed the back piece to Yahnis' cell phone and withdrew the sim card. Then he flushed the sim card down the toilet. Moments later he realized that his cell phone could've possibly been tapped also. The feds could easily review her call records and learn his number. A few seconds later, Baseer's cellular phone rang while that very thought was still in his mind. He hurried to his phone and saw that the caller was Peru. He answered "Yo" then Peru greeted him "Peace God. I just found out that my connect might have more than 20 bricks when we come through." "Be easy, don't talk like that right now." "Son, why do you sound like that?" "Like what? Worried?" "No. You sound like you have an echo."

"Word?" "Yo flush your chip son. Our phones are tapped!"

Baseer hurried to the bathroom to flush his sim card. As he was walking out of his bathroom, Cocaine and Heroin began barking again. Baseer went into his bedroom to monitor his surveillance cameras. That's when he learned what his dogs were barking at. The two men who were operating on the power lines were approaching his front door. They didn't realize that they were being watched. Baseer realized that something was wrong because his fence was locked. That means that the electricians had to jump or climb over the fence to enter his yard. That's when one of the men tapped on Baseer's front door. Baseer then switched the channel to monitor the camera that captured the entire front yard. He pretended like no one was home and continued to watch them on his TV screen. Next, Baseer went into his closet to remove his other two pistols. All of his pistols were fully loaded and he cocked each one of them.

Yahnis began panicking and asking Baseer to put his guns away. The two men continued knocking for three more minutes, so Baseer told Yahnis to go to the door and ask the men what they wanted. He walked her to the door quietly. He had the .45 in his right hand, the 9 mm in his left hand and the .380 was in his right pants pocket. That's when the men knocked three more times and Yahnis asked "Who is it?" Then a deep Caucasian man's voice answered "This is the Federal Bureau of Investigation." Baseer looked through the peephole and saw one of the men raising his badge up to the peephole. Then Baseer whispered to Yahnis "Ask them what they want."

When she asked them, they answered "We have a search warrant to search this residence." Then she said "Just one minute, I have to put some clothes on." Baseer looked at his TV screen and noticed four black Ford Crown Victoria's parking on the outside of his fence. Then he went to his bathroom to see if he could escape through the window. When he looked through the window, his dogs were barking and there were 3 armed Federal Agents standing in his backyard. At that point, he realized that he was completely surrounded. An entire minute passed before the agent resumed knocking on the front door. That time, Yahnis didn't answer. She had followed Baseer into the bathroom, asking him what she should do. That's when the agent yelled "Ma'am if you don't open this door in 30 seconds, we're gonna have to kick it down."

30 seconds later, the door was still shut so the agents knocked the door down. Three agents entered the house with their guns drawn, and the entire house was completely dark. Baseer had flipped the breaker off. The only noise that was heard inside of the house was the sound of the dogs barking outside. That's when one of the officers began making threats. He said "OK Mr. Watson, we know that you're in here. Just come out and make it easy on yourself." The three officers split up and began searching different areas in the house. One of the officers walked into Baseer's bedroom. He was using the infrared beam on his pistol to guide him through the darkness of the house. As soon as he entered Baseer's bedroom, two loud gunshots rang out and the agent collapsed to the floor. Baseer had been waiting on the side of his bedroom door and he shot the agent in his head at point blank range.

When the other officers heard the gunshots, they called out to their partner. When he didn't answer, they hurried back to the front door to exit the house. Then they went back outside where they joined 13 other agents and US Marshals. There were blue lights flashing all around the house and armed agents were standing around his entire yard. Baseer made his way to the bathroom by crawling on the floor, hastily. Yahnis followed him and climbed into the bath tub. They were in the bathroom for only a minute before they heard the sound of glass breaking in the living room. Then they heard the same sound of glass breaking in the the kitchen. The officers on the outside had thrown smoke bombs through the windows in those rooms.

Baseer reached into his pants pocket and grabbed the .380 to give it to Yahnis. As he handed it to her, he said "It's already cocked, all you have to do is squeeze the trigger." He then walked out of the bathroom and closed the door behind himself to prevent the smoke from going inside. He was going to his bedroom to retrieve his NY Giants gym bag from the closet. As he was walking into his bedroom, he stepped over the officer's dead body and proceeded to the closet. After he grabbed his gym bag, he began running back to the bathroom. He still had his .45 in his right hand, and the 9 mm was in his left hand. He carried the gym bag by the shoulder strap. As he was crossing over the dead agent again, he realized that he was wearing a walkie-talkie radio. Baseer then grabbed the radio and returned to the bathroom. He knew that Yahnis was nervous so he announced himself before he opened the door to return inside.

The entire house was smoked out with the exception of the bathroom. Baseer sat the gym bag down by the toilet and began examining the police radio to assure that it worked. He noticed that the volume was completely turned down, so he twisted the volume knob and turned it up. That's when he heard one of the Fed agents trying to get his attention over the radio. The agent was saying "Mr. Watson. Mr. Watson can you hear me?" Baseer looked back at Yahnis in the bathtub. He noticed that she was shivering because she was so afraid. That's when he pressed a button on the side of the radio and spoke into it. He said "This is Mr. Watson. Can you hear me?" "We hear you Mr. Watson."

At that moment, Baseer had a sudden flashback of the dream that he had about his mother and the baby. He snapped out of it and began talking into the police radio. He said "Listen up. I have your officer gagged and tied up. I shot him in his leg but he can live. This is what I want. Tell your squad to back the fuck up before I kill this pig in here. Plus, I've got this bitch in here and I'll blow her fuckin head off. Tell your people to back up and bring me a helicopter immediately. Have them drop the rope ladder near my front door. I'll leave the bitch here tied up and I'll bring your officer up on the helicopter with me. That's my only negotiation."

The officers hesitated for a few seconds then responded, "Your helicopter is on the way sir." Before responding again, Baseer decided to run back into the bedroom to remove the comforter blanket from his bed. Then he carried it into the bathroom with him and resumed talking to the agent on the police radio. He asked "How long is the chopper gonna take?" "It will be here in a few minutes. If you will look out of one of your front windows, you will see my officers retreating now." Baseer then began explaining his escape plans to Yahnis.

He said "Listen, they have a helicopter on the way. They think that I'm bringing the cop that I shot up on the helicopter with me. So, I'm gonna cover you with the blanket and I need for you to pretend to be him. I told them that I shot him in the leg so walk like you're wounded. When they lift us up, I'm gonna hi-jack that bitch and make them fly us to Cuba." As he was explaining his spontaneous plan, they heard the sound of the helicopter. Then Baseer spoke into the radio saying "I'm gonna be coming out and I have the .45 cocked and ready to blow your partner's brains out. Do what I tell you to do and he lives. If I see anybody besides you, he dies." Then the officer responded, "Everyone has left me. Don't hurt Agent Jones and don't hurt the woman sir. We've done what you asked us to do."

Baseer covered Yahnis' entire body with the comforter blanket. The smoke was beginning to clear since the front door was knocked down. Yahnis and Baseer slowly walked towards the front door because they noticed the rope ladder hanging in the driveway. Heroin and Cocaine were barking fiercely at the helicopter. Baseer had a gun in each hand and his gym bag was hanging from his shoulder. He pressed the button on the radio and said "I'm coming out." Baseer lifted the blanket to see Yahnis' face. She was crying and looked scared to death. Baseer gave her a kiss on the lips and said "Baby it's gonna be ok. Just walk slow like you've been shot and grab the rope ladder. I'm gonna be right there with you."

The two of them slowly walked out into the driveway together. Baseer carefully scanned the perimeter and he didn't see any additional agents or sharp shooters hidden around the house. He was completely exposed as he walked alongside Yahnis. He kept the barrel of his .45 touching Yahnis' head. The Fed agent was standing in the driveway with both of his arms raised in clear view. He seemed convinced that the person beneath the blanket was Agent Jones. There were three officers hidden on the other side of the house where there were no windows. Their police radios' frequency was on a different channel from the one that Baseer was speaking into. The agent allowed Baseer and Yahnis to continue walking towards the rope-ladder, then the agent grabbed his radio and switched the channel.

When the agent began speaking into his radio, he continued looking at Baseer as if he was speaking to him. Baseer couldn't hear him and he assumed that was because of the loud helicopter propellers. The agent was actually talking to the 3 officers that were hidden on the side of the house. He told them "The coast is clear, go inside and find the girl." The officers entered Baseer's house through the Kitchen window which was not in Baseer's view. Simultaneously, Baseer and Yahnis were starting to climb the ladder. When the officers walked into the house it only took them a few seconds to discover Agent Jones' dead body lying in the bedroom's doorway.

Baseer and Yahnis were about two tenths of the way up the ladder when one of the officers ran out of the house. Then he yelled out to the agent in the driveway and said "That's not Agent Jones up there!" In a matter of seconds, armed sharp shooters emerged from the patch of trees behind Baseer's house. Baseer saw them so he began firing shots at them with his .45. He held on to the ladder with his left hand. Yahnis, still covered, was directly above him. When the officers began returning shots, Yahnis panicked and dropped the blanket by accident. The helicopter was slowly ascending into the air. When the officers noticed the .380 in her hand, they began shooting at both of them excessively.

Yahnis had no other option but to begin squeezing her trigger and firing back along with Baseer. Yahnis' bullets didn't hit anyone, but Baseer shot two of them before finally getting shot himself. One of the sharp shooters shot Baseer in his left leg. Suddenly, Yahnis was shot twice in her side. That caused her to let go of the ladder, then she fell about 30 feet to her death. The fall caused her to break her neck. Baseer held on and continued returning shots into the direction of the sharp shooters. He was still carrying the gym bag full of money on his shoulder. After shooting out with the officers for almost 45 seconds, Baseer was finally hit in the chest. His first reaction was to drop his gun and cover the wound with his right hand. His left hand was still hanging on to the ladder. A few seconds later, one of the officers noticed Baseer's 9mm hanging out of his pocket. He fired another shot into Baseer's upper-torso and he plummeted 35 feet to the ground.

Baseer and Yahnis laid bloody alongside each other, motionless. Six armed officers surrounded the couple slowly with their guns aimed directly at them. As they got closer to Baseer, one of the officers noticed that Baseer's hand was covering a shiny chrome pistol on the ground. That's when Baseer raised the gun and fired three more shots at the men that were directly in front of him. One of the shots turned out to be a fatal one to one of the agents' heads. Then the other officers fired multiple rounds into Baseer's body lying on the ground. Baseer was shot a total of 16 times, and he died before the ambulances could've taken him to the hospital.

By that time, Baseer's entire yard was filled with police cars and SUV's. Blue lights were everywhere. After the dead bodies were carried away from the scene the investigators went into the house to take pictures and begin writing their reports of the incident. It took the officers about 5 minutes to find the breaker switch to turn the power back on. When they did, they split up into separate rooms and began collecting forensics. All of the cash in the gym bag was confiscated. One of the officers grabbed Yahnis' and Baseer's cellular phones only to find that they were without the sim cards. The officer in the living room decided to smoke a cigarette. While he was searching through the living room, he noticed an ashtray sitting on the bar. When he dumped his cigarette ashes into the ashtray, he saw a sheet of paper folded up beneath it. Then he unfolded it and began reading it.

After reading what was written on the sheet of paper, the investigator called out to two of the other officers in the house. When they walked into the living room, he said "Hey guys, look at this. It looks like he was expecting us." It was the second verse to the song that Baseer was writing, called Like I Want You. It read:

If you want me, you'd better bring the whole station

If you wanna try and shut down my operation

And I ain't sweating the raid

Cause I ain't takin no prisoners, even the news van's getting sprayed

The lead story headlining the tabloids

Task force team backed down by the bad boys

If they try to negotiate then I'mma talk shit

Better grab the yellow tape and the chalk stick

If you want me pig

Get it poppin right now don't taunt me pig

And you're wastin your breath telling me to freeze

I'll die running from the cops like Thelma and Louise

And let Jody sing it

Cause we can get it on anytime the police bring it

I know you want me, I want you too

I'll kill all of ya'll muthafuckin boys in blue

EPILOGUE

When the FBI notified Catherine of her son's death that night, she broke down into tears. Young Powerful was just beginning to get used to her and his grandfather James. Having the baby around made James consider rehabilitation from his drug addiction, and he restricted hanging out with his friends. Catherine called TK and Desire to inform them of the tragedy so that they could attend the funeral. Baseer's and Yahnis' funerals were to be held one day apart from each others. Baseer had an opened casket funeral and his entire family attended. Peru didn't attend the funeral because he was afraid of being apprehended by the police. He knew about Baseer's death because the report was all over the news in the Atlanta area. He decided not to rob his coke supplier. Instead he and Monique fled to Cuba with only $22,000 to their names.

Baseer's funeral was held at the Mt. Calvary Baptist Church in Fayetteville, NC. Everyone walked up to the casket to pay their homage with their eyes filled with tears. Baseer's ex-finance, Zanasia even showed up and shed a few tears for Baseer. Catherine had dressed Powerful in a 3-piece black suit with a white shirt. She also braided his hair. Desire was noticeably pregnant at the funeral. When she walked up to Baseer's casket, she placed a single rose on his chest and began crying. She also began whispering, "I'm so sorry Baseer." When Catherine carried Powerful to his father's casket, he didn't seem to understand what was going on. Instead of crying like everyone else, Powerful touched Baseer's eyelids as if he was attempting to wake him up from sleeping. Sadly, the baby had to attend his mother's funeral the next day.

After Baseer's funeral, Catherine introduced Young

Powerful to Desire and he shunned her immediately. TK also attended the funeral and he took Baseer's death really hard. So did Baseer's sisters and his father. When TK returned to NYC, he began working really hard on his music until he finally landed a recording deal. He is currently making a lot of money for his talent and he's keeping Baseer's name alive through his music. Keke, the correctional officer, was terminated from her job and arrested. After reviewing the prison's surveillance cameras the investigators concluded that she was involved in Baseer's escape. Catherine is in good health and she's raising Powerful in the suburbs of Fayetteville. She put away the $50,000 for the child to have when he becomes older. TK sends all of Baseer's distribution revenue to Catherine, and she also uses that money to buy the things that Powerful needs.

The End

Also available from this author...

WILD LIFE PUBLISHING

"RAW MATERIAL...
ORIGINAL, THOUGHT
PROVOKING AND VERY
WELL PLOTTED!"
-TERI WOODS
NEW YORK TIMES
BESTSELLING AUTHOR OF
TRUE TO THE GAME

Promise

A BLOODY LOVE STORY

A NOVEL BY

NOW BORN

AUTHOR OF *MOVING TARGET*